THE ASHES OF FOREVERLAND

Book Three

TONY BERTAUSKI

To the lost.
To the lonely.

SPRING

We all...

fall...

down.

AN INCOMPLETE LIST OF FOREVERLAND SURVIVORS

- ***Danny Boy***, *whereabouts unknown*
- ***Cyn***, *last known whereabouts Minneapolis, Minnesota*
- ***Reed***, *whereabouts unknown*
- ***Harold Ballard (The Director)***, *son of Patricia and Tyler, whereabouts unknown*
- ***Tyler Ballard***, *ADMAX Penitentiary, Colorado*
- ***Patricia Ballard***, *comatose at the Institute of Technological Research, New York City*

1

Tyler

ADMAX Penitentiary, Colorado

Tyler stepped onto the ledge.

The Italian marble was cold, his toes gripping the chiseled edge. The platform cantilevered from the roof a thousand feet above traffic. Taillights were strung throughout Central Park, starting and stopping, merging and turning, moving through the city like corpuscles.

He couldn't smell the exhaust from up there, couldn't hear the horns or the congestion, the shouts and whistles.

He held out his arms, Christ-like, tipped his head and inhaled the wind untainted by human grime, from the trash of selfish thoughts. Only the fierce breeze in his ears.

"Sorry to keep you waiting." Patricia crossed the portico.

Her loosely fit dress fluttered around her feet. The brightly lit glass walls of the luxury apartment—the only such apartment atop the Bank of America building—betrayed the layers of beige fabric that otherwise would hide her pear-shaped body. Her graying hair flowed to her shoulders.

"I can't stay long," he said.

She looked through him with those penetrating eyes, a smile reflecting somewhere in their depths. Her scent carried through the cutting breeze, her dress snapping like taut flags. He stopped on the bottom step.

"You don't have to leave."

"You know I can't stay, love."

A beige pile of fabric fell at her bare feet. Her naked body was without wrinkles; the sweep of her hips hypnotic. None of her curves were as alluring as the tight curls of her lips pushing into her cherub cheeks.

He watched her from the bottom step, watched her dive into the glass-bottom pool that was suspended over the thousand-foot drop. The water, crystal blue.

She hardly made a ripple, swimming beneath the surface to the other end. Her strokes were long, water beading from her fair skin. Tyler waited with a towel. He wrapped her as she stepped out, water dripping from her nose.

The taste of her filled his sinuses.

He pulled the towel over her shoulders. This time, it was he that turned away and climbed back onto the ledge. The night consumed the streets. Red lights flared; headlights glared. And there, on the horizon, between the stiff city edifices lining the streets like metallic offerings to an industrial God, just past the end of the road where the sun would rise in the morning, he saw the flicker of gray static. Nothing existed beyond that.

Stay? That would give me no greater pleasure.

But staying in this reality, this world that Patricia dreamed, would be so small. Despite her ability, she could dream up the city.

Stay, he could—he wanted to.

But stay and the human population would never know the true freedom of another reality—this reality.

Foreverland.

"The hosts?" he asked. "How are they doing?"

"You know your answer." Her shadow crept up behind him. "Hope is your albatross, dear."

Hope. It was indeed his bastard.

He was not so desperate to lay his future, his life, on the fragile ice of hope. But never had he thought he would be this old, this close to the edge of dying. He couldn't live forever. *Not in the flesh.*

Unless they found someone with the potential, the brain structure, to host a limitless Foreverland, one that went far beyond the city, past the horizon, one that replicated this planet.

This universe.

A new reality.

Patricia couldn't do it. Neither could he. Even Harold, their son, if he were alive, could only do so much. But someone out there could. There had to be. And that was why he asked, that was why he hoped.

Maybe they would find one before this flesh ended.

Her hands slid over his ribs, laced over his stomach. "I may have found one," she whispered.

"What?"

"A viable host."

"What do you mean? Why didn't you tell me?"

"Hope, dear. I didn't want to stoke it any more than you have. I'm taking a chance, but I've sensed her exceptional potential."

"You have her already?"

She nodded. "I've already had her. She is dreaming her own Foreverland and it is wondrous."

His chest fluttered. "She agreed to host?"

"No. She doesn't know...I had to take her, dear. She has no idea."

It was risky, but abduction was nothing new. "Why didn't you tell me?"

"I wanted to be sure."

"And you're sure?"

She kissed his chin. "A goddess."

Chance was a suspicious mistress, the harbinger of hope. And, try as he might to deny it, he was willing to gamble on a goddess.

Because a goddess is what we need.

"In order for her Foreverland to stabilize," she said, "we'll need her to sleep."

"How long?"

"A year."

A year? They had already squandered so much time on the other hosts. *Is this really our last chance to bring Foreverland to the world?*

He pulled her close.

Their lips met, warm and wet. The wind howled. He held her until it was time to leave her, to return to the physical realm, where his body of aging flesh waited. Her floral scent lingered in his nostrils, but a faint layer of decay sifted through it.

A year, he thought. *One more year.*

A point burned his forehead like a red-hot wire. He reached up, felt the slither, the sting of a wasp as the surgical steel needle slid from his forehead.

He stared through a blurry veil at a cracked ceiling.

A metal door clanged. Two prison guards stepped next to Tyler Ballard's bed and waited. He took his time, letting his feet touch the floor. He rubbed the thin spotted skin on his knobby hands for warmth.

The floral scent faded.

2

Alessandra

The Institute of Technological Research, New York City

"Ladies and gentlemen, can I have your attention?" someone shouted. "The tour is about to begin."

Alex put her phone away. Her husband had texted, wondering how long this visit would last. If he timed his exit from the Guggenheim, he could pick her up without parking.

Journalists crowded to the front. Alex dumped her coffee and moved along the wall, hands still shaking. A cold wave vibrated inside her like a chilled metal coil, a set of eyes scanning her organs. Her teeth damn near chattered, but she wasn't cold.

Nerves?

Through a gap of photographers, she saw the Institute's PR person standing in front of heavy double doors. Like the rest of the lobby, they were forest green, imbued with a sense of calming and healing. She had a sense that beyond those doors it was quite the opposite.

"I would like to welcome you." The small woman's name was Ellen; that's what the badge said. She was in her early thirties, her teeth flashing a white smile. "This is a very exciting day at the Institute of

Technological Research. You were handpicked to see our work up close, to ask our scientists questions. It's through you the public will know what we're doing."

She made it sound like they'd found golden tickets in chocolate bars when, in fact, they gave select tours all the time. But it was by invitation. Alex's invitation came as a surprise. She wasn't a journalist anymore and didn't work for a major newspaper like the others. She squeezed between a young photographer and the wall. Her black hair fell over her face.

She rubbed her hands. Her lips, cold.

"Before we do," Ellen said with her flashy smile, "I want to emphasize a few items. You have all signed a release and agreed to the abovementioned rules."

She held up a sheet of paper.

"Your enhancements, should you have them, will remain off during your stay."

There was a rumble of laughter.

"I know, I know. We're the pioneers of biomite research, but while you're inside the laboratory, we don't want to run the risk of interference."

The punchline wasn't *off*, it was *should you have them*. Every journalist on the planet had a certain degree of biomites—the recently invented and globally distributed artificial stem cells—seeded into their brain to help with memory, data processing and, for some, emotional regulation. And this was where biomites were manufactured. Alex had the maximum allowed by the government. They probably all did.

And that's why I'm cold.

She couldn't remember the last time she'd shut off her internal enhancements. In the last hour, it had become quite clear how much they helped regulate her emotions.

It sucked to be plain human.

"Your identification has an imbedded monitor." Ellen lifted the card around her neck. "Keep it on you at all times."

She added a few more pleasantries before pushing the doors open, leading the group down a stark white hallway. Alex worked her way to the end of the line. The smell of gourmet coffee was quickly replaced with sterilizing solutions and artificial clay—the distinctive odor of biomites. The place felt a bit too much like a 1940s asylum.

Scientists stood in doorways, wearing white lab coats, smiling and waving like they were extras hired to watch a parade.

"Alex?" The man in front of her had turned while walking.

"Oh, hey, Mason. Didn't recognize you."

"*¿Come esta?*" the balding man asked. *How are you?*

"*Muy bien.*" Being Latina, she often entertained bits of Spanish. "How have you been?"

"Soulless."

They had briefly worked together at *The Washington Post*. They caught up on gossip in between stops as Ellen briefed them on the function of the various labs—where new strains of biomites were being developed, how disease would be erased, how biomites would regenerate new limbs.

All the promises of heaven on Earth.

"What are you doing here?" he asked.

"Following the story, what else?"

She didn't want to tell him the truth, that she'd received an unexpected invitation to such an exclusive event. A man named Jonathan Deer. His name was a joke, but she'd done some research and discovered he was employed by the Institute and wanted her to see the new and exciting developments for herself. She was already writing about animal cruelty and was about to expose practices in all sorts of industries.

This wasn't even on her radar.

"Congrats on the book, by the way," Mason said. "Took balls to go into North Korea like that."

"That's what they say." Alex fiddled with her monitor badge.

"This your next project?"

She shrugged. "Maybe."

"Good luck, if it is. Getting inside information out of these people will make North Koreans look like old ladies. No offense."

"You calling me old?"

"Calling you a lady."

"That's a first."

His laughter was more of a grunt. Alex was in her mid-forties but turned heads like she was closer to twenty. Mason knew she was the furthest thing from a beauty queen. Those that didn't were quickly discarded.

They gathered at another set of metal doors. Ellen waited until everyone was crowded together. They were about to enter Wonka's factory, only there wouldn't be a chocolate river. Photographers held up their cameras; reporters lifted their phones.

"So far, you're disappointed." Ellen smiled and many of them laughed. "You didn't come all this way to be greeted by computer programmers and lab directors, or even get a history lesson on biomites, but it was part of the package deal. Now that's out of the way, we can get to the good stuff. I ask that you kindly find a seat in order for us to properly introduce the main thrust of our research. You will be allowed to explore once we are finished."

Someone raised their hand.

"Hold your questions," Ellen interrupted. "There will be time for that. I also want to remind you to avoid engaging in any degree of enhancement activity."

She paused, let that sink in, and then opened the doors.

There were exclamations of surprise, a storm of photography clicking and whirring. Alex could only see black walls above the group. They were reflective, like glass.

"You all right?" Mason was looking at Alex's chest.

She was holding the badge/monitor, but her hands were shaking almost violently.

"I'm cold." Her breath quivered. "Are you?"

He shook his head.

She rubbed her face. They shuffled ahead a tiny step at a time. Mason was the first to get a glimpse of what was around the corner and stopped. Alex bumped into him.

A scientist stood next to a lone table. His hair was unnaturally black; his face thick and square.

It resembled an operating table, but the surface was cushioned. An orangutan rested on it, his long orange hair contrasting with the green cushion, his weight sinking partway into it. There was nothing alarming about being so close to a sleeping primate.

It was the needle.

The long, surgical barrel was positioned in the middle of his forehead.

"Ladies and gentlemen," Ellen was announcing, "if you would kindly find a seat, we can get started."

It was a bit like herding kindergarteners away from an ice-cream truck, but the crowd eventually moved to a small block of chairs. Alex took the last seat in the back row, oblivious to the opposite wall's reflection.

"Good morning." It was the scientist who spoke, his accented English slightly broken. Russian, maybe? "I am Dr. K.P. Baronov, director and lead scientist at the Institute. I trust Ellen has answered your questions up to this point."

Ellen was sitting separate from the group.

"Very good. I know you have many questions, and I will answer them shortly. I also know you are very educated in this process, it was why you were selected for such exclusive tour, but I would like to update you on what we do here and why."

If he thought they were educated on needles in foreheads, he had been misinformed. Alex had seen pictures, but that was it.

"You understand, I am quite sure, that computer-assisted alternate reality, or CAAR, makes a direct connection with the organism's frontal lobe via a surgical probe."

He half-gestured to the orangutan.

"The subject's awareness, or identity if you will, is in some ways transported out of the body and into a dreamlike state. During the inception of such technology, the identity of the subject was put into a computer, but, as some of you know, that is no longer an effective means of creating an alternate reality."

"Why?" Alex's voice shook.

"Mrs. Diosa." Ellen half stood. "Hold your questions, please."

"It is okay," Dr. Baronov said. "It is very good question and why we brought you here. You understand that there are great many benefits that can occur through this method. We use orangutan because it is the smartest primate on earth besides humans. It is our hope that, with our research, this method will soon be accessible to all people."

"What about permanent damage?" Alex couldn't stop herself. Ellen's smile faltered, but the doctor nodded without hesitation.

"Of course, that is good concern," he said. "There was much to learn about this process and the obvious distress of the irreparable damage to one's psychology. It has taken much research to perfect the procedure, but I feel confident you will see the benefits today."

"How many test subjects did you kill? How many went insane?"

"We do nothing illegal at the Institute, Mrs. Diosa," the doctor said. "In fact, we have made tremendous strides in the process. For instance, it will soon be possible to link minds without the needle by harnessing the power of biomite-enhanced brains, like yourselves. Your brain biomites will operate like wireless computers. We strive to improve the quality of life in our test subjects."

Is that why our enhancements are off?

"In old method, the one discovered by Dr. Tyler Ballard, a computer was used to host an artificial environment, the alternate reality, if you will. The computer, though, is not efficient or suitable to respond to the soulful needs of a biological intelligence, like you or me. Or Coco."

He placed his hands on the sides of the orangutan's head.

"Coco is organic host, if you will. A network server, to borrow term from our computer friends. It is Coco that creates world in his mind for others to be transferred. He is host. It is his imagination that creates alternate reality."

"A dream?" Mason said.

"Of sorts." The doctor raised his hand. "Not anyone can become host. There is special quality to how the two hemispheres of the test subject's brain operate, a certain degree of openness and creativity that make him or her ideal candidate. It is this degree that will limit the world he or she can create. For instance"—the doctor waved his arms—"this room is extent of the world Coco can create. Beyond there is nothing, like limit of universe."

"And what do you hope to accomplish?" someone asked. "Some sort of virtual tourism? The animals, or test subjects, will pick up the tab of suffering for our pleasure?"

Ellen stiffened, but the doctor calmed her with an easy hand. "It is all right. I understand your apprehension. It is difficult to see organism with needle in forehead, but I assure you there is no discomfort. To answer question, what we have accomplished already is an improvement in psychological disorder. Test subjects emerge from altered states with increased intelligence and emotional stability."

"Is there really a need to network brains?"

The doctor smiled. "We are stronger and happier when we are united."

"In a new world?"

"Coco sets the rules of his world. It can be fantasy land or just like this."

"For who?"

"That is very good question, Mrs. Diosa." The doctor walked around the table and went to the wall. The black surface mirrored his expression as he reached up and knocked. It rang like glass.

The murkiness began to clear, revealing dark lumps.

The biting chill inside Alex gripped her whole body, pressing the air from her lungs.

Everyone reacted.

There were small cubicles on the other side of the glass walls, like boxes stacked to the ceiling of various sizes with test subjects laying still and prostrate—mice, rats, rabbits, chimps and gibbons. One large gorilla filled the square in front of the doctor. They all had one thing in common.

A needle.

"This is our community," the doctor said. "There is convincing data to show that while their bodies remain stable and alive, their identities are currently in Coco's world. And, more importantly"—the doctor raised his finger—"and this is very important for you to understand, they also contribute to Coco's world. It is like ecosystem, you see. They are integral to Coco and Coco to them."

"And Coco is god," someone said.

"Maybe." The doctor turned to face them. "We are still trying to understand how Coco creates the world's rules, if he even knows he has created them. In other words, are the laws of this virtual world locked into place as they are in our world? Or can he change them?"

"Can they go back to their bodies?"

The doctor chuckled. "Yes, Mrs. Diosa. They wake as if sleeping a wonderful dream."

"With no reality confusion?"

"There is some, yes. The dream state is very convincing. But that is the beauty, you understand. We have created a dream that is inseparable from reality, a dream where time is malleable, where time can go fast or slow. Imagine the possibilities to help soldiers suffering from post-traumatic syndrome? The handicapped can walk, the blind can see.

"The test subjects living in Coco's Foreverland, if you like to call it that, can experience entire lifetime in the span of one minute in flesh. Time, you know, is a dimension. We can live many lives this way, you understand."

"But they return to their bodies?" someone asked. "The right ones?"

The doctor glanced at Ellen, slowly nodding. "Yes, the correct bodies."

"But you said—"

"If you are referring to Foreverland body switches, I assure you there is nothing of that nature occurring at the Institute. It was unfortunate, indeed, that people have used it for such purposes, but such is the nature of many things. Bullets can be used for good and evil, yes?"

The doors opened. The scientists from the labs they passed earlier entered.

"And I think now would be good time to explore, yes?" He lifted his arms, staring at Ellen.

"You may look through the lab," she said. "You may ask questions. Please do not touch anything. As Dr. Baronov stated, this is a living organism."

The group moved slowly at first. Alex, too. Her leg muscles were stiff. She clamped her hands together to keep them from quivering. The journalists spread out and, little by little, cornered scientists with questions. Photographers were madly capturing the scene.

Especially Coco.

Alex hovered at the end of the table, working her way near the orangutan's head. The primate smelled earthy and damp. The cushioned table hugged him. Occasionally, the whir of internal rollers massaged his body, reducing the probability of bedsores. Unless he moved, his muscles would atrophy, the blood would pool.

How many lives have they lived already? Maybe years have passed.

She couldn't help wonder if the doctor was right: this could be the next step in evolution, a new revolution. *The reality revolution.*

Security stood nearby. If she gave in to the temptation and reached out to stroke the orange hair, to touch the eyelids or puffy patch of flesh around the surgical needle, she would surely be removed.

A bead of saliva glistened on the corner of Coco's mouth.

Foreverland. The doctor dared to use that word with what they were doing, but it was probably inevitable. If the public was going to embrace this technology, they would surely associate it with that word. He would need to reinvent it, to purge it of past associations.

Alex had read of Foreverland, of the boys and girls forced to visit a virtual reality. It was an odd name since it was anything but forever, a reality that was limited in space and the imagination of the host.

Unless the right host is selected. According to the doctor, it would then become forever, indeed.

"So he's dreaming?" A photographer was kneeling to capture the needle at eye level. He looked over the camera at Alex. "How do we know *we're* not dreaming?"

"Limits," she said. "There wouldn't be anything outside this room."

The young man raised his eyebrows, seemingly unaffected by the grotesque subject matter. They were in the belly of the experiment, surrounded by victims of research. All the photographer could think about while capturing all of this was the potential of the dream, his youth, his resilience.

"Have you done any human trials?" someone asked.

The many questions and answers bouncing off the hard floor and glass walls lulled. Many of them turned toward Dr. Baronov, waiting for his response to this particular question.

"We have not. We follow the law."

"What about Patricia Ballard?" a journalist asked. "Where is she?"

"Yes, she is here." He addressed the room as a whole, an answer he wanted to be clearly heard. "She has been here for quite some time, but I assure you there has been no experimentation. We are only serving to support her life. I believe you would agree we are best suited for such purpose."

"No research at all?"

"I believe you know her story, so I will not repeat it. It is very unfortunate what she was forced to do and we are respecting her life, as we were asked to do. That is all I will comment, thank you."

Alex noticed doors on the other side of the room, not the ones where they had entered. Guards stood in front of them. Judging by the lock, the guards weren't necessary. But, perhaps, what was behind them wasn't meant to be seen at any cost.

Coco's nostrils flared.

Alex swore she heard something guttural beneath his chin. The photographer was too busy reviewing his shots to notice.

"What about reports that Patricia is still hosting a Foreverland?" someone asked.

"The doctor will not comment further," Ellen announced. "We would like the focus to remain on the process and the future of this technology."

A few more voices chimed in. The journalists had what they came for. Now they were going for the great white shark, the jewel of this story: *Patricia Ballard, the only living human to host a computer-aided alternate reality*.

"Is she currently connected to a CAAR network?" someone asked.

Something moved beneath Coco's eyelids. His eyes moved back and forth as if, for the first time, he was experiencing REM. The saliva spread into surrounding wrinkles.

"How do you respond to reports of using synthetic brain cells on Patricia?" another person shouted. "Could she reach out to other people with brain biomites?"

"Is that why we're not allowed to use our enhancements?" somebody else asked.

"Any alterations we have implemented," Dr. Baronov said, "have been within our code of conduct, the law, and for the good of Patricia Ballard."

"Are you monitoring her inner world?"

"Can you communicate with her?"

"What does her world look like?"

The walls went black and the lights dimmed. The scientists were leaving. Coco's eyes continued to dance.

Alex ignored the chill down her back and leaned closer. Her scalp began to tingle. Warmth trickled from the top of her head, down into her chest, pushing away the chills. She didn't notice that she had stopped shivering.

"We will continue the tour through the staging area, where you will get a glimpse into Coco's inner world on computer monitors," Ellen announced. "Please, everyone, exit to the left where—"

The eyelids popped open.

Dark brown irises stared up.

Alex saw her reflection in the engorged pupils. But behind her she saw not the fluorescent lights or the black walls. It was something entirely different, something she didn't expect, not in a million years.

Palm trees.

"Oh!" Alex jumped back. Her fingers trembled over her mouth. Her chest was buzzing.

Her thighs filled with icy water. Her knees came unhinged.

Mason caught her before she hit the floor.

The energy shifted in the room. Several people ran to her. Mason laid her on her back. A red light reflected off the black walls. Ellen directed traffic. The journalists were ushered out of the room. Mason was the last one.

The red light and buzzing were coming from the identity card around Alex's neck. The monitor had been activated.

Her enhancements were engaged.

3

Alessandra

New York City

The waiting room was nearly empty.

Alex sat in a row of thinly cushioned seats that were linked at the armrests, staring at a properly dressed young man sitting almost statuesque. He was reading a *National Geographic*, an odd choice, so it seemed, for a kid with shoulder-length hair and clothing he likely found at a resale shop. The color of his hair matched the trunks of the palm trees on the front cover.

Later on, she would remember that.

She watched the traffic crawl, from the sixth-story office. Forty-Sixth Street was worse than usual. She attempted to ignore how long it would take to drive home, but her mind kept doing the math. She thumbed through emails on her phone.

Another one from the Institute.

Her lawyer had made it clear for them to leave her alone, that any contact be directed to her attorney. This health screening she agreed to had already eaten a day out of her life. They said she had violated her terms of agreement by engaging her enhancements while on tour.

She explained the nature of her condition, that she was prone to seizures and her biomites had auto-engaged when one was coming.

But the thing was this: she hadn't felt one coming.

If she thought about it, the whole auto-engage incident was nothing she had ever experienced. Even if she hadn't agreed to see a doctor, to document the seizure-induced auto-engagement, she would've gone to see him anyway.

Coco opened his eyes.

He woke up, she was sure of it. But when she told the EMTs, they assured her everything was all right. They even brought the photographer out, the young man that was snapping photos when she *went ape,* as someone said. Not a single shot with the eyes open.

"He never moved," the photographer said.

Her phone rang. "Hey," she answered.

"Still there?" Her husband's voice piped through the Bluetooth cells implanted near her auditory nerve.

"Still here."

"Have you heard the results?"

"No, not yet." She checked the time again. "They're running late."

"Okay." There was a long pause. "How you feeling?"

"Good." She told him about traffic and the rude receptionist that still worked for the biomite doctor. If the doctor wasn't so good, she'd go somewhere else. And, oddly enough, it wasn't far from the Institute. She could see the front door from the lobby if she stood to the right.

"Thought you'd be done," Samuel said. "We're back at the car, suppose we could walk around."

He said *we,* but she didn't catch that. She did notice his voice was a little off; it sounded like he had a cold.

"I'll text when I know, but it could be another twenty minutes or, I don't know, twenty-four hours."

He chuckled. "We'll just double-park. I'm sure the parking fairies will understand."

"We?"

"Mrs. Diosa?" the receptionist called.

Alex stood slowly and paused before walking toward the receptionist, making sure the floor was steady. That was the other thing she didn't tell Samuel, just how unstable everything felt. If she stood too fast or walked too quickly, the world felt...unreliable. Like walking on thin ice.

"You realize it's an hour after my appointment?"

The woman behind the counter pointed at the door to Alex's left without looking, her fingernail tapping on the iPad's glass. She wrinkled her nose like Alex wasn't wearing deodorant.

"Dr. Mallard got called out."

"Then who am I seeing?"

She sighed. "Dr. Johnstone."

"Who?"

Alex continued to stare. The receptionist didn't look up, pointing at the door instead. A sharp letter to Dr. Mallard was in order.

Enhance Your Life.

That was written on the only poster in the examination room, attached to the back of the door, an elderly woman beaming at children on a playground.

Biomites.

The medical industry introduced synthetic stem cells as the cure-all to human suffering, engineered to replace organic cells in the body, to regenerate damaged tissues, immunize cells and heighten senses. And now the possibility of wireless communication.

Some people seeded their legs to become better athletes; some improved a faulty heart. Others used them to replace skin cells; there were even rumors they could change the way they looked. The government only let you have so many biomites, so seeding your skin to look younger seemed more than superfluous.

It was idiotic.

But, hey, enhance your life.

The old woman looked so happy with her white teeth and wrinkle-free smile, like she would live forever and love every minute of it. Because that was what people wanted, they wanted to live forever.

Alex touched the poster, leaning in as if closer inspection would reveal the deep-down dirty secret. She had seen enough dark corners in humanity to know we didn't deserve immortality.

No one wants to live forever.

The door opened. Alex jumped and, regrettably, went, "Eeep."

Dr. Johnstone didn't notice. He was young, athletic and handsome. His hair was brown and curly, a little longer than usual for someone in his profession. And he smelled clean. Almost too clean, as if that was possible.

He introduced himself and apologized for the last minute substitution. She kicked the tires and asked for qualifications. He gave her a rundown.

"Have a seat." He gestured across the table. "Let's talk."

"That sounds serious."

"Everything's fine, Alex. There's nothing to worry about."

He docked an iPad on a round table. The glass surface lit up with an image of a naked brain. Her brain. He swiped his hand across it and various colors appeared. He began explaining how things worked, referring to methodology and seeding rates and recent biomite strains.

"You had a full scan with some biofeedback after your incident at the Institute and there's nothing abnormal. The majority of your biomites seeds are in your brain and the proliferation is proceeding nicely." He touched a thicket of red cottony growth near the frontal lobe. It looked more like a tumor. "Your cognitive functions are at peak performance for a woman your age."

"My age?"

"Mid-thirties, I'm guessing?" He smiled devilishly. He was only off by ten years. "Have you experienced an increase in performance since seeding?"

This was starting to sound like an erectile dysfunction commercial. "So why did I auto-engage?"

He shrugged. "The biofeedback didn't provide an answer, but that's not unusual."

She mentioned seizures, but he was doubtful.

"Have you ever done meditation?"

"No."

"You'll realize that we typically entertain more thoughts than we're aware of. There's all sorts of static going on in our minds, usually just below the surface. The subconscious is deep and mysterious. It's possible you engaged them without knowing."

"Wouldn't biofeedback show that?"

"In most cases. Or maybe you just don't want to remember."

She frowned. She didn't like to mix existentialism with her doctor's appointments. Stick to the facts, and the fact was this: Coco opened his eyes.

"Is there any chance someone could engage my enhancements?"

"What do you mean?"

"Some sort of wireless chatter that crossed over."

He shook his head. "Currently, there's no evidence of person-to-person mindjacking, if that's what you mean."

"But biomites can wirelessly communicate."

"Within your body, that's the extent."

She didn't mention what they said at the Institute, that the needle might become irrelevant due to biomite connectivity. Doubtful he would even believe the needle part.

"Subliminal messaging and thought hijacking are in the movies, Alex. Biomites are meant to enhance your senses, to heal injuries, and prevent genetic disease. They're not magic. You've got to take care of yourself—sleep right, eat right, moderate caffeine and sugar, lower your stress."

"My lifestyle never bothered me."

"Spicy food never used to bother me." He'd used that line before. Something told her he had this talk with a lot of his patients. He scribbled on the iPad. "I'm writing a prescription for anxiety. Take it for a month. It'll help you sleep, calm you down. Let's see how it goes. Come back in a month."

She nodded, but that was a white lie. "Just so we're clear, all the tests were normal?"

"Correct."

"I need an answer for the auto-engage, Doctor. I didn't do it." The doctor shook his head. "Can you at least recognize that I have a history of seizures and that there is a possibility of auto-engagement?"

"It's already in my report."

"And would you also include that there is a chance that biofeedback would not necessarily tell you it was auto-engagement that occurred, that a subconscious thought beyond my awareness could be responsible?"

"That's a small chance, Alex."

"Still a chance."

He sighed. She was gearing up for a lawsuit. "I can do that, if you promise me something. Slow your life down. Biomites don't make you invincible."

He looked at his wristwatch, a round antique with two hands and a second hand ticking across the numbers. *Strange choice for a man steeped in technology.*

"I'll see what I can do."

He left before she could ask about the wristwatch.

The waiting room was empty.

She didn't hesitate leaving the office, the receptionist busy texting or posting photos of quitting time. The hinges on the glass door squealed at a pitch that could shatter diamonds. It was unnerving and unacceptable and that would go in her tersely worded letter to Dr. Mallard, along with her reservations to continue as a patient.

The elevator doors were open and waiting. She punched the button and texted her husband, watching the traffic lights and endless line of brake lights.

Her toe caught something.

It was the *National Geographic* from the waiting room, the one the kid was reading. The corners were bent; creases cut across the tropical island and reflective waters. She picked it up as the elevator opened on the ground floor and rolled it into a tight cylinder.

Fifteen minutes passed. A produce truck had sideswiped a taxi and nothing was moving. The buildings' shadows grew longer and brake lights brighter. Cars honked; people shouted. An ambulance threaded its way down the street.

An hour elapsed.

Alex walked down the street and found the white Camry in the intersection of Forty-Sixth and Ninth. Traffic was slow enough that she climbed into the passenger seat, tossed her stuff on the floor and kissed Samuel on the cheek. Just as she was turning around, before she had a chance to look into the backseat—

Two headlights blinded her.

The driver's door collapsed beneath the bumper of a delivery truck, crushing Samuel's head.

Glass rained down.

Blackness enveloped her. Horns bled into angry shouts and the tinkle of glass. She spun in the darkness like a stuffed animal tumbling in a clothes drier...over and over and over—

"Oh!" Alex snapped her eyes open.

"You all right?" Samuel's voice was distant, almost like he wasn't there. "What's wrong? Alessandra, what's wrong?"

The car was fine.

There was no broken glass. No blood.

Not even a truck.

She climbed out of the car. Traffic angled to get around her, drivers raising their hands or giving her the finger. She stumbled against the car and looked up at the tall buildings, the sky bruised and crumpled. Anxiety lit her chest with dazzling tendrils. At the very same moment, lightning flashed across the sky.

Later she would remember looking at her hands, balling them into fists, and the city rushing past her like a raging storm. She would remember her husband's voice calling through cotton stuffed in her ears, even though the traffic was sharp and clear. Eyewitnesses reported she fell on her knees and pounded the asphalt.

She didn't remember that. Or the flashing lights of the ambulance.

Or seeing her husband.

4

Alessandra

New York City

Pressure.

Her head felt like an overinflated balloon, the rubber skin creaking with each stroke. And voices. There were voices out there.

So many voices.

Each one blurred like a bad recording. Each time, it joined a smudge of color, like blackness streaked with glowing lights, vivid smatterings of pigments that lingered for a moment, just a moment, then were swallowed by the dark until the next one.

Her own thoughts flitted in and out of existence, like an art film splashing random images. A few made sense, but none belonged to the voices. Just before the last stroke of the compressor filled her head, she saw a pair of brown eyes.

Coco.

The balloon popped.

A bright flash swallowed it all.

Alex was spared the pressure and the voices and haunting thoughts.

The world fell into place, all the pieces reshuffled and fit where they belonged. And the universe existed again.

It just existed.

And she did, too.

"We'll be suing," Samuel was saying. "Negligence, pain and suffering."

Through a veil of crusted eyelashes, the flowers were blurry. Brightly colored balls bobbed over them. Alex blinked slowly and the balls turned into helium-filled balloons tied to colored ribbon. She smacked her lips; the corners of her mouth stung.

"Got to let you go." Samuel hovered over her. "Alex? You awake?"

"Water."

He rushed out of sight and returned with a cup. She tried to lift her head. He helped her reach the bendy straw.

"Little sips." He took it away. "Give that a moment."

The water rushed into her parched throat and cooled her insides all the way to her stomach. He stared at her while she looked around the hospital room. His black hair was pushed back, his whiskers casting a shadow over the lower half of his face. And his smile glowed.

She smiled back, couldn't help it, but winced when her lips cracked.

He helped her with two more sips before setting it down.

"Are you feeling all right?" His voice was soft. She couldn't remember the last time it was like that. So soft, so caring.

"How long...have I been asleep?"

"Almost three days."

She lifted her arms and stared at her hands. There were no bandages. Besides feeling a bit shaky—she always felt that way when she was hungry—there didn't appear to be a reason she was in the hospital. Or sleeping for three days.

"They reset your biomites." He ran his hand through her hair. "Do you remember anything?"

The first thing was the pressure and streaking colors. But then the memory of traffic slowly rose from obscurity, the impact of a speeding truck and blaring horn that wasn't there.

And Coco.

"What's your name?" he asked.

She smiled. "Alex Diosa."

"Your full name?"

"Alessandra Diosa."

"That's my girl." He kissed her forehead. "I'll get the doctors."

He gave her one more swallow of water and put it out of reach. The muscles moved beneath his T-shirt. She collapsed on the pillow and watched him go. She was already tired, fighting sleep. She wanted to see the doctors, to see Samuel again.

The ceiling tiles had tiny perforations, like a white slice of the universe. The helium balloons drifted back and forth, crashing like soft metal.

A wave of static passed through the room, like a radio dial turned through a space of nothingness. It wasn't static. It was more like a conglomeration of words.

Voices.

She was suddenly thirsty. It took considerable effort to reach the cup. Her fingers brushed over the surface, finally grasping it. She took large sips, noticing the tracks her hand had left on the table.

And a circle the cup had left in a thick layer of dust.

Alex checked her email and answered voicemail, followed by a nap. There were more doctors and a thousand explanations. She felt partly numb, but that would change.

"What about the voices?" she asked.

"Voices?" the doctor asked.

She waved her hand around, as if this explained her experience. It was like a crowd in a distance, a stadium miles away, the roar swelling, the sounds blending, the voices indistinguishable from each other.

"What about that?"

The doctor nodded. They would run some more tests. Eventually, the voices would fade.

The next morning, she waited to be discharged.

A nurse was supposed to come with a wheelchair. Alex's belongings were already in the truck.

Except a ragged *National Geographic*.

It took a moment; then she remembered. It was on the elevator floor. Someone was looking at it in the waiting room. She was compelled to pick it up. Samuel must've thought she was doing research and brought it up to the room. It had been years since she'd read a print magazine.

The pages flopped in her hands. The cover was a tropical island set in the middle of the ocean, with swaying palm trees and a setting sun. *Not a bad place to be*.

The nurse finally arrived. Alex kept the magazine on her lap and was about to give it to an orderly when she noticed a piece of paper stuck in the middle. The end was torn.

An "A" was written on the end in green ink.

Chills crawled around her neck and tightened, reminding her of the cold chills in the Institute, not like a cool breeze or frozen rain. More like someone watching her.

Alex opened to the centerfold and the bookmark fluttered onto the floor. The nurse stopped to pick it up and handed it forward. She flipped it over.

Alessandra.

Few knew her birth name. Even fewer knew how to spell it. And there it was, written in block letters and wedged into a worn magazine. It wasn't Samuel's handwriting. And he didn't have a green pen, not that she knew. Not that any of that was impossible.

So why did she feel so cold?

5

Danny Boy

An island off the coast of Spain

An espresso waited.

A shirtless young man walked barefoot onto the veranda. He stretched, ribs protruding beneath pale skin, a patch of freckles across his shoulders and upper chest. He flipped the shag of red hair from his eyes and took the cup to the railing.

A tiny sip jolted Danny awake.

Jet lag still tugged at his inner clock, swishing in his head like water in the ears. Rarely did he fly back to the United States, but there were times when the situation was unavoidable. He spent the weekend in New York City and slept so hard on the flight back—a nonstop red-eye—that he hardly remembered boarding.

The Balearic Sea was spread out below, the deep blue water nearly glassy, cutting the horizon sharply where it met the equally blue sky. Beyond was the mainland of Spain and the port of Valencia. Once a month, he took the boat over to walk the open-air markets and meet with people for lunch, maybe dinner.

Business. Always business. And unusual for a sixteen-year-old. But very few sixteen-year-olds owned a thirty-million-dollar villa in the Mediterranean.

His name would not appear in Forbes or any other lists. His money was hidden, dispersed amongst various accounts and names. Danny had good reason to remain anonymous.

He finished the espresso, but it did nothing to clear his head. Maybe yoga would help. He looked more like a skater than a wealthy acolyte of meditation: lanky and rail thin. His breath was slow and purposeful. He could feel the sea below him, the birds above.

A breeze cooled him, sifting through his thick curls, as if God breathed with him. Through him.

Lilac. I smell lilac.

Lying in the corpse pose—the final pose—he thought that was odd since there were no lilacs growing on his property, yet it pervaded the atmosphere, saturated each breath. He heard a bone-china cup placed on a marble table beneath the portico. Sweat beaded across his chest. He exhaled then retreated to the shade.

Another espresso waited.

He took a moment to listen to the birds, to bathe in the mysterious lilac scent before tapping the low-set table. The morning reports danced across the surface in high definition. Life on the island was peaceful, almost solitary. But technology made distance irrelevant.

He sat back and sampled his drink, rubbing the knot on his forehead while scanning the newsfeeds. It itched this morning. The hole had healed, but a scar reminded him of Foreverland. Even if he could forget the itch and ignore the scar, his dreams took him back to the tropical island, put him back in the dark and dank cell where the needle waited. Two years in his past and he still fought the temptation to reach for the needle in his dreams.

We never left the island, someone once told him.

He left the island. He just went back there every night.

He had escaped the island with the seed money to invest in the villa. For that he was grateful but, given the choice, would trade it all to erase those days from his past.

"*¿Quieres algo más, señor?*" Maria stood near the open doors.

"*No, gracias, Maria.*"

"*Muy bien. El correo está sobre la mesa.*" *The mail is on the table.*

"*Gracias.*"

She smiled and began to close the doors.

"Maria, wait!" Danny waved to stop her. He retrieved the colorful bag that he had placed beneath the sink a week ago. She shook her head while he held it out.

"*Para su hijo,*" he said. "*Feliz cumpleaños.*" *For your son. Happy birthday.*

As she stood with one hand over her mouth and the other over her chest, Danny hooked the handles over her fingers. Her son had been in an accident. Danny was paying the medical bills, but the boy might not walk again.

"*Gracias,*" she muttered. "*Gracias, gracias, gracias.*"

He returned to the kitchen. The veranda doors were still open, the curtains dancing as the breeze picked up. He searched the refrigerator for a late morning snack, cutting cantaloupe and pineapple into chunks. The wind scattered the mail across the floor. Danny took a bite and started for the basement, where more business waited.

A thick envelope rested between his feet.

Danny Boy was written on it.

He nearly dropped the bowl. No one had called him Danny Boy in years. Two years, to be exact.

Not since the island.

There was no return address, just a stamp in the corner. The handwriting was shaky, the ink bright green. He held it up to the light, as if it might ambush him. He could feel something inside it, something circular and heavy.

Danny tore it open.

It was a disc about the size and shape of a DVD but as thick as a slice of cheese. The edge was blue, but the reflective surface was scattered with a hundred pinholes. Maybe a thousand. He turned it at angles, watching his blue eyes cross over the constellation. A sticky note was attached to the back. *Build the bridge, Danny Boy.*

A single sheet of lined paper fell out of the envelope, the writing in the same green ink as the address and sticky note. It was four lines:

The Earth I tread

Upon leaves and loam
I fly alone
Where the sand is home.

He read it at least a dozen times and promptly tore it up, and would spend the coming weeks trying to forget who sent it.

Danny woke in heaven.

The clouds floated around him. His stomach rose into his throat, and then he remembered he'd taken a meeting in the immersion room —a hemispherical domed projection room—and fell asleep. He had been dreaming of, what else, the island. Just before waking, he was flying like they often did in Foreverland.

But now he was awake.

He wiped the drool off his lip and called the effects off. The polished wall went blank and he stared at his reflection in all directions.

It must be late; he was still tired. He'd gone for a swim that morning, maybe that was it. He started for the outline of the door.

A bundle of letters was on the floor.

Maria must've dropped them off after seeing him snoozing on the lone chair. This wouldn't have bothered him had his name not been spelled out in big green letters.

Danny Boy.

The foggy remains of sleep blew away, replaced by a shiver. He considered whether to open it or just throw it out like he'd done the first letter. He didn't want to be reminded of the island. He'd escaped that tropical hell with Reed and Zin, but they'd all split up soon after and hardly kept in touch.

To start new lives.

And now this.

The Earth I tread upon leaves and loam could be any of them. For a time, they'd all wandered around lost. *I fly alone* could be Reed because he was an introvert, a loner. When they were on the island, he didn't mix with the other boys, didn't do what he was told. Everyone on the island knew that.

Where the sand is home.

That was the clincher. Only three people in the world knew where Reed's body was buried—his teenage body, the flesh he was born into. That body was dead. But Reed had transferred his identity, his awareness, into Harold Ballard's body when they erased Harold's identity. They did so without guilt, without shame. He was the one doing it to them; he had it coming.

Reed was a teenager in Harold Ballard's old body.

Reed's bruised and broken teenage body was buried on the beach. *Where the sand is home*. Only three people knew that. Danny was one of them. Reed and Zin were the other two.

But why so cryptic? Why the handwritten letter?

Zin was unreachable. The last Danny heard, he was on a vision quest somewhere in India where phones and computers didn't exist.

Reed, though, had moved back to the States. It had been a year or so since he last saw him. Even then he was a little off, dealing with survivor's guilt. They all were. No one could survive the island and be normal.

Maybe someone from the island had located Danny and was preparing to blackmail him. This thought crossed his mind. After all, Danny, Reed and Zin escaped with Harold Ballard's money and left all the boys on the island to be rescued by the Coast Guard. Maybe someone wanted a cut.

Danny could let that happen.

If that was the case, he wouldn't arm himself with a battery of lawyers. He would just walk out of the house and disappear. Money could always be made, but freedom was different. Have that taken away and you realize money means nothing.

The island taught him that.

Danny slid his thumb under the envelope's flap. Another disc fell out, the same as before: a blue edge and reflective sides with hundreds of pinpoints. The holes, he noticed, weren't simply poked or drilled through the thick plastic, they were angled on the inside, conical but at different degrees.

A note was attached. *Build the bridge, Danny Boy.*

Inside the envelope, there was a tri-folded paper, one edge still had ragged tags left from a spiral-bound notebook. Four lines in green ink.

We all dream the same,
A dream that feeds in the dark.
My demons are different than yours,
But we all have them, just the same.

He read it three times. He doubted no more.

We all have demons, Reed once told him. It was the last thing he said before leaving Spain. Zin went on a vision quest to vanquish his demons. Danny threw himself into innovation. But Reed was different.

My demons are different than yours, he told Danny.

"Maps." The immersion room came to life. "Find Reed's last known location."

Reed never left an address, but Danny had tracked the IP address on his emails, cross-referencing his point of access and snooping through his activity.

He was good at that.

The image of Earth rotated on the immersion room's spherical wall and floor until Boston was beneath him. His stomach lurched as the clouds soared up and the city zoomed toward him. His feet were directly over Holworthy Street in Roxbury, an everyday neighborhood with tall, narrow homes.

"Street View."

The details twisted and formed a three-story house, the siding beige, the door new. A white van with a missing hubcap was parked out front. Reed was living on the second or third floor.

Why here, in the middle of the city?

Danny walked near the still form of a man on the sidewalk captured by Google's roaming Street View vehicles. He was wearing a blue sweatsuit, white stripes down the legs. His pit bull was caught sniffing the curb.

"Zoom."

He pointed at the third-floor window and the view pixelated for a fraction of a second before enhancing. Danny clutched at empty space, turning the view to the side of the house. Nothing of interest there, he went up and down the street and got as far as four blocks before returning.

He might not even be here anymore.

He began to call the immersion room off, couldn't waste the day deciphering an amateur poem and wandering the streets of south Boston. But a small detail caught his eye. It was the second story. The curtains in the window were crumpled.

A small flash had been captured, like a reflection. But the angle was all wrong for the sun to be reflecting off the window.

Danny pulled the view closer. The window zoomed but pixelated. It took a few moments for the computer to process the details.

A jar.

He pulled the view so close that the window towered over him, warping across the domed ceiling's curve. He stepped closer. There was something beige inside the jar, hidden beneath the hot flash. At first, he thought it was blurring across from the house's siding. When the details finally crystalized, he recognized the contents.

Sand.

6

Danny Boy

Valencia, Spain

"*Por favor.*" Danny raised his cup.

A waiter arrived, minutes later, with another espresso.

Santiago, a plump Spaniard with bristled mustache and thinning hair, sat opposite Danny. Always dressed impeccably, he kept his collars unbuttoned, where a tuft of curly black hair emerged. His attention was buried in his phone, his thumbs busy. Another email to answer, another report to read. He would stop to rub the birthmark high on his forehead that resembled the state of Florida.

Danny cocked his head. There was something off about Santiago, something he couldn't quite place. *Did he trim his mustache? Dye his hair? Maybe he lost weight?*

He meant to ask him, but forgot. Much later, he would understand what had changed. And why.

From where they sat, Danny could smell the port and see the beach, the flat line of the ocean's horizon. It smelled different, more fragrant. Like a flower. Lilacs again. Children were laughing somewhere. This was a good place to do business.

A good place to live life.

The Spaniard excused himself. Danny crossed his legs and watched a ship cross the horizon before pulling the reflective disc from his pants' pocket. It was too thick to be a DVD or a Blu-ray. There were no grooves or inscriptions. He tried inserting a pencil into the holes, attempting to turn the disc like a template but they were too small. He even compared the pattern to various constellations, but nothing matched.

All he saw when he looked at it was his reflection. *Build the bridge, Danny Boy*.

He couldn't build a bridge with a disc, unless it contained plans that he hadn't figured out. Maybe Reed would send a special disc reader, but why all the clues? He only needed to pick up a phone.

Santiago was across the restaurant. Danny sank the disc deep into his pocket. He was nearly finished with his drink when Santiago returned with a tall American woman. "*Señor Daniel*," he said, "*esta es María*."

Danny stood.

"Mary." The woman reached across the table. Her grip was strong.

She dropped the leather bag slung over her shoulder. The waiter was at the table before she could sit. In Spanish, she ordered a drink. Her words tumbled off her tongue like misshaped stones, as if she looked it up in a translator only moments earlier.

Santiago asked about her trip, how she like Valencia so far. She answered with a bright, white smile, looking at Danny more often than Santiago. Her blonde hair was short and smooth, the kind you'd see on a billboard. Danny found himself smiling.

She returned his grin. When she did, her eyes sparkled like a car was behind him, the headlights forewarning him.

"How old are you?" she asked.

"Does it matter?"

"My clients are about to invest a billion dollars with your company."

"I don't need their money."

Santiago laughed nervously. "Danny's record is well established," he said in his most affected English, an accent that was effectively sophisticated. "His age, I assure you, is of no consequence."

She nodded while smiling. She'd flown the better part of a day to negotiate when they could've met in the immersion room. *How do Americans say?* Santiago had said to Danny when he arranged the meeting. *We meet old school.* She wanted to sit in front of him, look him in the eyes and sway him with charm, perhaps nudge him and later bully him with facts.

The waiter returned with a drink.

"Danny Jones." She used his full name, the name he now used. Danny Jones owned a thirty-million-dollar villa off the coast of Spain.

Danny *Forrester* left the island.

"The wonder boy with no past," she said. "The boy with no family, a teenager that, according to Santiago, learned Spanish within months of arriving."

Danny looked at his companion. Santiago shrugged. He did become fluent in Spanish, but she had it wrong. It was two weeks.

"You've invested extremely well and managed to stay out of the spotlight for a sixteen-year-old. What was it you said, Santiago? He is the reincarnation of Einstein with a taste for technology instead of stars."

"I, uh..." Santiago rubbed his birthmark.

"He's right." Danny lifted his cup. "And would you do business with Einstein at sixteen?"

Her smile was less flashy, but genuine. Had she sized him up already? She lifted her coffee.

All three drank.

"I suggest you drop the name 'Danny'," she said. "Sounds like a kid I went to summer camp with."

Santiago filled the awkward silence with the wonders of Valencia while Señorita Maria nodded, occasionally flicking a glance at Danny. He was sixteen years old; she was right about that. And most sixteen-year-olds were full of hormones, enslaved by them.

Not Danny.

There was a famous study called the Stanford Marshmallow Experiment that measured children's intellect with a proposition. The experimenter put a single marshmallow on the table. If the child could wait fifteen minutes without eating it, he or she would get two marshmallows. Those that waited the longest had grown up to be more intelligent.

Danny would've outlasted them all.

"I would love to see your city," Mary interrupted Santiago, "but I'd like to discuss a few matters with Danny."

She launched into her presentation with ease—nonchalant and conversational. Her clients were aiming to become the largest manufacturer of biomites, not just in quantity but innovation. They saw the artificial stem cells as the future of humankind, the next step in evolution, the perfecting of the human body.

Immortality was in reach.

Danny watched her present the facts of cost and production and risk. He wondered how old she was. How many biomites had she already injected into her face, smoothing out the wrinkles and glossing over the rough spots, waxing her intelligence to become one of the world's best—and most beautiful—negotiators?

Her eyes were magnetic blue, the kind of blue reserved for the glassy sea on a clear morning. Her lips were perfectly painted, her teeth pearly white. Her eyelashes fluttered. It was hypnotic. Give her enough time, and perhaps every man would melt.

Eventually, there was a flicker.

It was a small change in the way the light danced in her eyes, like the headlights behind him turned on the high beams. He turned around. It wasn't a reflection. There was no light behind him.

It was as if a piece of color had gone missing, a pixel of blue absent from her left eye. This cancerous gray dot bled out to the surrounding iris just to the side of the pupil, bleaching the pristine color.

It continued into the white.

The gray pixilation oozed over her eyelid and consumed her eyelashes, up into the hollow of her eye socket and over the bridge of her nose. Danny slid his chair back and refrained from recoiling as it soaked outward like an inky stain of gray static, eating a hole through the smooth complexion, turning Mary's face into a mechanical faceplate spouting words that were just sounds, data that were just numbers.

She glanced at Santiago.

The gray spot wasn't eating her face. It was chewing a hole in the fabric of space. As if she wasn't there. As if nothing was there.

Nothing at all.

And it was nothing that howled inside him. He felt it in his gut, heard it deep in his subconscious, calling like wolves. Calling him to be with it. To be nothing.

To be Nowhere.

"Señor Danny Boy?"

Danny snapped back into the present moment. Santiago stared with wide eyes. Mary was beautiful again, not a spot on her cheek or in her eye, as if nothing had happened, the fabric of space just as it should be.

They were looking at someone next to the table.

"Señor Danny Boy?" a boy asked, then dropped a letter on the table. This was a standard-sized envelope, the kind that would contain a letter, not a disk. Danny was transfixed by the green lettering.

Danny Boy.

"Hey!" He shoved away from the table. "*¡Espera!*"

"Danny." Santiago swiped at his arm.

Danny jumped out of reach; the chair clapped onto the floor. He leaped over the stone wall onto the sidewalk. The messenger was already pumping the pedals on a beach bike, bouncing over the curb and around a building. Danny leaped around traffic, swinging his arms with the letter squashed in his fist. He was gaining on the young man, whose coarse black hair fluttered over his shoulders.

He cut down an alley.

Danny gave chase through a crowd and emerged on the road running parallel to the beach. His side stitched with stabbing pain; he struggled to breathe. The boy was gone.

He looked at the wrinkled letter damp with sweat. *What is happening?*

Had someone tracked him down? One of the old men, perhaps? They certainly would want revenge. Danny had taken everything from them. *Everything.* But if one of them had survived, managed to elude the authorities that arrived when Danny, Reed and Zin had escaped, they wouldn't bother with poems or clues; they would've come straight away, kidnapped him while he slept. And even if they did send letters, they wouldn't know what to write.

The sand is my home.

Danny sat on the beach, watching sailboats slice across the horizon, the gulls hover over the water. Children ran past. He tore the letter open.

Another four lines. Another poem.

He read it over and over, hoping repetition would ease the cold fear rising. Like those days on the island, trapped in the cold concrete room of the haystack when the needle dropped from the ceiling, when he felt like crying.

When sometimes he did.

He didn't go back to the restaurant, didn't conclude business. He walked to the port where his ship waited. His captain took him back to the house. Santiago would later call him, but he wouldn't answer, wouldn't return his messages. Mary would stay in Valencia another week before returning to the United States, and her clients would refuse to invest with an unstable teenager, no matter how bright and promising.

But none of it would matter.

Every question contains its answer,
When the children sing and stare,
When you look into the blue,
And see the endless Nowhere.

Nowhere was the opposite of somewhere. But for those that survived the island, it was more than that. It was the place where existence ceased, where space became a maddening array of gray static, complete chaos.

He saw it in Mary's eye, felt it howl inside him. It beckoned; it threatened.

As Reed knew it would.

7

Danny Boy

An island off the coast of Spain

Danny swiped the bathroom mirror. Beads of condensation raced to the sink. His irises were blue with dark bands radiating out like spokes. No gray.

No Nowhere.

He held the note, the edges damp in his hand. *When the children sing and stare.* Just before someone was sent to the Nowhere, they had a blank stare. Is that what it meant? *When you look into the blue.* Did he mean the blue in her eyes? The blue on the edge of the disc.

What bridge?

He shook his head and took a deep breath. He was reading too much into it. The symbolism could mean anything.

Every question contains its answer.

"*¿Señor Daniel?*" Maria knocked on the bedroom door. "*Señor Santiago es aqui.*"

"*Un momento!*"

A small scar was centered between his eyes, an inch above his eyebrows—the mark was innocence lost. Danny knocked on the mirror and stared at his hands. Ever since he returned from New York, everything felt a little off. Was it his imagination? He had the sense of skating on a frozen pond when spring had already arrived.

And he could feel the ice thinning.

Danny got dressed to meet his mentor on the veranda.

A cloud of smoke hung around Santiago's head.

He was admiring the million-dollar view. Danny watched him from beneath the shade of the pergola. The smoke polluted the ever-present smell of lilac. He hadn't seen the Spaniard since he abandoned them at the café. Santiago sensed the eyes on him and turned.

"Cigar?" Santiago waved the Cuban. "You are too young to smoke, forgive me."

His laughter cut across the wind.

"Sit in the shade?" Danny said.

The heavyset Spaniard shuffled beneath the pergola, the cigar clenched between his teeth. Maria stood in the doorway. Danny asked for water.

"Scotch," Santiago said. "Neat."

They sat opposite each other. Santiago's laughter rumbled on for no apparent reason. He did this for one of two reasons: he'd been drinking, or he was nervous.

And one never occurred without the other.

"Danny," he said. "Danny, Danny. *¿Cómo estás, mi amigo?*"

"*Muy bien.*"

"*¿Huh? ¿Si?*" His laughter faded. He rolled the cigar between finger and thumb, the smoke hanging over the Florida birthmark. Something was off. It was like two images that didn't quite line up.

"I worry about you, Danny. I worry."

"*Pero innecesario.*"

"Oh, I think it very necessary, *amigo*. You are so young and the world so big. You grow up so fast, and I worry. You have everything ahead of you, Danny—whatever you want. *¿Comprende?*"

Danny nodded. *I understand.*

Maria brought their drinks and a bowl of fruit. Santiago took tiny sips, sighing. He worked the cigar like a child casually hitting a pacifier. Danny took an ice cube and ran it across his forehead. They spoke about the stock market, about potential investment opportunities as well as the current ones.

When lunch arrived, Santiago shook his empty glass. When Maria brought a second drink, he bit a grape in half. "There is the matter of Mary and her investors."

Danny winced. It took a moment to comprehend what caused it. His forehead tingled. He connected the sensation to a word.

Investors.

The Investors, they were the old men that brought them out to the island, the old men that meant to steal their bodies. That word would always sting. He put on sunglasses, the world feeling a bit too bright.

"You see, your escapade"—he waved his knife—"the running you did at our meeting has caused...consternation, Danny. It was childish. People do not care to give money to a child."

"I won't explain myself, Santiago. There will be other investors, you see. Entrepreneurs are interested in one thing—money. They don't care who makes it for them."

"May I ask, what was the letter?"

"A girl, in town." The lie seemed fitting, less secretive. He was grateful for the sunglasses.

"*¿Amiga?*" The laughter slowly rumbled. "This is what I mean, Danny. *Amigas* are for boys, not men."

"Then the world is run by boys!" Danny's laughter was louder than Santiago's.

"Perhaps this is so. But, lucky for you, I saved this meeting with your investors. Mary will meet again on the promise you wait to chase your *amigas* after lunch."

"How do you work such magic?"

Santiago shrugged. "They know me, Danny. They trust me. I tell them to trust you because I believe in you. Since day one, I believe in you."

"Why?"

"I know a jewel when I see one. I recognize talent."

"*¿Cómo?*" Danny pressed. "What talent do you see?"

"You always ask the right questions, that's what I like about you. You make good choices." He pointed with the knife, chewing with his mouth open. "You are one in a million, Danny."

When lunch was finished, Santiago pushed away from the table and lit a second cigar. He took a cappuccino from Maria and puffed blue rings.

"No more running, Danny." He pointed with the cigar wedged between his fingers. "The investor will meet us tomorrow at the same restaurant. No more letters and such, no interruptions or we meet right here, on the veranda." He thumped the table. "They want your ideas, Danny. You are visionary. You will help bring a new world into one that is tired and old. *¿Comprende?*"

New world?

This was a new pep talk. Santiago was always about enjoying the fruits of life. By fruits, he meant wine, he meant women. Not a tired world or a new one.

It was getting hot, even in the shade. Maybe it was the smoke. Danny rubbed another ice cube on his forehead.

"Everything is yours, Danny. And when you are old enough, we will enjoy cigars together and talk of our triumphs. We will drink good liquor and live very long. A new reality."

Reality? "You mean new world?"

"Same thing, Danny. You have everything you want. *¿Comprende?*" Santiago's laughter returned. He lifted his cup. "*¿Por qué nunca dejar?*"

Danny choked.

Santiago didn't notice. His head was back, a column of blue smoke streaming from his lips. It reminded Danny of something long forgotten, a chimney on the tropical island that belched smoke when one of the old men had successfully stolen another body. *Smoked* is what they called it. *Someone just got smoked.*

"What did you say?" Danny said.

"*¿Que?*"

"What did you say, just a second ago?"

Santiago thought a moment, dashing his ashes. "*¿Por qué nunca dejar?*"

It was an innocent phrase that sank its knuckles so far under Danny's ribs that it robbed his breath. He gulped small bites of air, tears brimming behind the dark lenses.

"The bathroom calls." Santiago excused himself.

Danny raised a hand but didn't wait for the Spaniard to return before going to the patio's wall. He ran the last couple of steps, vomiting over the edge. He rinsed his mouth, wiped his eyes and tried to appear normal.

Those words, the very same words, had been uttered before.

He'd heard those words on the island, long ago, to describe Foreverland—the imaginary land where he and all the boys were forced to go, where their dreams had come true, where they got everything they wanted so they would never return. They would leave their bodies behind, empty of awareness.

Foreverland was the trap they couldn't resist, so wonderfully everything a boy could want. The old men told them so. They said exactly what Santiago just said in Spanish.

Why would you ever leave?

"Lunch tomorrow, Danny?" Santiago waved from the house. "I come pick you up."

Danny agreed.

It was the second lie he told that day. He wouldn't be there when the Spaniard arrived. He wouldn't go to lunch. Reed sent those letters.

Now he had to find him.

8

Alessandra

Upstate New York

"*¡Hola! ¡Hola!*"

The front door opened, followed by rustling bags and heavy footsteps. Alex wiped her hands on an apron and turned just in time to see a petite woman come at her with arms wide open.

"Ooo," the woman dressed in brown moaned, clenching her daughter in a long hug that betrayed her inner strength. "*¿Cómo estás?*"

They hugged beneath a rack of stainless steel pots and pans, an embrace Alex tried to relinquish twice.

"*Bien, Madre. Bien, bien, bien.*"

Madre pulled back and stared at her daughter, searching for the truth. Alex took the old woman's hands and kissed them like she did when she was a child. Madre's eyes teared up. She held Alex's hands to her cheeks and kissed them over and over while muttering prayers.

An unsteady march came down the hall.

"Ah, there she is." Her stepfather, a retired farmer, limped into the kitchen, the uneven gait the result of a tractor rolling on top of him. He wore boots made for cutting wood because you never know when a pile might need tending. The only thing bigger than his boots was his belly and, of course, his personality.

"Can I get an autograph?" Hank asked.

Alex hugged him. His beefy hands were cut from bucking bales and manhandling ornery hogs. He lifted her onto her toes.

"*Bonita.*"

"*Gracias.*" She laughed. "You're early."

"No traffic," he said. "Your mother fell asleep."

"So you drove 100?"

"Not quite."

Alex took the paper bag and placed the bottle of wine on the island counter. Hank went to find a comfortable chair and a television because, as he always said, driving makes you tired.

"You are cooking?" Madre asked.

"I follow the directions on the box."

"But that's still good, you know. The apron and everything is good." Madre patted her hand like before, this time without the prayer.

Alex began cleaning dishes. She could only take so much of that look, the one Madre lovingly saddled onto her children. *Look what you do to me,* Madre would say when something bad happened. Her brothers, perhaps, deserved as much, but none of the guilt stuck to them. And Alex, the fallout of her older siblings fell on her like ashes of a well-tended fire that had once burned fiercely.

It took three years of therapy for Alex to unwind the weight of Madre's suffering. That was why Samuel didn't call her from the hospital, why Alex didn't contact Madre until she was home, when everything was normal. The old woman no longer said those words, not to Alex. But her eyes still spoke them, the creases on her forehead were very clear.

Look what you do to me.

Alex lifted her hand halfway to her head before stopping. She thought the voices were beginning to swarm, but it was just the lawnmower. That strange crowd of voices, young voices like children, still came in waves. If she listened for them, they were always there, in the distance. The doctors had no explanation, just to be patient.

Hank came back into the kitchen and asked for a corkscrew. Madre refused to let him open the wine. They argued while he pulled the cork out.

Cheese and crackers were served and nearly gone when Samuel finished mowing. Madre's worry lines had faded in the warm glow of red wine. Now there was just laughter, and a warm feeling infused the room, like sunshine beamed from the light fixtures. The last time Alex felt like that she was very young, before she was saddled with worry and declarations.

A sunbeam sliced through the window; a heavy cloud of dust danced in the light when she noticed the distant chatter, like a crowd on the other side of the fence, the garbled words muffled in the trees. She paused at the sink and looked into the backyard until the voices faded.

Samuel had turned the yard into paradise. Almost everything was blooming yellow, her favorite color. Butterflies and bees and dragonflies came to visit and never seemed to leave. And the scent of her favorite shrub filled the kitchen, violet flowers in full bloom.

Lilac.

Hank dropped the last card on the pile and they added up the points. Alex wrote down the scores while Madre gathered the cards to shuffle. Samuel excused himself to find another bottle of wine.

"When are you going to start writing?" Hank asked.

"When I'm ready."

"Well, how long does that take?"

"I'll know."

"You know what they say about getting back on the horse?"

"Wear a helmet?"

Hank bellowed laughter like a distant relative of Santa. Madre arranged the cards all in one direction, tapping the deck on the table, and began the ritual of shuffling exactly seven times. She placed the deck in front of Hank.

"Whatever happened to the piece you were working on, the one on animal abuse?"

"Hank." Madre knocked on the deck. "More cards, less talk."

He nodded and dutifully cut the deck. Madre began dealing. Alex didn't answer. She didn't want to talk about writing or hospitals or accidents. She caught Samuel's cards before they slid onto his chair, and waited for his return.

"What's done is done, Alex," Hank said. "You can't fix the past."

A cantankerous old fart, Hank liked politics and drama. Not the usual modus operandi for someone that grew up in the country. *If you're not pushing buttons,* he once said, *you're not living.* Hank insisted that stones were not meant to sit and rest, but to turn over to see what was hiding beneath. Sometimes that meant you had to throw a few.

"I'm not trying to fix the past, Hank. Just leaving it where it belongs."

"But you're not writing. Sounds like the past is still in the present."

"Stop," Madre hissed. "Talk is over, old man."

"I'm just saying." He gave his patented shrug and leaned back with a slight smile. It was the equivalent of a boxer taunting an opponent with his chin. "Alex is a writer. She's not writing. So is she Alex?"

"Bones don't heal overnight," Alex said.

"Or maybe they're not broken."

"You still limp."

He patted his hip. "That's hard living, *chica*."

Alex bristled. He only called her *chica* when he was bored, his way of saying she hit like a girl.

"You could get it fixed," she said.

"It's not broke."

"Then why do you limp?"

"Old men are supposed to limp."

"You're saying your past makes you who you are? Sounds like someone isn't present."

"I'm saying I'm exactly who I should be. Old men die and babies suck on mother's milk."

"Enough." Madre slapped the table. "No more talk of *niños*. Look at your cards before I take them."

Lines carved her forehead, but these were different than the ones

Alex feared. This expression Madre reserved for her husband, when he forgot to take out the trash or pushed arguments too far.

He scooped up his cards, adding a twinkling wink that said meet me out back later and we'll finish this. Samuel came back with a fresh bottle and filled all the glasses. The game resumed; cards were played.

Jazz streamed through the speakers and somewhere outside children were playing. Samuel began to whistle and Hank asked him to stop and Madre told them to behave themselves. The hand was almost over when someone said.

"Don't forget who you are."

"What?" Alex said.

"Your play," Hank said.

"No, what'd you say?"

The others looked confused. "It's your play, Alex," Samuel added.

"No, he said something else." *Don't forget who you are.*

Alex waited. She wanted to push more, but Madre's lines of impatience could turn to worry, so she dropped a card. Madre smiled, played her trump cards, and the hand ended soon enough.

Samuel corralled the deck.

Alex noticed the subtle tracks on the polished surface, a light dusting. She dragged her finger across the table, wondering where all the debris was coming from.

"Some things you can't forget," Hank said. "Or shouldn't."

But when she looked up, the old man was finishing his wine. And Samuel was eating a cracker. Madre tallied the points.

She didn't ask him to repeat it. Instead, she excused herself to the bathroom.

Madre didn't need to see her breakdown.

Alex went to the bathroom then hauled the recycling out to the garage.

She didn't explain why she felt compelled to do it before the card game was over, just called out from the kitchen and walked out before anyone could argue.

Hank got to me.

The old man never argued with Samuel. Maybe because Samuel was a lawyer, a damn good one, or a man. Or maybe because Hank knew Alex would give him a good fight but, in the end, he'd get the final word. She couldn't recall anyone ever winning a debate with Hank, whether it was politics or Chinese checkers.

But she'd never heard him pretend not to say things.

She didn't imagine that. He wasn't pretending. He couldn't have said it because *he had a throat full of wine.*

She took a deep breath, made a detour through the backyard, and cleared her mind. Despite the cloudless sky, it was brisk. She hugged herself against the chill and wished she would warm up. She needed to clear the clutter in her head. Maybe a nap. Sleeping had been doing her good lately. She always woke up refreshed and happy.

And happy wasn't a word she wore often.

She dumped the recycling and crossed the driveway. The neighbor across the road waved from his mailbox. Alex waved back and slowly made her way out to the curb.

The street was lined with mature elms that arched overhead. Despite the dappled shade, it was warmer out there, almost ten degrees. She already felt good inside and out. Must've been the fresh air. *Sometimes a short walk is the remedy.*

There was a wad of envelopes stuffed in the mailbox; she sifted through them on the way back, half of it junk. The garage door was still open. She tossed all of it into the recycling bin but noticed the address on a large envelope.

Alessandra.

A wave of gooseflesh raced down her arms. Alex looked around, even at the blue sky. She'd done a story once, when she first started as a journalist for *The Washington Post*, on paranoid schizophrenia. One of her subjects insisted there were cameras always watching, satellites that recorded everything. He described how he got this feeling when the spies were watching him, how his joints tickled and the back of his throat itched.

She never forgot that.

She tore the envelope open. Several glossy sheets fell on the concrete. It was from a travel agency. The fliers advertised package deals all over the world with illustrious beaches, endless sand and swaying palms on uninhabited islands.

She flipped the pages over, admired the views and, one by one, dropped them into the recycling bin. But they seemed familiar. *Where have I seen these?*

It was the last page.

White sand was on one side of the island and cliffs on the other. The view was from above, taken from a helicopter or a drone. *Maybe even a satellite*.

She'd seen this photo, seen this island.

"Alex!"

She dropped the photo. Samuel was on the back porch.

"You all right?" he asked.

"Yes, sure. Just...picked up the mail."

"You want to finish the game?"

"Yes, of course."

How long had he been standing there? Was that what she felt?

She wadded up the page and tossed it. Of course she hadn't been there. She'd never been to a remote island in her life. She'd seen a thousand photos of beaches. She climbed the steps and noticed the red tulips in the bed Samuel had mulched.

He stood with the door open. When she turned around, the tulips were yellow. Maybe she needed to schedule another appointment with Dr. Mallard or Dr. Johnstone. She wasn't just hearing things.

She was seeing them, too.

9

Alessandra

Upstate New York

The tulips' petals had fallen.

They rested on the mulch in various degrees of yellow, faded by sunlight and age, signaling the end of spring. Alex snipped the tulip stalks. She had plans for the backyard. A row of fruit trees against the fence and a vegetable garden in the corner.

She entertained thoughts of moving to upstate New York or even western New Jersey, where they could purchase acreage. Samuel could still get to the city and, should she decide to write again, she could get to her agent.

For now, she just wanted to be home.

There was a hole in her glove and dirt was getting under her fingernail. She went to the garage and found another pair, almost new, in the bottom of a bucket, but they were too small even for her hands. They were for a child.

Alex searched under the workbench for another pair of gloves. She noticed her briefcase stuffed inside a plastic bin. It was on top of a stack of papers, empty cups and sweaters. Samuel must've cleaned out her car.

It had been months since she drove her car. In fact, she hadn't even left their property.

The leather smelled like work. Life was smooth now, like gliding over black ice. She hadn't seen her briefcase since getting out of the hospital, hadn't even thought about it. Half-written notes and unsigned contracts were mixed with traffic tickets.

The small raincoat was at the bottom of the plastic bin. She pulled it out and something fell. It was the *National Geographic*, the one from the doctor's office. She hadn't seen it since the hospital.

The bookmark.

She'd forgotten about that. Her name had been written on the piece of notebook paper in green ink. It was rather shocking at the time. No one ever used her full name, not outside the family at least. Now it was gone.

She smoothed the wrinkles on the cover. The island was small and isolated in an endless ocean. A sense of déjà vu passed through her. The issue was a few years old, which would explain the wear. She licked her fingers and flipped to the cover story.

Places You'll Never Want to Leave.

The piece was dominated by photos of remote tropical islands. *Heaven does exist*, said one blurb. *It's just hard to get to*.

The photos were stunning, but the centerfold resolved the sense of déjà vu. That was the one from the travel agency, the piece of mail she'd opened when Madre and Hank were visiting.

The exact same photo.

There were no credits. She turned to the front, went through all the names where the photographers were properly recognized, but nothing was credited for the tropical island.

"There you are."

Alex dropped the magazine. Her heart thudded. Despite the clear sky, thunder faded in the distance. Spring showers were coming.

Samuel had the mail in one hand, a tall glass of tea in the other. He handed her the glass and shuffled through the mail, dropping most of it in the recycling after ripping the junk in half. One of them was a large white envelope addressed with green ink, her name in big block letters.

Alessandra.

"You all right?" he asked.

"Did you clean out my car?"

"Someone had to."

He began searching the shelves for car wax. Alex remained in the garage, staring at the recycling bin. The return address was a travel agency. She couldn't remember the name of the other one, but they had to be the same.

It was getting hot and stuffy. The afternoon heat was picking up fast. She pressed the glass of iced tea against her forehead.

"Where'd you get this?" Samuel held up the *National Geographic*.

"It was with my stuff."

He thumbed through it, frowning. His complexion turned a shade darker, eyebrows protruding. She felt the heat of his anger and took an involuntary step back.

"I didn't put that in there."

She shrugged. "I didn't clean out the car."

"Where'd you get a three-year-old magazine?"

"It was from the doctor's office. I had it with me in the hospital, remember?"

He fanned through the pages. The bookmark fluttered out from the last couple of pages. It landed on the workbench, her name staring up at him in green ink.

Green ink. The travel agency envelope was also lettered in green ink. Samuel grunted. Something twisted inside her when he made that sound, like predators were nearby.

"You do this?" He held it up.

Did he not remember the magazine? He had to bring it from the car to the hospital room.

But that didn't mean he read it, didn't mean he pulled the bookmark out. But the way he was holding it, the way his eyebrows protruded told her he didn't. And he really wanted to know who did.

"Yes," she said. "Just marking a spot."

"When did you start using your full name?"

"I was playing around."

"Playing?"

"Yeah."

"With your full name?"

"I don't remember a lot of what happened then, Samuel. Is something wrong?"

He was nodding. It wasn't her handwriting, and he knew it.

"Where'd you get a green pen?"

"It was at the hospital."

She avoided stepping toward the recycling bin. Half the travel agency's envelope was turned up. He'd obviously forgotten about it or wasn't paying attention when he ripped it.

"Just seems odd you would write this," he said.

"I'm a little confused. Is there something you should be telling me?" She found her footing, like she sometimes did in the middle of a debate with Hank. Sometimes a good offense is a good defense. "It's an old magazine, Samuel. Here."

She placed it in the recycling bin, perfectly covering any trace of green ink. "You keeping that for evidence?"

He was still pinching the bookmark. When he didn't move, she snatched it from his fingers and threw it away.

"Could you haul a bag of mulch to the tulip bed?" she asked. "My back is a little achy."

He thought about it, then smiled. It was a forced smile, one that never quite reached his eyes. She pretended to search for gloves while he took a bag out to the yard. She quickly grabbed the junk mail and hid it on a shelf of old paint cans, making sure the magazine stayed in the exact same position.

The spring shower that, minutes earlier, sounded nearby had cleared up.

The sky was cloudless and blue.

Alex quickly tore the large envelope open.

More vacation fliers. She quickly found the one she was looking for. It was the overhead view of an island with white sands on one side, cliffs on the other.

She could've held it next to the *National Geographic* centerfold; they would be identical. *National Geographic* wouldn't use stock photos. Unless the agency pilfered it, this was highly unusual.

The Land of Forever, the title said in the corner. *Why would you ever want to leave?*

Later that night, she and Samuel watched a movie with a bottle of wine. They slipped into bed. She waited until he was snoring, and then waited another half an hour.

The old wooden steps creaked on the way up to her office above the garage. She turned on the computer, the first time in months, and typed a search.

Land of forever.

The result was at the top, the number one hit.

A gust of wind hammered the house. The windowpane creaked.

She swallowed a hard lump, looked at the door and listened. A familiar sensation buzzed in the back of her head, sending up the small hairs on her arms. Her journalist instincts lit up. Something was about to happen.

She clicked the link.

Foreverland.

10

Tyler

ADMAX Penitentiary, Colorado

Gramm raked his fingers through his hair and counted the stray follicles. He always counted, sort of a way to show his respects to his receding hairline.

A former chemist, his hair used to be thick and wavy and fall over his ears, curled just above his eyes. He was known as *the surfer scientist.* But twenty years in the United States Penitentiary knocked the surfer out of him. Now it was thin; now it was gray. Now he watched the surfer scientist disappear one follicle at a time.

He started up the metal stairs, his footsteps clanging on the treads. Two pairs of footsteps trailed behind him. Gramm waited on the third floor.

Melfy, a short, heavyset African-American guard, carried a tray with a bowl of soup and a carton of milk. Her tight curly hair was cut close to the scalp, but there were signs of gray mixed in. Gramm noticed those things.

Drake, the second guard, pulled himself up the steps, his boots clobbering the metal treads. The six-foot-something, pasty-white male still smoked on his days off. He wheezed on the top step.

Gramm stared at the flabby piece of work, raking his hair five times. It would cost him twenty follicles. They passed through a checkpoint without pausing. Green metal doors were on each side, the paint chipping from the surfaces, white numbers painted below sliding slots. The stringent odor of cleaning supplies stung his nostrils.

They stopped at the last green door.

"Hold on." Gramm raised his hand.

He took several slow breaths. His heart rate only became more violent. It didn't matter how many slow breaths he took, it wasn't going to slow down.

He nodded.

Drake threw the door open, the scent of potpourri wafting out. Beneath the floral aroma was the smell of old skin and decay, like something dying a very slow death.

One that was thirty years in the making.

A cafeteria tray sat on a cluttered desk, the food cold and untouched. Gramm waved Melfy inside. She replaced the tray with the one she was carrying, the soup still warm and spilling over the edges.

There was a bed against the wall. It was thick and wide and humming. Gramm took the chair from the desk and sat down, facing the bed and the old man sleeping on it. Dr. Tyler Ballard looked to be one hundred years old, but Gramm knew he wasn't quite eighty.

The old man wore a gray uniform with a number stitched over the right breast. It was loose and wrinkled, oddly matching the thin skin that sagged from his cheeks and chin. Even his eyelids were paper-thin, the bulge of irises moving beneath them.

Gray and withered, only the slow rise of his chest and the fluttering of his lower lip suggested he was alive. Only the rosy flesh around the needle in his forehead was other than gray.

Drake, the fat guard, wheezed like a long-distance runner finishing a marathon, his lungs wet like a recovered drowning victim. He stepped forward with that rheumy gaze, the long-term effect of a mental hostile takeover, a man with a biomite brain that had been hijacked years ago. The imbecile was dull and trainable, which made it that much easier for Dr. Ballard to take over the fat man's biomite-laden brain and reprogram his thoughts to do whatever Gramm needed. Still, the oaf couldn't follow directions.

He reached for the old man and Gramm yanked him back. *You don't wake him.*

They watched and waited. Gramm raked his scalp. Twelve follicles were lost before the old man's chest began to swell, a long, deep breath. He smacked his lips.

His eyes fluttered.

His fingers began to crawl. The bed whirred, internal rollers kneading the aged body.

Dr. Ballard's hand rose like invisible strings lifted it. His hand hovered over his face and stalled like the puppeteer wasn't sure what to do next. Dr. Ballard focused on his fingers and the lines creasing his palm, then reached for the needle.

He pulled it out.

Gramm squeezed his hands together to avoid squirming, to keep from pulling his hair. That lone feeling of the needle plunging in or out of the brain was cold and foreign, tasted like metal, an inch and a half of surgical steel that glistened.

The old man propped himself up on one elbow and threw his weight to his side. Gramm and the two guards watched him slowly work his way into a sitting position. They didn't attempt to help. He had made that clear long ago.

The bed continued to thrum.

The old man leaned on his knees and contemplated the needle like script was written along the gleaming shaft. Then he broke it off and threw it away. Three deep breaths with his eyes closed, he hummed upon exhalation. When the paper-thin eyelids fluttered open once again, blue eyes with sharp edges aimed directly at Gramm.

Gramm's head hummed with a cold touch.

"Tell me," Dr. Ballard said, his words long and drawn, "why she is searching for Foreverland."

Gramm fidgeted. He couldn't help it. He uncrossed his legs, dropped both feet on the floor but didn't answer. It wasn't time to answer.

"What rekindled her interest, Gramm? Answer."

"I...I don't, don't know. No one has sent emails or texts or called. Samuel has been with her the entire time and, and given her everything she wanted."

"Hank's behavior didn't seem odd to you?"

"He was a little feisty, but that's been his personality, the way she knows him. If he changed, she'd notice."

"But we don't need him goading her back into writing, either. We need her happy, content. We need her to sleep, Gramm. Not motivated."

Gramm allowed his hand one pass through his hair.

Dr. Ballard didn't ask about the magazine and the photos of the tropical island. He would bring it up later, discuss whether this was another coincidence or a pattern. No need to pile on.

There's bigger news.

He rubbed his face with both hands and stared at the floor. Gramm could feel the old man's thoughts churning. Give him enough time and he would have a solution. But that was the problem.

Time.

The old man didn't have much. He insisted on letting his body wither like a husk of harvested corn.

"I don't like this." He raised his hands.

Drake and Melfy took them on command and helped him stand, waiting by his side to let the world balance beneath his feet. His elbows were bruised. Gramm suspected there were bruises on his buttocks and back as well, despite the specialized bed.

The old man shuffled to the desk and drank a bottle of water without pause, wiped his mouth with the back of his hand and stared at Gramm. The queer coldness was in his head again, starting in the core of his brain where a patch of biomites had been seeded. The sensation crept out like frozen tendrils.

Dr. Ballard sensed the worry. "What is it?"

Gramm could barely feel his legs when he stood. He didn't want to say it, not out loud. If he thought about it, concentrated on the image, the doctor would just know it as if it was his own thoughts. But the old man just returned from Patricia's Foreverland; he was still adjusting to physical reality.

Gramm would have to say it.

"The boy. We've lost him."

"Danny?"

"He...left the villa. Didn't tell anyone."

"Where did he go?"

Gramm shook his head. That was all the old man needed to know. It was obvious now that he said it out loud. Hank's badgering, the *National Geographic*, Alex researching Foreverland, and now Danny had disappeared.

This is no coincidence.

And there was no time for complications.

The old man dropped the spoon and pushed the tray away. Melfy guided him into the hallway. Drake and Gramm followed them out to the yard, where the doctor would spend the next half an hour walking and thinking and returning to the world of flesh.

He would decide how to address these changes.

And fast.

SUMMER

A snake sheds its skin.
To be born again.

"What do you have to offer, Mr. Deer?"

"Call me Jonathan."

Mr. Connick glanced at his notes and shook his head.

He blinked, his eyes closing an extra beat, considering whether he should throw Jonathan out of the office, have him arrested. His name was a joke, but in a meeting like this, no one showed their true face.

Jonathan reached into his jacket and revealed an index card sharply folded. The other sheet, the one with a list of names, would remain in his pocket for now.

"You can speak freely," Mr. Connick said.

The office was soundproof, tamperproof, completely isolated from eavesdropping. Still, Jonathan slid the card across the polished desk. They stared at the steepled note.

Mr. Connick bounced his fingers, perhaps considering, once again, throwing him out. He leaned forward and read what was written on the inner portion of the fold.

"This is what you want. I asked what you have to offer."

"Can you deliver?"

Mr. Connick tapped the rigid edge of the note on the desk, staring at Jonathan's eyes. They were green for this meeting, and slightly narrow. He'd reshaped the bridge of his nose and extruded his brow. Only a few people in the world knew his true identity. But no one, no matter how much technological power they had, would be able to match Jonathan's identity with facial recognition.

Not even Mr. Connick.

He got up and paced along the spacious window with a view down Chicago's Adam Street. The lake was visible between the buildings. The note bounced between his fingers, his hands clasped behind his back.

"Audacious, Mr. Deer." His voice reverberated off the glass. "What could you possibly have to offer me for this? Money? Information? Power? I assure you, whatever it is, there is not enough to get what you're asking. Nothing even close."

He flicked his wrist. The note skidded across the desk, landing on its side, open for Jonathan to see his own handwriting.

"What could you possibly offer us?" Mr. Connick said.

Jonathan leaned back. "Your very own universe," he said. "Foreverland."

11

Danny Boy

South Boston

The rental car was still running.

Danny adjusted the vents. The sun had moved behind him, the glare no longer in his eyes, but it was still blazing hot. No one was doing much of anything outside. Every thirty minutes, a stringy woman would come onto the porch to smoke. She'd stare at him until she finished, flick the butt onto the lawn and go back inside.

All the deals he put together in Valencia had fallen apart by now. Santiago would try to delay the inevitable and convince the investors their millions of dollars were in good hands. But Danny had turned off his phone and left everything behind when he flew out late one night.

The emaciated woman was coming out for another smoke, her tenth of the day, when Danny opened his door. Cicada song welcomed him to the summer furnace. He locked the doors and walked down the cracked sidewalk, feeling the eye of a neighborhood watch sign follow him to the corner house.

The neighborhood had the smell of trash—sour beer and rotting eggs. Beneath it all, he noticed the faint hint of lilac. It reminded him of his villa off the coast of Spain.

He climbed the porch and walked to the staircase built into the side of the house. The wood was relatively new, the steps leading up to a platform on the second floor and another on the third.

His heart rate grew louder.

The door on the second-floor platform was locked. There was a peephole but nothing for Danny to see inside. He looked around before lightly tapping with a knuckle. He waited a full minute before doing it again and thought about trying the third floor when he noticed the digital lock.

It was brand new.

He rapped one more time, staring at the distorted reflection on the numerical pad. Someone had scratched four letters into the gold-plated trim.

GRAD.

Danny punched the numbers that corresponded to the letters. Nothing happened. He rubbed his finger over the etching, the lines smooth and tarnished. Someone had done it quite some time ago. Assuming it was Reed, why would he put that there?

Was it a clue?

Grad was short for gradient, such as slope. That could be converted to a number, which could be the combination. Reed's letters led him here with clues from the island, but there was nothing that corresponded with slope—nothing on the island or anything since. He couldn't even guess.

Grad could also mean graduate. *Or graduating.*

Back on the island, when a transition was complete, when one of the boys had permanently vacated their body, the chimney would smoke. That was when the old men said someone graduated from the island, that they were healed.

They got SMOKED.

Danny punched the corresponding number: *766533.*

The lock whirred. Warm, stale air seeped out—

"What are you doing there?" A man stood on the bottom step. He was wearing flannel bottoms and no shirt, his stomach overhanging the drawstrings.

"Looking for a friend."

"And you just walk in?"

"He gave me the code." Danny pushed the door open.

"Don't mean you can walk in."

"I'm meeting him. He gave me the code so I didn't have to wait in the sun, you know."

The man pushed his fingers through oily black hair.

"Is there a problem?" Danny added.

"I don't know, is there?"

"My friend up here making noise?"

"Why?" The man's second chin jiggled.

"He doesn't pay his rent sometimes." Danny reached for his wallet. "Do I need to square up for him?"

"Yeah, sure."

"Look, is he paid up or not?"

"None of your business."

The man looked away. Reed was paid up, but it was hard to tell if he was the landlord or a nosy tenant.

"Have you seen him?" Danny asked.

"Not in a while."

"Like a week? A month?"

"Something like that."

"Which is it?"

"What do you want with him?"

Danny grimaced. "I'm worried about a friend, that's all. He doesn't feel good most of the time. If he's not here, which I don't think he is, then I'm just going to wait inside for a few, all right?"

The man rubbed his gut in a slow circle like he was comforting an unborn baby.

Danny walked inside, pulled the door closed and waited. When there were no footsteps up the staircase, he began to look around.

All the blinds were closed. A couple of the windows were covered with sheets, throwing the apartment into dim gray light. A fan rotated on a coffee table, the whirring blades pushing dead air around the room.

Danny turned on a short lamp. There was a couch and a couple of chairs. The pillows were perfectly arranged, almost intentionally, as if someone dressed the place up or never sat down. A kitchenette was to the left and a cluttered desk straight ahead.

Danny stood perfectly still.

It smelled like a vacation, like sand and sunscreen. Reed always had the scent about him, like he showered in the ocean. Danny sometimes wondered if there was a strange connection to the island, if somehow Reed had been infected with the false promises of Foreverland, saturated with the tropical allure.

A television blared from downstairs. The ceiling creaked from footsteps above him. Inside the apartment, ghosts of desolation dared him to come inside, to look around. Light sliced through a bend in the blinds.

He reached through the plastic slats and grabbed the Mason jar. It was nearly full of white sand, the kind that would sift through an hourglass. *Or found on a tropical island.*

A green ink pen had been stabbed into it.

All doubts fell away.

A jar of mustard was inside the refrigerator, along with a block of hard cheese, an egg and a bloated jug of milk. It had been expired for six months.

The bed was bare, the mattress thin and frayed. A round cushion was in the middle of the floor, a zafu for meditation. So he was meditating, just like Zin taught him.

A few clothes were folded beneath the bed. Danny pulled out jeans and T-shirts. He was braced to find a tropical shirt—something Harold Ballard wore on the island—but they were solid colors. That's when he realized one of his nagging fears: somehow Harold Ballard had returned from the ethers of the Nowhere and reclaimed his old body.

He folded the shirts and noticed a black cable. Danny fished it out, pulling something heavy from the dark corner. Straps were attached to the end. A cold chill shook through his arms. The leather straps formed a headset with a knob that would center over the forehead.

Inside was the needle.

The last time Danny saw the headset was on the island, when the needle would flick out like a stainless steel tongue, find the hole in their head and transport them away from the suffering.

To Foreverland.

But Reed never took the needle, not until they forced it on him. He was the only boy on the island that refused Foreverland. So why now? Even so, there was no host to create Foreverland. It was Harold Ballard's mind that created Foreverland. And he was gone.

Where would he go?

The other end of the cable had been cut. Whatever it was connected to was gone. And Reed had left the rest to be found, to let Danny know he was using it.

Just above the naked pillow, scratched into the wall with the same instrument used on the digital lock, were tiny letters.

Danny leaned closer.

Build the bridge.

He wondered if he left his home to follow the ramblings of a madman, an addict to the needle, a broken mind fighting to get back to Foreverland. Why would Reed go back to Foreverland? Even when they were on the island, when all the boys couldn't wait to punch the needle, he knew it was a trap.

Why go back now?

There was no computer or television, no sign of anything electronic. In the front room, the desk was buried beneath memos and office supplies. An article had been trimmed and taped to the paneling. It was the only thing on the wall, a printout from *The Washington Post* announcing the opening of the Institute of Technological Research in New York City.

That was Danny's last and only trip back to the States.

Spiral-bound notebooks were stacked in one drawer, their pages filled with poems and run-on sentences, no periods or commas, just page after page of words, like a prisoner trying to relieve his loneliness by spilling his thoughts.

With green ink.

A sketchpad was at the bottom. Every page was covered with a face drawn in pencil, shadows smudged for effect. It was a girl with short hair. Despite the grayscale, Danny knew who the girl was. She had bright red hair and green eyes.

Lucinda.

She was Reed's girlfriend, his love. If it wasn't for her, they never would've escaped the island. None of them could thank her enough, and none of them could forget her.

Especially Reed.

The folders stacked on the desk were organized in a way only Reed might understand. There were photos that appeared to be all the teenage boys that had been on the island and a list of names. *Incomplete list,* it said. As if there were still victims to be discovered.

There were meticulous notes on the back of each one, written in green ink, some describing their past and what happened to them. A photo of an old man was attached to each boy's photo.

The Investors.

Was he hunting them down?

It would be impossible to find them. The wealthy bastards disappeared after leaving the island in their boys' bodies. They might even get plastic surgery, hide in remote places. Money could get you lost and never found.

Danny knew that all too well.

There was another folder with teenage girls, accompanied by the same type of notes and similar Investors, these old women. This was the other Foreverland, the one with cabins in the middle of Wyoming. Danny knew about that one, too.

The Wilderness.

While the boys were on a tropical island, the girls were stranded in cold desolation. Harold Ballard's mother, Patricia Ballard, was the host. She was the one that created Foreverland for the girls, sucked their identities out and made room for the old women to steal their young and able bodies. But when Harold Ballard's Foreverland was destroyed, his mother began to malfunction.

The girls had it so much worse.

They lived in squalor, forced to wear rags and crap in the woods while the boys slept in dormitories and played video games. Reed had photos of the survivors shortly after the girls were saved. They were beautiful with short hair that had been shaved when they arrived, but the memories haunted their eyes. They would never forget.

None of us will.

The girl on top, Danny remembered her. She was the one, they said, that saved them all. She had somehow escaped Foreverland, woke up to pull the needle out of her head. But when the other girls wouldn't wake up, she volunteered to go back inside. She was blonde with blue eyes. He flipped the page over.

Cyn. Her name is Cyn.

It would take months to go through all Reed's notes. Danny couldn't carry them out without Flannel Pants seeing him. He couldn't risk anyone calling the police, either. He could come back in a week, go through them more carefully. There must be a clue hidden in the text.

He checked the other drawers, found several pencils and a new box of green pens. The lid was open. One of the pens was missing.

Only one.

Danny looked at the window, the green pen stuck in the sand like a cigarette butt. He sat down on the couch with the jar, pulled the pen out, and stirred the sand like thick soup. He went to the kitchen and brought back a bowl to empty it.

Nothing but sand.

Danny raked the contents, swirling it in circles, sifting it between his fingers. There were no prizes, no clues. Just fine particles of sugar sand.

He thought about things to take, ways he might stuff them down his pants, a notebook or stack of papers, take them to the hotel and study them. He began pouring the sand back into the jar. Something was inside.

My body lies beneath the sand.

That was in the first poem. Danny assumed it meant Reed's teenage body, but maybe it meant the sand in the jar, also.

A square of paper was glued down, grains of sand stuck to the bottom. His fingers were too fat to reach it. He used the pen to swipe at the edges until it broke loose. The folds were intricate and numerous. It unfurled into a narrow strip with tiny green letters. He held it up to the dim light.

It was an address.

12

Alessandra

Central Park, New York City

Alex was tired.

In her younger days, she could go days on a few hours of sleep. Now she was always tired, napping at least twice a day.

She found an empty bench and sat back to record her senses. This moment—the green smell, the birds singing—was a keeper. She opened a new biomite function that would play the moment back with all these sensations on a later day.

Ever since the biomite reset following the accident—the accident that never happened, she reminded herself—life had been good and the weather perfect. She was truly blessed.

A couple jogged around a twenty-something college student. Her coat was out of season, along with her stocking cap. She approached with her head down, seeing only the concrete in front of her, carrying a to-go cup of coffee in each hand.

Exactly what Alex wanted.

"*Hola*," Geri said.

"Good morning."

"*Caliente*."

"You read my mind."

Geri dropped her bag between them. "How are you?" she asked with a trace of Chicago nasal.

"How are things at the magazine?" Alex asked, tired of responding to Geri's inquiry, a question everyone asked her nowadays. It was never in a flippant manner, like *hey, hi, how are ya?* It was very serious, very concerned. Like they all knew about the breakdown, the reset.

"Good," Geri answered. "Seven years of college and a ton of student loans might get me minimum wage."

"But you love what you do."

"Can't get enough."

"And Jeff?"

"A pain in the ass."

Geri looked over her rectangular glasses at Alex, studying, looking for an answer to her first question.

Alex touched her hand. "I'm fine. Thanks for asking."

It had that *Let's move on* tone. Geri got the message, unzipped her frayed bag, coffee stains down the side, and dropped three folders on Alex's lap, each an inch thick.

"There's everything on the Foreverland projects. I can dig up more if you plan to write about it. Which I don't think you should."

Alex frowned. *Enough, already*.

The plain folders were unlabeled and loaded with printed photographs and documents with tiny font. Most of it was public knowledge, but some of it was exclusive stuff that Geri was good at finding. It's why Alex paid her to do the preliminary work. Sorting through the chaff was tedious.

"There are two documented cases of Foreverland body snatching. One was somewhere in BFE, where a bunch of girls were kept in dirty cabins with a wood-burning stove and candles while rich old ladies lived in luxury. Their host was a comatose woman." Geri looked over her glasses. "I think you know her."

Alex opened the folder and saw a photo of mountains and rolling hills and an old cabin. It could be the middle of Montana or Wyoming. She was familiar with the story, knew the girls were teenagers. The wealthy women kidnapped them, used Foreverland to suck their identities out of their bodies and then, voilà, an old woman moved in. It was like buying a new car—a young, healthy car with smooth skin and perky breasts and another sixty years of life.

Alex lifted a photo of an old woman that looked like a shrunken version of a full-sized person, like God left her in the oven too long.

Patricia Ballard.

"The other folder has to do with the first Foreverland, the one on the tropical island. They were doing the same thing, the body-switch stuff, only with boys. They had it way better than the girls." She grunted. "Figures."

There were photos of the boys and old men, of the buildings and grounds. It was more like a resort.

"What happened to the kids?"

"What do you mean?"

"Was it like their brains were erased and reformatted? Where did the personality go, I guess is what I mean?"

"That's a good question." Geri flipped through the pages and pulled a photo out of the stack. "The survivors said there was some gray cloud beyond the sky, like outer space. That's where their minds got shredded and mixed together."

Dios mío.

"They called the gray space the Nowhere. But here's where it gets weird." Geri put down her cup and slid the bottom folder out. "The guy that ran the tropical island Foreverland was Harold Ballard. He made a zillion dollars and went missing when the whole thing collapsed, probably sipping mai tais in a Mediterranean bungalow somewhere. He was, or is, the son of Patricia, the host of the wilderness Foreverland."

Harold looked more like a vagrant with a tropical shirt than a mai-tai-sipping zillionaire. There was a smile behind the dull gray beard, she could see it in the squinting eyes.

"Patricia Ballard is married to Tyler Ballard," Geri said. "Or was. Are you still married if your wife is a vegetable? I don't know, maybe she's not in a coma anymore, who knows where she is. In fact, I don't think anyone knows."

"At the Institute."

"Did you see her?"

I felt her. Alex flinched. That thought slapped her hard. *She was at the Institute when I was there, when I was looking into Coco's eyes.*

"I'll bet you didn't see her," Geri said.

Alex shook her head. No, no, she didn't.

"That's what I mean. They say she's in the Institute, but no one ever confirms it. You ever hear of her husband?"

Again, Alex shook her head.

"He invented the whole computer-aided alternate reality thing."

"Foreverland?"

"Yeah. He used it to experiment on his wife, turned her into an overcooked vegetable and went to prison. And then guess what happened? Harold followed in daddy's footsteps and started experimenting on anyone he could get his hands on, pretending like he was healing minds when he was just buying property and tropical islands to serve the insanely wealthy. The bastard put his mother in the wilderness and they played their messed-up alternate reality games while they made billions."

"What happened to the money?"

"What?"

"After the rings fell apart, what happened to the money?"

"Authorities got it, mostly. Used it to set up a Foreverland fund to help the survivors. They're a little cuckoo with the hole in the head and everything."

Geri put a finger gun to her forehead.

"Where's the rest of it?" Alex asked.

"Rest?"

"You said 'mostly'. Where's the rest of the money?"

"Some of it went to fund the Institute." She avoided looking at Alex, knowing that was where things got weird, and flipped through the pages on her lap. "I got it noted in there somewhere. There were also a number of accounts that went missing, which they figure was moved when Harold disappeared."

"How much?"

"Millions." Geri flicked the photo on Alex's lap. "Twisted pups, right?"

Alex heard the rumors, she knew the story about the Ballard family, but no more than the general public. Most of it sounded like science fiction and the family no more than characters with split personalities. If pressed, she didn't believe most of it. It was tabloid fodder.

But now it was sitting on her lap. There were documents from reputable sources, things no one would know, from people she trusted.

A quiver of fear shot through her midsection and lit up the nerves in her arm. Her hands began to shake, coffee spilled through the lid. She pretended to sneeze, clasping her fingers together.

Geri looked at her phone and explained freelance work was picking up. She threw her bag over her shoulder. "I can still do some research for you, if you need me."

"I need to pay you."

"I'll bill you with PayPal."

Alex looked at the folders, careful not to release her hands. They would shake if she let go. *What's wrong with me?*

The trees began to quiver. A rogue breeze swept through the park. Alex slammed the folders down before the papers ended up littering the park. A crowd roared somewhere, but she knew better. There wasn't a crowd.

She closed her eyes.

Geri sneezed as the dust rode past them.

Alex was staring down, waiting for the wind to die, but losing track of time. Time seemed to be doing that—speeding up and slowing down. Had she been staring at her lap for one minute or one second?

"What happened at the Institute?" Geri was still there. "If you don't mind me asking."

"Getting old. I don't recommend it."

"I heard a rumor about you. Want to hear it?" She waited, but continued without Alex's consent. "Rumor is you tripped out, tried to activate some enhancement during the tour that short-circuited your senses. Like pushing 240 volts through a hair drier, you know."

Alex chuckled. She didn't respond because it was stupid. But then the time lapse thing happened again and she lost track of how long she'd been chuckling, how long Geri had been standing.

"Why do you want to do this?" Geri pointed at the folders.

"What do you mean?"

"This is heavy. Why do you want to get involved? You're getting old, like you said."

There was a time when that would've pissed her off. Now she couldn't disagree. She was sitting in the park trying not to let someone see her hands shake. *Why am I doing this?*

"You ever feel an untold story?" she said.

"What?"

"It's a journalist's gut feeling, a sort of sixth sense you develop when there's more to a story than what's being presented, a piece that wants to be told, that wants you to know it. That wants you to tell others."

"That's what this is all about?" Geri tapped the folders.

"Yes."

"Seems pretty open and shut to me. Old people with money and poor people with something they want. A tale as old as time."

Alex wasn't sure about that. She was letting her instincts lead the way because something was out there, an untold story that even the secrets didn't know. She felt it at the Institute, a wave welling up in the ocean, something just below the surface. A monster in the deep and she was sitting directly over it in a little boat.

The wind had died.

Geri said goodbye. She was running late for another appointment. Alex sat with the folders on her lap until her coffee was cold. She opened her briefcase and placed all of Geri's research on top of the torn travel agency photo and *National Geographic*.

She stopped.

It took a moment to find the photo in Geri's folder. She placed it on the bench, side by side with the travel agency photo and *National Geographic*.

The exact same island.

The monster in the deep.

13

Alessandra

Upstate New York

The backyard felt like carpet. Deep, lush green carpet.

Alex slid her shoes off, wiggled her toes, turned her face to the sky like a sunflower and listened to her call go to voicemail.

"This is Shane Lee, director of photography at *National Geographic*. I can't take your call right now. Please leave your name and number. Thank you."

This time, she decided to leave a message. "Shane, this is Alex Diosa. We have a mutual friend, Amy Ferris at *The Washington Post*. I had a question about a photographer in one of your back issues. I won't take much of your time, please give me a call."

She continued her walk to the vegetable garden while thumbing a text to Mr. Lee. If she didn't hear back by the next day, she'd call again. Some folks never returned a call until after the third message.

How did he get that shot of the Foreverland island? And why was a travel agency using it, a travel agency that wasn't returning her calls, either?

First, find the photographer.

The lilacs were spent but still fragrant. Weeds choked the garden. A month ago, it was as clean as the driveway. That was before Geri delivered a gold mine in Central Park.

Alex rolled her shoulders. Knots were bunching up beneath her shoulder blades and a perennial ache took root in her spine, keeping her awake when she did make it to bed. She didn't need a chiropractor. She fell on her knees and sank in the composted soil; puffs of organic dust filled her nostrils.

Just a little horticultural therapy.

The weeds easily came out. She crawled to the next row and recalled playing in the garden while her mother pulled weeds, setting up dolls and rolling cars between the stalks. She'd sit in the shade of sweet corn and pretend it was a forest.

She was halfway down the third row when she noticed something yellow tucked between the tomato plants. Sweat stung her eyes. She wiped her face with the bottom of her shirt, but everything seemed a little out of focus.

Samuel's car rolled up the driveway.

"Hey." His tie was loose, his collar open. He dropped his leather briefcase on the ground. "What are you doing?"

She got up and wiped her hands on her thighs.

"Got a call from the Institute today," he said. "Know anything about it?"

"What?"

"They said you were dropping the lawsuit."

"I...I told you, Samuel, I don't want to sue."

"Nah, nah, nah, that's not what this is about." He tugged the knot on his tie. "You're angling."

"What?"

"What are you up to?"

"Samuel, I don't like the way you're talking to me. I told you in the hospital I didn't want to sue."

"You're trying to go back there."

She stepped out of the garden and pushed all the weeds together. The ground swayed. *Am I dehydrated?*

The Institute wasn't supposed to tell him she was negotiating an interview with their executives. *We drop the lawsuit, I come back for another tour. And this time I see Patricia.*

It was a long shot.

"We're not doing this," he said. "You're not going back. Write whatever you want, you're not going back to the Institute."

"Don't tell me what to do."

"I'm worried." His hands were on his hips, jaw set. The words didn't match the body language. For a second, he looked like someone entirely different, like a man ready to break something in half.

"I need some water."

She went into the shade of the garage. Samuel came out with a bottle of water. He set up a chair and watched her drink until she waved him off.

"I'm all right. Get out of your suit; we'll talk later."

He paused, unsure if she would be all right. Or just didn't trust leaving her alone. Eventually, he went inside. Alex finished the water but still felt wobbly.

Her phone buzzed. Alex took it on the third ring.

"You busy?" Geri asked.

"No, I'm fine. What do you got?"

"I got more weird for you."

Something squeaked. Samuel was rolling the wheelbarrow into the backyard, the axles squealing for oil. He loaded the mound of weeds, significantly more than she thought. *Have I been out there this long?*

The sky had cleared, clouds on the horizon. Everything was back in focus and she felt good again. Normal. Just needed water.

"I'm sending over more notes," Geri said. "This Ballard family is a bunch of dysfunctional geniuses. You should consider writing a book on them. At the very least, a novel. They're like characters out of a science-fiction movie."

Alex had been through her notes. She was having the same thoughts.

"The father's been in a maximum-security prison for over thirty years. He was only sentenced to twenty years."

"Twenty?"

"Yeah, twenty."

“So, why is he still incarcerated?”

“It gets a little murky there. Best I can find is that his sentence was extended twice, but there’s no reason.”

“Even bad behavior doesn’t extend your sentence.”

“See what I mean?”

“Can I get an interview?”

“I made some calls, talked to a few people, but it doesn’t sound good. He doesn’t take visitors.”

Samuel stepped into the garden to grab another pile of weeds. He waded to the end of the row and stepped between the tomatoes.

“You want me to submit a request?” Geri asked.

He picked up a yellow object, the one that was nestled in the weeds between the tomatoes. He kept his back to her and quickly threw it over the fence into the neighbor’s yard.

“Hello?”

“Yes, yes,” Alex said. “File a request. I want to interview him as soon as possible. Tell them whatever you have to. I’ll sign whatever, promise whatever. Let’s get it started.”

“Done.”

Samuel stepped out of the garden and dumped the wheelbarrow in the back before going into the house, sweat stains on his shirt.

Alex stared at the fence.

Those neighbors were good people. They had two dogs, but no kids. Alex swore she saw him throw a plastic truck.

A little yellow plastic truck.

She was feeling dehydrated again.

14

Tyler

ADMAX Penitentiary, Colorado

Tyler stood in front of a wide window, watching inmates play basketball and walk the track. The threat of rain sank into his joints like cold drips of mercury.

The door opened behind him. A middle-aged man in a starched white coat stepped into the room and docked a tablet next to a computer. Harvard educated, perennially optimistic and a believer in reform, he was a good man. A good doctor.

"Body of an old man," he said. "Engine of a teenager."

The good doctor patted the exam table. His eyes were sleepy, whiskers a few days old. He washed his hands, humming as he dried them, gently inspecting Tyler's forehead. The hole appeared to be an empty blackhead, but the surrounding flesh was puffy and red. Gramm was concerned about infection. The stent had been in place for over twenty years and there had never been a problem.

But his body was twenty years older.

"You need to stop with the needle," the good doctor said. "You don't need it."

"Don't lecture me."

"Your current brain biomites are fully capable of digital transmission. There is a new biomite strain with improved frequency. It would only take a little training to make your...*connection*...without it."

The good doctor always stuttered on the topic of Foreverland, as if the word only surfaced in his consciousness long enough to leap off his tongue.

Tyler winced when he touched the stent.

The good doctor apologized, but that's not why Tyler reacted. He liked the needle, had grown accustomed to it in the same way a long-distance runner enjoyed the burn.

Or a junkie craved the spike.

The good doctor tapped the tablet a few times. An image of Tyler's body—slightly hunched and crooked—illuminated on the wall monitor. The good doctor stared while tapping his lower lip.

He began to say something. Then froze.

Caught with an awkward expression, like a sneeze was coming, a sneeze flash-frozen on his face while his biomite-laden brain seized. It waited for a command.

Waited for Tyler.

The old man closed his eyes, drew a deep breath and let his thoughts sink into the good doctor as if he was clay. Tyler's thoughts were the fingers of an artisan penetrating his canvas. A violent shiver vibrated between his ears, an electric arc that made his brain itch. This always happened when he synced up with one of his people.

My people, he thought. *The people that run this prison, the people that voluntarily seeded themselves with biomites. The people I own.*

My people.

Tyler had hijacked them one at a time, recoded their brains like programmable processors, left suggestions in their subconsciousness, secret words that turned them catatonic, that opened their minds and allowed him to pick their thoughts like fruit. Afterwards, they had no idea a thief had run through them.

Life was so much easier when people did what you wanted.

The new biomite strain the good doctor mentioned was experimental, more research was needed to assess their stability and function. And that would take time.

Tyler didn't have time.

He didn't like experimenting. He was old and vulnerable. He was also nearing the maximum biomites allowed by the government. *No human being could be composed of more than 49.9% biomites, lest they be considered more machine than human.*

The penalty was swift and eternal.

He didn't need the government sniffing around the prison. There were rumors of illegal biomites, ones the government couldn't monitor. These could be used to go over the 50% mark. In fact, an entire body could be made of them. But they were rumors.

There was no time for rumors.

"Seed a microliter of biotype Q into the brain," Tyler said.

"Seed a microliter of biotype Q into the brain," the good doctor repeated.

"Bypass brain-blood barrier via mucosa."

The good doctor waited, eyes wide like a car accident was happening. "Bypass brain-blood barrier via mucosa."

Tyler turned his attention to the wall monitor and focused on the colorations filling the brain. The right hemisphere, the creative half, the land of imagination—where Foreverland was born—was vivid and varied.

"Program a 100 ppm proliferation in the right hemisphere."

"Program a 100 ppm proliferation in the right hemisphere."

The good doctor turned to prepare one microliter of biotype Q that would increase Tyler's brain capacity. He inserted the seeder up his right nostril.

Hot tracks remained on Tyler's cheeks.

The good doctor sat on a stool, staring at the window. The wide-eyed shock was gone, but blankness still haunted him.

Gramm waited at the foot of the table.

Tyler lifted his hand. Gramm helped him sit and gave him a few minutes to sit quietly. The new seeding would need a few days to integrate. He expected more efficient wireless transmission of his thoughts, a more seamless transition into Foreverland. Still, he wasn't ready to give up the needle.

Rain streaked the window.

The good doctor maintained a glassy-eyed stare, his zombification proof that, little by little, Tyler was carving away his identity. The good doctor would return to normal, regain his own self within the hour. But there was always a little missing.

Tyler didn't hijack Gramm. He enjoyed the old-fashioned camaraderie. At the very least, he didn't want him to end up an empty glove like the good doctor.

"Alessandra has requested an interview," Gramm said.

"What?"

"She's moving forward with her research."

"I thought we took care of this, Gramm."

"Her assistant keeps providing research, keeps her interested."

"Where's she getting it?"

Gramm shook his head.

"Put a stop to it."

"Certainly." Gramm cleared his throat. "In the meantime, the interview..."

"Deny."

"I think you should reconsider—"

"Deny her, Gramm. I don't want her coming here, not now. We need her to focus on normality. Acceptance. Once she realizes how happy she is, how perfect her life has become, then she'll sleep. That's all I care about."

He trusted Gramm. His assessment was always unfiltered, unbiased and accurate. But this wasn't the time for Alessandra to know Tyler. More adjustment was needed. More acceptance.

She's our last hope, the one person capable of hosting a new reality, an endless Foreverland. Humankind will give eternal thanks for her sacrifice.

The gray sky was a smear of charcoal. A thunderhead was crawling over the distant mountain range. The men returned inside.

"Danny is going to Minnesota," Gramm said.

"Duluth?"

"Yes."

He turned at the shoulders. Gramm stood like a noble soldier. The good doctor remained on the stool, lower lip glistening with saliva.

"Interesting," Tyler said. "He's looking for Cynthia."

Gramm nodded.

"Why would he be doing that?"

"I…I don't know. I suggest we stop them both."

"Stop them?"

"Permanently."

"You want to terminate them?"

Gramm raked his hair and stammered. "We don't need them. Keeping them alive can only be trouble. Cynthia is, you know...contaminated."

Tyler watched the former chemist pull the stray hairs from his fingers, watched his lips silently count. Uncertainty pained him. He was a scientist at heart; he liked control. Having the ability to eliminate Danny and Cynthia at will was too much temptation.

Tyler knew better.

Those two kids had potential. They couldn't host a Foreverland like he and Patricia wanted—certainly not like Alessandra—but they were not useless. And despite Tyler's willingness to sacrifice with callous decisiveness, he was not a cold-blooded murderer.

"No," he said. "We'll not end them, Gramm."

That moment of compassion would eventually be his undoing.

"Where did you find Danny?"

"He arrived in the States undetected," Gramm said. "But we located him at Reed's last known residence."

"Interesting. Why is he searching for Reed all of a sudden? Why now? Why in secret?"

"He spent an hour and a half inside the apartment. When he came out, he began driving and hasn't stopped."

"How do you know it's Minnesota?"

"He programmed Cynthia's address into the GPS."

"Where'd he get her address?"

Gramm stuttered without an answer.

Tyler turned at the sound of thunder. The skyline was hazy. "He found something in the apartment," Tyler muttered. "Has he been in communication with anyone?"

"Nothing out of the ordinary. Every email, text and phone call has been verified, nothing to suggest a secret code or otherwise."

"Reed?"

Gramm hesitated. "Reed is gone, sir."

He wanted to say more, to argue there was no way Reed could be behind this. They knew that the boy named Reed, the one that took Tyler's son's body, no longer existed. Reed was dead.

Tyler had the proof.

The sinus on the right side of his face was beginning to throb. He was already feeling the euphoric effects of the new seeding. His thoughts felt crisper, his body thrumming with good intentions.

"Someone is guiding Danny," Tyler said.

"There's no evidence—"

"He leaves his home, breaks communication with Santiago and goes directly to Reed's apartment? That is all the evidence we need; someone is guiding him. The young man does not take an interest in a long-dead friend out of the blue."

"We need to stick with facts, sir. Reed is nonexistent; we have verified that. There must be another explanation."

"Or we've missed something."

Underestimation was not the mistake Tyler wanted to make. It seemed impossible that Reed was alive, but so did hijacking this entire prison. *My people.*

"Why would he go to Cynthia?" Tyler mused.

Gramm offered suggestions, but the old man wasn't interested. This hardly seemed threatening. It might even be beneficial. Cynthia was the girl that survived Patricia's Foreverland; she had trouble acclimating to normal life. Danny might be exactly what she needed. Maybe she would become an asset after all.

Still, why is he going? Why now?

Tyler started for the exit.

His newfound stamina was not to be wasted on pointless arguments. They would watch Danny and Cynthia, not let them out of their sight again. But now, real work needed to be done. Gramm followed him to the elevator.

They descended to the basement.

15

Cyn

Duluth, Minnesota

Cyn didn't open letters.

There was a stack next to the coffee machine and another in a wicker basket. The bills were taken care of through a trust fund established by the Foreverland Survivor Fund, assets acquired from the old women that kidnapped them.

Cyn wasn't a survivor. She was a fighter.

But she was tired of bleeding.

The curtains were drawn, blotting out the afternoon sunlight. The television droned in the background, electric light dancing on the ceiling. She hardly watched the programs, just wanted the sound to drown out the chatter in her head.

Not chatter. Just a voice.

She had thoughts that she called her own. But she also had someone else's thoughts in her head. That was the voice she was attempting to mute.

She dropped her foot on the floor, a sandbag thudding on the carpet. It took a minute to pull herself out of the swishing slumber.

The cracks of light streaming around the front door told her it was daytime. The clock told her to get going. A meeting started in twenty minutes. And if she wasn't there, someone would come for her.

It was better, she learned, to act like a normal addict than someone with a special affliction—an identity crisis that no one would understand, that no one knew existed.

Then just kill yourself, the voice told her.

Cyn pushed her short hair from her eyes. In the dusty light, it looked more muddy than blonde. She shoved a magazine off the low table, found the plastic prescription bottle under a newspaper and tapped out a white pill. A tiny pill.

A voice-dulling pill.

Shut up.

The voice had a name. It wasn't a name Cyn gave it because it wasn't just her imagination. The voice was someone that had a name, a name Cyn refused to acknowledge. She tried to ignore the ghost that lived in her subconscious, the identity that, without the pills, would rise to the surface like a leviathan, an old woman distorted by her nightmares, a demon with a massive maw, with row after row of teeth that wanted to devour Cyn whole.

I have a name.

Cyn wasn't bipolar. Not crazy, not unstable. The voice in her head was the old woman that kidnapped her, that dragged her out to the wilderness to steal her body.

Barbara.

It was bad timing that put the old woman in her head. But Cyn was a survivor.

Barb, Barb, Barb.

Living in the ashes of Foreverland.

The chalky pill stuck to her tongue. She washed it down at the kitchen sink.

"Now shut up."

She pulled the towel from the window and squinted in the daylight. The postal truck was at her mailbox.

The pill bottle slipped from her fingers and bounced on the

linoleum. She bent over and picked it up near the oven, the glass door covered with three layers of wax paper to obscure any reflections.

Pull the paper off, Barb whispered. Her voice was fading in the pill's haze. *Look at my reflection.*

Her arm ached to rise; her hand itched to do what she said. Cyn never did, but hated the compulsion to do so. Barb was confused. The old woman thought this was her body.

Cyn's cell phone vibrated somewhere in the front room. She found it beneath a pizza box. A text from Macy.

Meeting in 20. Picking up in 10.

Cyn chewed at the side of her thumb, nibbling off a fresh lump of skin before working on her fingernail, staring at the text. The prescription haze settled around her, picked her up and carried her to a place where she didn't care about anything.

A place where she could survive.

Where she didn't hear Barb.

She could stand there for a half hour if she let the haze have her, until she was ready to sleep again. But then Macy would knock on the door, force her way into her life and save her again, like she did six months ago.

And then she'd have to explain the pills.

She'd have to explain she wasn't really clean, that she couldn't live without the little white saviors, the slayers of Barb. She would have to explain something that no one would understand.

I don't hear voices. I have an old woman inside me!

She chuckled, despite the fog.

Quickly, she picked up the empty sacks and pizza boxes, filling three trash bags that went out the back door. She went to the fishbowl and noticed Teddy doing the backstroke.

Teddy got flushed while the shower ran.

The water pushed away the fuzzy veil.

If she could live in the shower, where the guilt would be washed away, where her tears circled the drain, she would never step out. She would let her skin pucker, she would scrub away her sins, let her mind be clean.

New again.

But nothing is ever new again.

The doorbell was ringing.

Cyn watched the last of the water seep into the drain, listened to the showerhead drip. The ringing turned into thumping. Cyn stepped out, her flesh soft and pink. She dried off in front of the sink; three towels covered the mirror.

Teddy was still floating. She forgot to flush.

"Cynthia?" The voice was muffled.

More knocking.

"Coming!"

Cyn answered the door in a robe, hair still dripping. Sunlight knifed across her face. Macy was on the front step, arms crossed, skin as black as her tightly cropped curls.

"You just wake up?"

"Shower. Be ready in a sec."

"Better make that half a second. I don't like being late."

"Sorry."

Cyn left the door open and ran to the bedroom to get dressed, pulling clothes from a pile. She pinned her hair on top of her head and brushed her teeth, bending over a small corner of the exposed bathroom mirror, where she saw her teeth.

But not her eyes.

She walked out to a bright front room, sunlight streaming through all the windows. Macy pulled aside the last curtain, her black skin flawless, smooth.

"What'd I tell you about the windows? Relapse lurks in dark corners."

There are other things in the dark.

"Your mail." Macy tossed a bundle in the wicker basket. She palmed a glossy flier and shoved it in her back pocket, sort of hiding it.

Cyn didn't need to see it to know what it was. The same flier came every week. And Macy took it every week.

Biomites.

The evil advert for biomedical technology, here to cure hormonal imbalance, heal your pain. Here to save the human race.

Biomites, the scourge of addicts everywhere.

Feel how you want to feel? Think how you want to think? That's just another drug, Cynthia, only this one is on the inside, one you can't turn away from. This one turns you into a drug.

Live life on life's terms, Cynthia.

Let go. Let God.

There were a hundred more lines she could quote from the Big Book—Macy beat them into her head like ten-penny nails—but none of that wisdom could exorcise the demon from her head.

Can biomites make you new again?

Cyn knew the answer.

In the spring, she'd gone to New York City to find out. She'd been invited to participate in the new healing at the Institute of Technological Research. She didn't remember much about the trip; those were the using days, soaked in alcohol and popped by pills. She got so hammered that she'd fallen off a curb and cut the back of her hand. Blood was dripping off her elbow. The people at the Institute took her to the hospital and got her stitched up.

She didn't remember much of that either, but the scar on the back of her hand was proof. She did remember the biomites, though. They had those. She didn't get any, but they had them.

That was almost five months ago.

She remembered that because the day she got home was the first day she went to a meeting, the day she got clean, the day she met Macy.

The first day of the rest of her life, Macy told her.

Macy held the door, tapping her toe, staring at her blank wrist because late addicts were relapsing addicts. Cyn grabbed a banana, noticing the envelopes in the basket, the one written in green ink. She hardly noticed the name on the front. It wasn't addressed to Cynthia.

Later, when Macy dropped her off, she would scramble to find her pills when she picked up the thick envelope and read the name no one had called her since leaving the wilderness.

Cyn.

Recovery happened in the back of a bowling alley.

When addicts opened up their lives, displayed all the warts, the wars, the bleeding souls and unhealed wounds, they did so to the rumble of pin setters and rolling thunder.

Cyn swam to the front row.

Macy took one look at her and whispered, "We got to talk."

Her eyes couldn't hide the pill's haze. Cyn was drowning in it. How could she explain the pills weren't the water filling her lungs, they were the lifesaver she clung to.

Cyn. It was addressed to Cyn.

It was a bulky envelope containing more than a message. It was thick and round, maybe a DVD. But she didn't find out. It went straight into the trash.

She received another one a week later. A third one arrived a week after that. Both of those went into the trash, unopened. She doubled down on the pills to dull the voice, but the little white saviors couldn't stop the envelopes from arriving.

Let go. Let God.

Several regulars of the bowling alley AA meeting told their war stories about the days in the trenches with the drink, the drugs, the high. They listened without response, nodding as the details rolled out. They all knew how the stories went. And how they ended.

Cyn nodded, only to blend in.

She often made up reasons for why she turned to drugs and alcohol, things like abusive parents and uncontrollable boyfriends. Maybe they weren't too far from the truth, she didn't really know. She didn't really trust her memories. Maybe what she remembered really did happen to her.

Maybe not.

Didn't matter.

The pain was real. And that was what she talked about, the pain. That was what everyone nodded along with.

The ache.

That was real.

"Anniversaries?" Josh took the podium. "Anyone?"

Macy raised her hand, waving it on her way to the front. Maybe she didn't know about Cyn's pill haze that day. If she did, she wouldn't be holding an anniversary chip, wouldn't be smiling down on her.

"I want to recognize six months, y'all. Six haaard-earned months to a brave girl that fights the fight each and every day, here and now. Eighteen years old, you're the youngest recovering addict in this room, congratulations, girl. Six months."

Macy started the applause.

The room joined in.

Some stood up.

The love cut through the numbing pill haze and reminded her why she got up every morning, why she fought the fight, that when clouds covered the sky, there was still a sun behind them, shining its light on everyone. The good and the bad. The unclean.

The broken.

You should kill yourself, Barb whispered in her head.

Cyn took the chip, squeezing it like a lifeline, clinging to it like a rope dangling over a pit that had no bottom. Drugs and alcohol had thrown her into their depths once before, plunged her into the cauldron of despair.

It was these people, this chip, her loving sponsor that reminded her pain was inevitable, suffering was optional.

If only Barb would die.

I die, Barb whispered, *you die.*

"Anyone else?" Josh asked.

Cyn didn't hear the next round of applause, just realized the world was out of focus from tears burning her cheeks. She wiped her eyes to see the newcomer.

"One day clean," Josh said, shaking the boy's hand. "Looks like Cynthia's no longer the youngest."

Long red hair, the body of a skater.

"How old are you, Danny?" Josh asked.

"Sixteen."

"Welcome to the rest of your life."

There was a standing ovation, a long line of recovering addicts shaking his hand, hugging him, patting his back. The boy was all smiles, the glowing grin of newfound redemption. She remembered what that was like, the smell of hope, the promise there was more to life than the high.

Fred, the three-hundred-pound security guard, a longtime sober member of the bowling alley chapter, applied his welcome hug: a vicious embrace that lifted the new member off his feet amid a chorus of laughter and good cheer. He squeezed the chip from Danny's hand.

Fred dropped him. Danny bent over to pick it up.

Cyn froze.

She had stood to welcome him in a much less dramatic fashion than Fred when the long red hair fell away from the back of Danny's neck.

A lump over the fifth vertebra.

The plastic chip dug into her palm. She backed away, resisting reaching up to massage the lump on her own neck, the same size and shape that covered the fifth vertebra. It could be coincidence, but there were no accidents in this room. Everything happened for a reason. That lump could only mean one thing.

Through the pill haze, through the love, through all the happiness in the room, a cold chill filled her legs.

He's been to Foreverland.

The leash.

The clamp, the lump, had been surgically installed to bite the nervous system should any of the girls go where they didn't belong. It was an invisible fence for humans.

The doctors said they couldn't remove it, that it was too risky. But it was safe; it was deactivated. Nothing would happen.

Except remind her of the wilderness for the rest of her life.

Cyn stopped going to meetings.

The windows were covered, the doors locked. Macy called, texted, hammered the windows. Cyn feigned illness, insisted she hadn't relapsed.

Just pills. But I need these. You don't understand.

The days were bleached in the haze. She stopped checking the mail, but Macy left it on the front step. Through the window, she could see the green ink, the name on the envelopes that kept coming.

You should kill yourself.

Meeting adjourned, Cyn watched the bowling alley chapter leave through the back door.

Skater boy was there.

He would have a one-week chip by now. Or was it a month? The pills had smudged time into one long blur.

She watched them get into their cars, watched cigarette smoke stream out cracked windows. Danny, however, walked past the front doors of the bowling alley and went to the diner at the end of the strip mall.

From a safe distance, she saw him sit in a booth. The summer asphalt baked the cold chill from her chest. She paced behind a McDonald's, wiping the sweat from her face.

He ordered.

The waitress arrived with two coffee cups.

He sipped from one.

The diner's air was cold.

The waitress didn't ask to seat her. "He's over there," she said.

She could see him across the room, sitting in a booth, eyes cast down as if he was reading. A cup of coffee was in front of him, the other waiting for her.

The noisy kitchen competed with the chatter in her head, Barb rushing out of her subconscious, whispering in her ear with that deep, scratchy voice scarred by a lifetime of smoking.

Get out of here, Barb whispered. *Go home. Be alone.*

She closed her eyes until colors splashed in the dark, tears seeping through the cracks and wetting her eyelashes. The floor beneath her disappeared.

And she was falling.

Get out.

"Hon?" The waitress was drying her hands. "You all right?"

"Yeah."

"You're looking for the boy over there, right?"

Cyn nodded.

"Well, he's waiting. Unless you want me to tell him you didn't show. I don't think he's seen you."

She could walk out, go back to the house and close the windows, hide in a scalding shower until she couldn't feel the emptiness, take pills until the falling stopped and she just hovered over the pit.

"That what you want?"

"No."

She fell once before and found her way out. She could do it again.

"Who are you?"

He didn't look up.

There was a folder to his right, a stuffed manila folder with ragged corners. He was clutching the table, his knuckles white. She thought he was having a seizure, but then he let go and slid the folder across the table, next to the cup of coffee. That was her cup, cream already stirred in.

Just like she took it.

She could ask him again, but he wasn't going to answer. The answer, it seemed, was in the folder. He sipped at the coffee cup, eyes cast not at a phone or an iPad but the blank slate of a cheap diner tabletop, breath streaming in and out like a metronome.

Do I know you?

There were photos in the folder. Glossy paper and dark colors. She didn't sit in the fake red leather bench across from him. Not yet.

She dragged her fingers across the table, let them rest like twigs on the coarse folder before pulling it closer. There was a stack of about twenty photos inside, all printed on full pages. She didn't need to see them all.

Just the first one.

The rolling hills and a dilapidated cabin.

She knew the inside of the cabin, the beds and the marks on the wall she had scratched to count the days where she woke up—where all the girls woke up—with a shaved head and no memories.

Foreverland.

"I've been there," Danny said.

A tear streaked over her cheek. Because she knew what he meant. He knew. He hadn't been to the cabin or the wilderness. But he had been *there.*

He'd been to Foreverland.

Silence, for once, filled her head. Barb receded into the darkness of her subconscious.

"I was on a tropical island," he said. "We all woke up without our memories, were told we were sick, that we would be healed. Old men gave us everything we wanted, as long as we took the needle."

He looked up, his blue eyes clear, placid.

"We never thought about where the girls came from, but it only made sense that you were coming from your own Foreverland, but not from a tropical island."

He spread the photos on the table.

The luxurious brick house where the old women lived. The garden where Jen's body was buried. The little cabin where Patricia slept. It was nothing like a tropical island.

Nothing but suffering in the wilderness.

"We were the ones that crashed Foreverland," he said. "A few of us escaped the island, left the old men for the authorities. We didn't know there was another Foreverland. Didn't know you were still in it."

"Do you remember me?" she asked. She searched his face, begging for recognition.

"No."

"But we went there? With you?"

"I don't remember much." Weakness trailed in his voice. "I try not to. It brings back too much..." He shook his head.

"How did you find me?"

"A friend of mine—one I escaped with—he told me to find you."

"Why?"

"We might be in trouble."

Despite the ominous tone, the dire warning, the threat that Foreverland might still be out there, she didn't shake or shiver. Not a quiver touched her insides or hummed in her head. For the first time she could remember, she felt alive and present.

Because he was there. He knew the suffering.

I'm not alone.

Cyn dropped into the seat.

She came eye level with the fair-skinned redheaded boy, a ginger with a slight build and an unshakeable presence.

"What kind of trouble?"

"It might not be over."

"What?"

"Foreverland."

"How...how is that possible?"

The little bell over the diner's door rang. Danny looked over her shoulder. He said without taking his eyes off the front, "He wrote me, told me to find you."

"A letter?"

"Yes."

Finally, she shuddered. She didn't have to ask the color of the ink. "Why?"

"I don't know."

Danny gathered the photos and dropped them on the seat next to him, out of sight.

"There you are." Macy stood at the table. "I'm worried about you, girl. Why aren't you taking my calls?"

Cyn didn't look away from Danny. His gaze lingered. *Keep this quiet.*

"Sorry, Macy. I got a little mixed up in the head."

"You all right?"

Did you relapse? Are you using? Do you need me to run this punk out of town? Because you've been acting strange ever since he arrived.

"I'm good, yeah."

There were pleasantries passed back and forth, thank you for the coffee and the conversation. Danny really helped clear her head, get back on track. Macy hummed and nodded. That wasn't his job, not without the group, not when he had less than a month clean.

Cyn left him at the table. When she reached the parking lot, the whisper returned.

By the time she got home, it was more than a whisper.

You will kill yourself.

16

Danny Boy

Duluth, Minnesota

The coffee tasted like dishwater.

Danny cradled the mug, staring at the brown swirls as the tingling faded from his arms and legs. He'd never felt it that strong before. When she sat down across from him, it was like inhaling a steady stream of nitrous. He had been clutching the table to keep from floating away.

Now that she was gone, he sank into the red leather bench.

When he saw her the first time, he'd experienced something like that, but it was faint. He'd chalked that up to the new environment and nerves. He always sat in the back of the room, never got closer than ten or twenty feet to her. But when she sat across from him, within arm's length...

Wow.

It wasn't until the initial rush settled that he noticed the fragrance, a scent that clung to the back of his throat. He assumed it was something she was wearing, an essential oil or something. Even now it hung over the table thicker than usual.

Lilac.

She was beautiful, no surprise. She was stunning, even from a distance. She had the gait of a cat, lithe and dangerous, but fragile at the same time. If she missed a step, he was afraid she might shatter. He got lost in her blue eyes, suppressed the urge to reach out and take her hand. When their fingers brushed, a tingle sent him toward the ceiling again.

It made no sense, but this was the right place.

He thought the photos would jar something loose. Maybe she could explain why Reed sent him. It was just a guess. But there was nothing. All he saw was the ghosts in her eyes—the same ghosts that haunted his dreams.

The memories of Foreverland.

He ordered another coffee and read the newsfeed. He caught up on daily events, counted all the missed opportunities since leaving the villa. He'd stay in Duluth until he figured something out. There was only one certainty: he wasn't going back to Spain.

Not until something makes sense.

The diner's bell rang as the door opened. Danny was thumbing through a story on biomite halfskin laws when he sensed Santiago, could smell the Spaniard's musky body odor, the trace of a cigar.

A strong, slim figure was walking toward him. The backlit glare obscured her features. A slight sense of vertigo turned the table as Santiago's presence got stronger.

Macy dropped into the booth.

He rubbed his eyes. The smell of Santiago didn't match up with the glaring dark-skinned woman. It took a moment for his senses to reset.

Her eyes were almost all pupils, the irises dark brown. Unblinking, she folded her bony fingers on the table. The waitress stopped by. Macy dismissed her without breaking her deadlocked stare.

"What are you doing?" she asked.

Danny didn't answer. She was asking something else.

"Huh?" she grunted.

"Living one day at a time."

"Cute." She nodded. "You drive a rental into town and shack up in a hotel and decide to clean up in the back of a bowling alley like our chapter is some holy grail."

Danny stiffened.

He'd been careful to keep quiet, never went directly to the hotel that he'd booked several miles away. He hadn't sensed anyone watching him, no one waiting in the parking lot or following him.

"You come for her?" she asked.

"You know who I am?"

"I can spot an addict a mile away. You ain't no addict, son."

A chill raced beneath his ribs. *Son.* That's what they called each other on the island, it was their slang. They didn't say *man* or *boy* or *dude*. Everyone was *son*.

"Give me the folder."

The photos were still on the seat. He didn't move. She already knew too much.

"I will tear this place apart and beat you with a table leg if you don't get a move on." She leaned over the table, never breaking eye contact. "Give me the folder."

Someone once told him that you didn't have to be stronger or meaner than your enemy, you just had to out-crazy them. He didn't stand a chance.

He put the folder on the table.

"Is this a joke?" She spread the photos out. "You trying to make her relapse? Push her over the edge?"

Danny didn't respond.

"Who sent you?"

That was the question she wanted to ask. That's what she wanted to know the second she sat down. She was trying to disguise it in all this concern for Cyn's sobriety, but the subtle change in expression—the slight shift from hard rage to hopeful curiosity—told him she was angling for something else.

"I'm going to ask you again." She leaned in. "Who sent you?"

"No one."

She looked around, perhaps considering trashing the place to beat him with a table leg.

"Out of the blue you travel across the world to get clean? Is that what you want me to believe, that you just got a wild hair to leave your life to ruin my girl?"

"She's a Foreverland survivor. You know about Foreverland, right?"

"I know about survival."

"There's not many of us left."

"Maybe she doesn't want to remember."

"None of us do," he said. "But we can't forget."

"I don't care about you or any of the others. Only one survivor I do and you can bank on this." She shoved the photos into his lap and stood up. "You break her and you better keep running, son. *¿Comprende?*"

She hovered over him. Her breath was humid with a faint trace of smoke and lilac. Danny met her challenging gaze.

"*¿Por qué iba yo a dejar?*" he asked.

She began nodding, a dangerous smile touching her eyes. Cold fear clenched Danny's chest. Macy shoved away from the table and backed toward the front door before turning to leave.

His coffee was cold.

He needed to find out why Reed sent him here. *They* knew he was here. And Danny didn't know who *they* were, but Reed was sending cryptic poems and planting clues along the way. So there had to be a *they*.

Why would I leave? Macy knew exactly what he said in Spanish.

There was definitely a *they*.

17

Cyn

Duluth, Minnesota

A slick of sweat.

The air conditioner running, the ceiling fan blowing. The heat coming from inside her, a furnace churning hot coals.

Get up.

Electric light swam through the fan's blades, shadows flickering over textured ceiling. Shadows painted the corners while a late night pitchman demonstrated a waterless mop.

Wake up, darling.

Cyn's elbow sank into the cushion. Her head a dead weight. Mouth stuffed with cotton.

You're nothing. You don't exist because you're nothing—

"Shut up." She weaved her fingers through her hair, squeezing the sides of her head. "Shut up!"

It was better not to engage, not to recognize her. It only made her real, gave her substance. Brought the old woman closer to the surface.

She searched a pile of clothes, swiped papers off the coffee table—photos of the wilderness fluttered in front of the television, photos she wanted to ignore but couldn't escape. A glass of water soaked a *National Geographic* crumpled on the floor, the cover photo a puckering tropical island. A magazine that just showed up in the mail.

Her prescription bottle wasn't there.

You're nothing. Stop wasting my time and kill yourself.

"Shut up!"

It didn't make sense that Barb would want Cyn to kill herself. Where would the old woman be without the body? They were both in it. If Cyn killed herself, they'd both be dead. *Right?*

Laughter echoed.

These were the dark moments Cyn thought about suicide, to just end all this, to get it over with. What was the point? She lived alone. And every night was a battle with sanity.

With no end in sight.

But it was these dark moments when Barb came so close, when thoughts of suicide rose up that Cyn chose life. Because she knew the moment she swallowed enough pills to end this, Barb would win.

And Cyn was a fighter.

You silly girl. Silly, silly girl, Barb whispered. *You are a mistake, a hapless floundering mistake. You always have been, and always will be. You cling to nothing—*

"You did this!" Cyn kicked over the table. "You should've died! You lived your life, you old diseased bitch! Your life was over. You lived it! This is my body; now get out!"

You were nothing when I found you. A broken young girl with so much potential, wasting away while your body—your young and able body—was trashed and scorned. You didn't want it, so I took it. Now...let...GO.

"This is my body. My life."

Your life? And who are you?

Cyn crawled into the kitchen, searched the cabinets, pulled spices out of the cupboards, fumbled through empty containers and old prescription bottles.

Memories? Is that who you think you are...memories? Silly girl.

She searched for an answer, told herself not to engage, not to answer the old woman. But if she wasn't her memories, then what was she? She couldn't answer.

Memories were all she had.

She woke up in the Foreverland cabin, sixteen years old and a shaved head. She struggled to survive with no identity and none of her memories. It wasn't until her memories returned that she felt real, that she regained her youth and innocence. Even the memories—the abusive parents, the drugs and homelessness—they were better than none at all.

She went to the bathroom and searched under the sink. The towels hung off the corners of the mirror, a slice of her reflection looked back.

A wrinkled cheek.

Bright red lipstick.

"No."

Her lower lip quivered. That was her reflection. *But how...*

You wasted your life, didn't you?

Thoughts bubbled to the surface.

Cyn stood under the harsh light of a bare LED bulb, staring at the beige towels hanging over the mirror, recalling memories of a young girl that got a horse for her tenth birthday.

Of being elected high school president.

Graduating Princeton cumma sum laude.

Vacations. Marriage. Children. Grandchildren.

Yachts.

Cancer.

"Sweet Jesus." The words slipped out.

She hated it when that happened. That wasn't what she would say, never in her life. That was *Barb's* displeasure forming on her lips. Those were Barb's memories, that was her standing on beaches, living in mansions, wearing diamonds—

"No, no, no." She pulled her hair. "Get out of my head. Get out!"

The memories poured in like sewage.

Shhhh. Just close your eyes, darling. Just go to sleep. That's what you want. That's what the pills are for. Just sleep.

Her back ached. She did want to sleep, wanted to close her eyes and drift into bliss and never wake up.

You were never meant to be here.

Barb had taken her body. She had expelled Cyn into the Nowhere, cast her identity into the nothingness, into the eternal grayness, never to inhabit a body again.

But she did. Cyn came out of the Nowhere to find her body that they now shared already inhabited by Barb.

"This is my body."

Not for long.

"Get out."

Just sleep, darling. Shhhhhh.

A cold rush of fear gushed through her. Her grip on this moment was slipping.

"No!"

She slammed her fist into the towel, felt the mirror spider beneath it, the satisfying crackle of shards across the sink.

She ran into the front room, turned up the television and covered her ears, singing along to an infomercial that promised everlasting peace with one dose of biomites. She sang all her favorite songs.

And realized she'd never heard them before.

Shhhhhhh.

An old woman was watching her.

Wrinkles across her face, lips bright red. Jagged pieces missing from her torso.

A chunk of time was missing. *How did I get in the bathroom?*

The mirror was shattered; the fractured reflection of an old woman looked back, hypnotic eyes snaring Cyn, the truth swimming in their blue depths.

Barb was in the mirror.

A bottle rattled in Cyn's hand. The lid was off. Thirty pills inside. She had the impulse to pour them in her hand, to tip her head back and swallow.

"No."

Invisible strings tugged her hand. The jagged reflection watched her empty the bottle into her left hand and smiled. Cyn's jaw felt pried open, her head pulled back. Pills danced on the floor.

Most of them landed on her tongue.

Close your eyes. It'll all be over shortly.

Her cell phone was on the sink. She had no memory of putting it there.

You can't kill me, Cyn thought, *without killing yourself.*

Shhhhhhh.

You can't kill this body without killing yourself!

The invisible strings pulled her arm, this time toward the phone. She felt herself reaching for it, sliding her thumb over the glass. She would call for help after she swallowed.

And help would come. Help would come.

No, please.

Barb was close to the surface, her thoughts slipping into the light. Paramedics would pull her back from the brink of death; they would save the body. But Cyn would be unconscious. Barb would rise from the deep and snatch her up, would shove her into the dark subconscious where no one would hear her again. When the paramedics revived the body, Cyn wouldn't open her eyes.

Barb would.

Please don't throw me into the Nowhere, Cyn begged.

She hated herself for giving up, hated herself for letting Barb win, but she was willing to trade places with Barb, to be a prisoner in the dark subconscious if she just promised. *Not the Nowhere.*

Cyn swirled her tongue and managed to get three pills to fall out. A fourth stuck to her lip. The rest continued to melt.

Why are you doing this?

Barb didn't answer, just watched her slide down the glass door of the shower—phone still in hand—meeting the cold tile floor.

Danny, Cyn thought. *It was Danny.*

The old woman remained quiet, feeling the saliva pool under Cyn's tongue. It was in the diner, when Cyn was near Danny, that Barb went quiet. Somehow Danny's presence pushed her deep into the dark subconscious. He was a threat.

Barb knew it.

Danny! Cyn thought.

Her thumb slid across the phone. Numbers glowed beneath the glass. She attempted to throw the phone, but her elbow barely flinched.

No, you don't, Barb said.

She pushed the pills against the roof of her mouth, chalky residue squeezing between her teeth, saliva dangling from her lower lip. Cyn squeezed her eyes until sparks danced, and focused on her arm.

This time the phone bounced across the floor.

It hit the door jamb and ricocheted into the front room. The screen cracked. The numbers cast an eerie glow on the back of the couch.

She was kicked by an invisible boot. Her face slapped the floor. Half the pills were involuntarily spit out, but the rest were stuck inside her mouth. Her hand, moving on its own, scooped the slimy white mess back into her mouth.

The slurry began to slide down her throat.

She was forced to crawl into the front room. Her tongue swelled. She collapsed on one elbow. Her knees continued moving, sliding across the floor, hand extended, fingers stretching for the phone.

Closer, she moved.

Her legs lost feeling. Her hands tingled. Cyn willed herself to give into the numbing. She was quitting. Her body heard the white flag of surrender and answered.

Her hip thumped the floor.

The strings were cut. Barb pushed it, but she only squirmed like a poisoned animal. The phone was a mile away.

Get up, Barb hissed. *Get up, damn you.*

Half a smile curled on her lips. The pills would eventually go down. But without the phone, the paramedics wouldn't arrive. Cyn would die.

But so would Barb.

18

Danny Boy

Duluth, Minnesota

The foliage was thick and dewy.

The edges cut Danny. He ran blindly through the thicket. The tickle of hot breath was on his neck. Something crashed through the canopy. He didn't look back.

Nails dug into his back.

Leaves and dust swirled in the air. Despite the pain, there were no talons piercing his flesh, no predator above him. Just an invisible force lifting him into the clouds. He knew what would come next, what always came next.

Pelting sand.

Voices.

No sun above the clouds, no blue sky or stars. Just the endless gray of the Nowhere—

Danny!

He surged awake, jumped off the sweat-soaked bed, chest heaving, pulse thumping.

The hotel. He was in the hotel room.

Someone had shouted his name. There were people outside his room, but that's not where it came from. Someone called for him in his sleep. But the dream was always the same, never interrupted, never changed.

Someone needed him.

Heart still racing.

The moon illuminated his faint exhalations. Danny hesitated in the driveway. Cyn's house was nestled in the dark, the windows dark, a television splashing light from the corner.

Danny didn't believe in fate, didn't believe destiny was predetermined. He didn't believe in soul mates or the alignment of stars. Danny believed in free will.

But she needs me.

He cupped his hands to the window, risking looking like a complete creep. The porch was dark, the shadows hiding him from the street. The couch was empty. The microwave threw faint green light across the kitchen. If he rang the doorbell, how would he explain what he was doing there after midnight?

It already seemed like he was stalking her. Because he was. This would make it all too obvious.

He was about to turn around when something caught his eye. He pressed his face against the window. The microwave light revealed a sickly green arm from behind the couch.

Danny burst through the front door.

Cyn was curled up on the hardwood, convulsing, clutching an empty prescription bottle. A shiver shot through him.

She's laughing.

It gurgled in her throat. A hoarse, gravelly laugh crawled out of her. Her cheek lay in a pool of saliva; a white pill stuck to her lip. He hooked his finger under her tongue and pulled out a lump of half-melted pills. There were more. He dug deeper and she gagged.

Panic.

Did she already swallow them? Should I make her puke? Call for help?

She planked against the floor, vibrating like a bare wire pumping voltage through her legs. Something was grinding, like two stones under tremendous pressure. Her jaws were clenched.

He had to call someone, but in the rush out of the hotel he'd forgotten his phone. He had to do something. Run outside, pound on the neighbor's door, scream in the street...*something!*

A phone!

He scrambled over Cyn and grabbed the cell phone. The glass was shattered, but it lit up. He didn't need her code, just needed to press the *Emergency* icon.

No!

Her eyes snapped open, the whites on full display.

Danny crawled over to her. He took her hand, a long scar bright and raised across the back of it. Her fingers were stiff, her arm a rigid bar. He slid his palm against hers and cupped her hand between both of his hands. That sweet feeling he experienced in the diner returned, melting through his arm, lighting him up with peaceful warmth.

And something broke. Cyn fell limp.

He felt it when he squeezed her hand, like he'd triggered something. He felt it flow through his arm. Her eyes closed; her head rolled to the side.

"Cyn?" She stiffened when he started to let go. "Can you hear me?"

She panted. Hair plastered to her forehead. He brushed it aside and noticed the small scar where a needle had long ago carried her into Foreverland.

The phone began dimming. He debated. If she swallowed the pills, there was still time to pump her stomach. But when he took her hand, something stopped. He stroked her cheeks, flush and damp.

She squeezed back.

Her fingers tightened, just once. Like someone calling from the other shore, waving a flag. He squeezed again. Moments later, she squeezed back, a bit tighter, a little longer.

He leaned against the couch and pulled her head on his lap. She was so limp, burning hot. He wanted to get a damp rag to cool her, but every time he loosened his grip she would go rigid.

He couldn't explain why he didn't call for help. It was just a hunch.

He didn't believe in soul mates, didn't believe in fate. But he believed —for now, right now—she needed him.

Sunlight cut the outline of the front door.

A morning chill crept inside the house. The furnace kicked on, but the floor was cold. And hard.

Danny woke with a start, pain stabbing his neck. He'd slept on his side without a pillow. His hip and shoulder were bruised; his fingers, still laced with Cyn's, throbbed.

She breathed easy.

Her temperature was normal. They made it through the night. If she'd swallowed the pills, she wouldn't look so normal. But if he was wrong... *Why didn't I call for help?*

Slowly, he slid his hand away from her, folded her hands over her stomach and waited. She rolled her head, moaning. He almost reached back when she fell back to sleep.

Quickly, he went to the bathroom.

Towels were piled on the floor, shards of the mirror lay across the sink. Pills were scattered around the bathroom. It looked like suicide.

But why would the pills be everywhere?

It looked more like someone poured the pills down her. And what magic did Danny possess? He held her hand and it stopped. Then he realized what had happened to him.

No dreams!

He had fallen asleep and didn't dream. He couldn't remember the last time he wasn't cast into the nightmare. Each and every night he ran for his life, sometimes across the sand, sometimes through the jungle.

Always on the island.

Danny brought pillows and blankets to make her more comfortable. He'd stay until she woke up, make her breakfast. They could talk, really talk about what was happening, what all this meant and what they were supposed to do. Reed sent him for a reason.

He began picking up trash and cleared a place on the couch. If he could pick her up without disturbing her, she could sleep on the cushions. He noticed the envelopes. It was a stack of unwanted mail in a basket. It was mostly junk, and Danny wouldn't have given it a second thought had he not seen the green ink.

There were three large envelopes. Two more were under a pizza box, another one halfway beneath the couch. They were the same size, same thickness. The stiff outline of the disc was evident. All unopened.

He looked at her sleeping soundly.

She knew what was inside, knew that Foreverland was coming. And she wanted to forget.

But Foreverland came calling. He didn't know how or why, he was just glad he'd reached her in time.

Danny ripped the flap open.

The disc rolled out. The pattern of pinholes looked the same as the one he'd received. The only difference was the thick edge. His was blue, hers yellow.

A folded sheet of lined paper fell out.

Danny picked it up and held it to the light. There was nothing about building a bridge, just two lines written in green.

43.58039085560786

-107.24716186523438

He recognized the numbers. They were coordinates.

Raised letters had been pressed through the paper from the other side. He flipped it over to see the poem.

He put it in his back pocket.

Danny put her on the couch. He lay next to her, reciting the poem, dissecting and examining every word. He had to be sure.

Half an hour later, he backed the SUV into the driveway, loaded it with blankets and winter clothing and all the food and bottled water in the house. It was still very early when he carried her to the SUV and laid her in the passenger seat. No one saw them drive away.

Danny passed the hotel, but didn't stop. There was nothing he needed. He was thinking about the poem.

Where once there was light on a dusted rim,

When day followed day, now a night-filled sin,
Turn back your sight to where your steps begin,
And return to the root and fall again.

He programmed the coordinates into his GPS. That's why Reed sent him, to take her back to where her steps began.

To fall again.

19

Alessandra

New York City

The trees were turning.

It was still early September, but fall had begun showing its colors.

The waiting room was filled with children. Most were there for physicals, a little biomite boost to maximize their ability, to make them better athletes. Better students.

Just better.

A trail of taillights lit up the street, another day in traffic hell. The Institute was down the street on the corner of Forty-Sixth and Seventh. Tourists walked past without a glance into the prestigious research center, no clue that the world was being changed inside those doors. She considered making a surprise visit, tapping the intercom and asking for Dr. Baronov.

Today's not a day I want to be escorted away by security.

After her appointment, she'd call Kada. She used to be an editor for Penguin before becoming a freelancer. Kada took on a project here and there, even consulted with Alex, because she loved the business as much as she loved the city. And if she wasn't working, she was on Broadway.

And a show sounds good.

Someone yanked on her pant leg. "I think she wants you."

A little girl pointed across the room. The receptionist stared at Alex, eyebrows pinched, waving her over. Alex took her time.

"Anything wrong?" the receptionist asked.

"Just a checkup."

"I called your name five times."

She'd been doing that more often, getting lost in thought, losing track of time. It was just a few minutes here and there, but when she'd blanked out for an hour, she decided to make an appointment.

The receptionist tapped her computer screen with a long fingernail. "The doctor is waiting."

Alex went to the back room and stared at the inspirational poster of a grandmother watching children at play because biomites make life better.

She checked her phone, sat back and stared at the poster again, remembering a time when she was younger, when her parents would take her to the park and she'd play on the equipment for hours. Summer smelled like cut grass and tasted like sweet tea.

Ah, summer.

"*Hola.*" Dr. Johnstone opened the door.

Alex dropped her phone. She looked for her bag, but she'd left it in the waiting room. There were no new messages, but another time lapse occurred. Twenty minutes gone.

Damn it.

He washed his hands. Long curls of brown hair hung over his eyebrows. "How's the book going?"

"It's in a holding pattern."

"A little delay?"

"Something like that."

Her interview requests with Dr. Tyler Ballard had been rebuffed. Interviews with his doctors, lawyers, investigators and grocery store clerks had been denied, too. The Institute not only denied her access but filed a restraining order, citing her prying had damaged their research and if she was caught on or near the premises she would be arrested. Samuel wanted to restart the lawsuit, but Alex held out hope. If they sued, she'd never see the inside again.

"Well, you can't work all the time." The doctor checked his wristwatch. "Got to save some time to smell the flowers."

"I suppose."

"Just another day in paradise. Why would you ever want to leave?"

"What?"

"Mmm?"

"What did you say?"

He looked up. "Pardon me?"

"I'm sorry, I don't mean to sound defensive. You said something that sounded familiar."

"Another day in paradise?"

"The other one."

"Why leave?"

She nodded. It was something like that. *When life is so perfect, why would you ever want to change it? Or leave it?* Everything was perfect—perfect house, perfect marriage, perfect job. Perfect life.

Why would she ever want to leave?

Has it always been this way?

She didn't think so. Didn't her marriage suffer? Didn't Samuel have an affair or something? Those things sounded familiar, but what did any of that matter?

And isn't there something missing?

She wondered that every day, like there was an enormous hole below her, covered by the thinnest of materials, a cap that creaked with each step. She didn't want to know what was down there. If she did, she'd fall.

And everything was perfect.

"You having any problems?"

"No."

"No more episodes like last time?"

"No."

"Any unusual events, such as phantom car accidents?"

"Nothing."

"Anything suspicious?"

"Suspicious?"

"You know, out of the ordinary. Anything that might strike you as odd."

He doodled with the image on the desktop, of her brain lit up. There was a lot more red than the last time, most of it still in the right hemisphere. In fact, the entire right hemisphere was enflamed.

"Alessandra?"

"What?"

"Are you all right?"

"What did you just call me?"

He frowned.

"You called me Alessandra."

"I think I said Alex. Is there something else you prefer?"

Her knee was bouncing. She kept it hidden beneath the table. Maybe she should let him see it. If she was going to have an episode, this was a good time. She suddenly had her doubts about him, not sure she trusted him.

Then why am I here?

"So anything unusual?"

"I'm sleeping a lot."

"How much is a lot?"

"Twelve hours." *With naps, it was more like fourteen.*

"That's more than usual?"

"I think it's more than usual for anyone, don't you?"

"Not necessarily. Everyone's different. You said you weren't writing as much, you're working in the garden more often. Maybe your body is just catching up."

She didn't remember telling him about the garden.

"Listen," he said, "everything looks fine, Alex. In fact, your numbers are perfect. If I wasn't in the biomite technology field, I'm not sure I would even suspect you were seeded, that's just how perfect you are."

Her phone vibrated. A text arrived.

"How happy are you?" he asked.

"What?"

"On a scale from one to ten, how happy are you?"

"Eight."

She had no problems, no irritations. She had everything she could ask for. Isn't that what life was supposed to be? Shouldn't that be a ten?

Why did I say eight?

"There's a biomite update available, if you're interested." The doctor began washing his hands. "Nothing invasive, just a sync treatment to prevent any potential mutations. Not saying you're susceptible to a malfunction, it's just good to stay on top of things, stay preventative. All the trials for this new strain have been excellent. I fully recommend it. It'll take five minutes and then you're out of here."

She nodded. Her life was an eight. She wanted it to be a ten. *Doesn't everyone?*

He squeezed her shoulder and left the room with an adios.

Alex checked her phone. *Geri?*

For a moment, she couldn't recall the name. Then she remembered and it was clear. How could she forget her free-soul assistant? She hadn't heard from her all summer. Geri hadn't returned most of her messages, and when she did, she was too busy.

"Got something for you," the text said.

Alex texted back, "What?"

A minute later. "You in the city?"

"Yes." She stopped from texting back, *How did you know?*

"Meet at Bella's Deli at 4."

That was right down the street. She could walk there. In fact, Kada's apartment wasn't far from that. She could leave the car in long term.

A nurse arrived.

Alex leaned back and let her insert the seeder into her right nostril.

"Mrs. Diosa!" The receptionist held up a handbag.

Alex stopped at the door. That was her bag, the one she left in the waiting room. She was careful to watch her step on the way back, still a bit woozy.

The receptionist smiled. “Thank you.”

Alex wasn’t sure why she was being thanked. Everything had that double-vision feel, like the lenses were still being focused.

On the elevator, she checked her phone. It was past five. She’d been in the back room almost two hours. She thumbed her phone and Kada answered on the second ring.

“Come on over,” she said.

There was something else she was supposed to do, but there were no voicemails or texts. In fact, the only text she’d received that day was from Samuel. She decided to call him.

She really missed him.

Alex saw five Broadway shows that week.

She went by herself to see *Wicked* a second time. It was night when it ended. A drizzle wet the asphalt and beaded on the hoods of taxis. Despite the chill, she decided to walk back to Kada’s, maybe catch a cab on Forty-Eighth.

She enjoyed the lights, especially the way they stretched over the wet pavement, the way they sparkled on the buildings. It was the sound of cars honking, people shouting, the smell of exhaust that tingled her bones. It was all around.

It was the city.

My city.

She felt like she owned it. There was a connection deep in her core, a feeling that everything tugged at her heart, emanated from her soul; a connection that was seamless and unbreakable.

Even when someone coughed from a doorway and began following her, she was unshaken. She felt the gap in his teeth, the wet hair beneath his hood, the withdrawal shaking his hand. He didn’t harm her, didn’t ask for change or a handout. He just stopped following her at some point.

She should’ve found that odd, but she was connected. Didn’t everyone feel this?

This must be a ten.

She left Friday morning.

The traffic wasn't bad and it wasn't long before she was cruising through the hills. The phone rang.

"Where are you?" Samuel asked.

"Not far."

"I miss you."

She smiled. It felt much longer than a week. She foraged in her handbag for chapstick while steering with her knee. A manila package slid out, spilling its contents on the seat and floorboard.

"I'll leave work early," he said. "See you for lunch."

Alex waited for the next stoplight, glancing every so often at the cache spread across the floor mat. There were folders and photos and paper-clipped reports. Mail, too. When she caught a red light, she unbuckled her seatbelt and grabbed a handful.

The reports were from Geri.

There was a vague memory of wanting to meet her in the city. *Wasn't I supposed to be at a deli?*

A quick skim revealed loads of inside information, photos of a young Tyler and Patricia Ballard, stuff Alex could only dream of finding. *How does she do it?*

She'd have to give her a bonus when the book published.

The mail, though, wasn't addressed to Alex and it didn't belong to Geri. It wasn't a letter, it was a flier. One of those small glossy cards. It said, *Have you seen this boy?*

There was a photo.

A car horn blared. The light was green.

The postcard slipped from her fingers and fell to the floorboard. She drove the rest of the way home, reading random sheets of paper pinned to the steering wheel, whatever she could grab while driving through the countryside, occasionally driving off the road or crossing the center line.

Tyler Ballard was a young neuroscientist. Patricia was a psychologist. Both were tenured professors at an Ivy League university, career-minded people intent upon helping the world.

Then Patricia was diagnosed with early onset Alzheimer's. The story of the couple was well documented. The public empathized.

Until the holes appeared.

Tyler was researching his controversial technology that involved brains, computers and needles in the brains of rats and mice, but was not given permission for human trials. The couple attempted to cover the evidence, but was quietly placed on leave with pay.

He took his research to the basement.

There were pictures of Patricia in the basement with a needle protruding from her forehead, Tyler in his basement lab with eyes that hadn't slept for days.

And a photo of them lying in bed, holding hands.

If she didn't know how the story ended—Foreverland kidnapping youth—her heart would ache.

Alex threw the papers on the kitchen table and shuffled through them like gold coins.

The postcard was on the bottom.

She held it up as if it was hard to see. Even under the light, it felt dim. It was a picture of a twelve-year-old boy. He was Hispanic with short black hair, his eyes large and brown. His smile sly and knowing.

The back door slammed, but no one was there.

The room began turning.

She needed water. Dehydration caused room spins. She stood at the sink, downing a tall glass of water when the music began.

It was upstairs.

"Hello?"

It wasn't a radio. It was more bells and tones, something more soothing, like a lullaby.

A crib mobile.

"Samuel?"

She put one foot on the bottom step and the room suddenly turned her toward the couch.

There was a box of crayons on the floor, paper on the end table, but not the papers from the car. These were pulled from a coloring book with bright faces and purple lips and yellow eyes.

She threw herself against the wall and followed it through the kitchen, made it to the back door in time to puke over the railing.

The petunias were a mess.

A car pulled up as she heaved round three, this one squeezing her gut like a wrung towel.

Samuel jumped out. He was by her side for a moment, running inside the house. She sat down and closed her eyes, the acrid taste of vomit in her sinuses.

The Tilt-O-Whirl began to slow.

"What happened?" Samuel put a wet rag on her forehead.

She didn't know, explained the room-spins, the sudden nausea. She thought he was home, that he was upstairs playing...*music*? What the hell happened?

The biomite sync.

She'd been fine all week. Better than fine, in fact. She'd been perfect.

A ten.

When she was ready, when she trusted her body to stand up, she made it inside the house without assistance. The floor didn't spin, the walls didn't turn. She just wanted a warm shower and a nap.

On her way past the dining room table, the papers were neatly stacked. The front room was clean, no coloring book pages scattered on the floor. And no music.

It was later she thought something was missing.

A postcard, or something.

20

Tyler

ADMAX Penitentiary, Colorado

Tyler's bed didn't creak, just gently squished under him.

He reached beneath the mattress and stared at the surgical steel needle encased in a tube of gel. He broke the seal—his arthritic hands knobby in the joints, the thin skin spotted—and admired the perfect symmetry of the needle, the silver gleam and dangerous point.

Anticipation wet his mouth.

Pins rolled beneath the mattress, massaging his legs, back and buttocks. He positioned the tip of the needle near the stent. The leathery flesh began to throb. Sometimes, he rammed it into his head and his consciousness would be slung into another dimension.

He kept his eyes open, breathed deep the musty odor of the prison's painted walls and slid it slowly into his forehead. The cold spike sank its fang.

The ceiling swirled into the sky, the walls fell apart.

There was no sensation of travel, no illusion of space. *The needle's kiss.*

His reflection looked back from a ticket kiosk. He was wearing khaki pants and a navy blue blazer. He ran his hand through thick wavy hair the color of honey and straightened his open collar, a gold ring glinting in the theatre's lights.

The city smelled like a cleansing rain. There was no exhaust, no trash—just the sterilized version of a perfect society. *A perfect reality*.

The usher opened the door.

A few people milled through the lobby in tuxedos and long gowns. Beyond another set of doors, a tenor bellowed opera.

An escort led him to a grand tier box with two seats. Below, *Phantom of the Opera* unfolded. He sat next to Patricia, reached into her lap and took her hand. She held him tightly, her other hand holding a tissue to her chest.

She would sob when it was over.

She always did.

Patricia slid her hand over the brass rail.

The theatre was empty. The crowd had dispersed, leaving in their cars or calling cabs, heading back to their supposed homes. In Patricia's Foreverland, they were just illusions of her own mind, but he often wondered if she replicated them from actual people in the city.

The details of the theatre, the opera singers and the custodians sweeping the stage were flawless. Her ability to absorb these details from the space around her physical body, as it lay in the Institute, and project them into her Foreverland was as uncanny as it was unexplainable. Her mind was an ethereal sponge.

Is the physical world any more legitimate than Foreverland? Under what pretense is physicality the gold standard?

That was the question he begged all of humankind to answer.

"Tyler? Are you listening?"

"I'm sorry, lost in thought. You were saying?"

"I'm concerned."

"And what are your concerns?"

"Your body, for one. I was looking at the results of your latest physical."

He didn't want her to worry, frequently hiding the dire conditions he encountered in physical reality, but it was difficult to hide his thoughts or emotions when he came here, where all was on display.

"I want you to consider using the good doctor's new biomite strain. It will stabilize your health, guarantee longevity."

"It's too much risk."

"Your health is far too fragile to argue. If you lose your body at the wrong time, then where will I be?"

"I fear government intervention is more to be worried about than my health. Abusing biomites will set off alarms. We don't need the authorities watching us too closely."

"What about undetectable biomites, the ones Gramm spoke of?"

He shook his head. "You speak of things far more risky. My body is old, yes. There are aches and pains, but it will last as long as we need it to last. And when the time comes, we will cross over into Alessandra's eternal Foreverland. Don't worry yourself, please."

She drummed her fingers on the brass rail, watching men push brooms across the stage. "Perhaps you should stay here, then. We'll cross over when she's ready."

She didn't look at him when she said it.

He could feel her loneliness when he was gone. Living in this Foreverland, within her own mind, knowing these were merely reflections of people in the physical world and not actual beings was distressing. No matter what shapes and sizes and colors she looked at, no matter how human they seemed, they were all projections of her mind.

She needs me.

"I can't leave my body," he said. "Not yet."

"But she is almost ready."

"That's not it. I need to be here, in the prison. There are still matters to attend."

"And Gramm cannot do them?"

He trusted the former chemist, but he was weak. His mind was too open, his taste for biomites too strong. Tyler feared his assistant could be overwhelmed by the wrong person too easily. And that he could not risk.

"Perhaps it's time to abandon the prison," she said. "It's always been a risk. And now that the Institute is fully functional, there's no reason for you not to come here."

He cocked his head. "What's really bothering you, dear?"

She wiped her eyes and stuffed the tissue in her purse. Perhaps the opera jarred loose long-held emotions she didn't want to face, or didn't know were there. *There is so much in the subconscious that a thousand lifetimes could not uncover the secrets we keep from ourselves.*

"I don't think Alex will sleep," she said. "There have been too many disruptions."

"Anomalies."

"More than anomalies, Tyler. Someone is purposefully enticing her to remember."

She refused to name him, as if uttering *Reed* would somehow summon him into being.

"She won't remember her past. And even if Reed is behind this, he won't succeed. Her life is perfect, darling. She'll soon forget everything and sleep."

He floated a thought into this world. Unlike physical reality, a thought here could become a wish that, falling into the right context, was fulfilled. Tyler envisioned a man dressed in black and called him to the stage.

Moments later, a man dressed in black strode across the stage, his face partially obscured by the white mask. The custodians continued sweeping as he lifted an arm and his voice carried into the empty theatre.

"Think of Me", he sang all alone.

It tugged at the emotion welling just beneath Patricia's eyes.

Tyler held out his hand. There was no more talk of biomites and host, no more worry about the future. Everything was going near enough to plan that Tyler pulled her close for the remainder of his stay.

In the grand tier box, they danced.

He opened his eyes, a concrete ceiling above him, a dull wall beside him. And all the aches and pains, the stiffness of eighty years surrounded him.

He extracted the needle.

It slithered out and left behind an antiseptic sting. Tears involuntarily welled up. He hated to leave her, to come back to this plane. If hell existed, it was in the physical world, not some distant make-believe. He no longer doubted that.

The opera still echoed in his head.

He wiped his eyes. The throbbing continued.

An infection was setting in. Soon, it would alter the function of his brain and, in turn, the quality of his mind. Even if he avoided the needle and went to wireless brain biomites, the infection was already there.

Have I already failed you, dear?

He blinked away the tears. More had pooled against the bridge of his nose. Patricia trusted him. It was her vision to create Foreverland, to build a new reality. She was the one that conceived of it in the very beginning, not him. She knew, long before biomites were ever conceived, that all the minds in the world could be linked, that human singularity was possible, that the illusion of separateness could be dispelled.

And peace would reign.

While astrophysicists searched for new worlds in faraway solar systems, she knew that a new reality was not light-years away, but the distance of a thought.

It's here. We *are the new reality.* We *are the endless possibilities. We are heaven, we are hell.*

And she trusted him to bring her vision to fruition, trusted his technology, trusted him to plug her into the needle first. It nearly killed her. Had it done so, he would surely have taken his own life, not strong enough to bear the guilt, not brave enough to go on without her.

But now there was little sand left in the hourglass for him. Time was the god that meted out each grain with methodic timing and refused to sell more. Time was a cruel god that promised eternity.

But delivered only the past.

His bare foot found the floor. Slowly, he slid his feet into slippers and opened the cell door. Moonlight cast his shadow. He passed a guard holding the elevator open at the end of the hall, and pressed a button on the panel.

Tyler's stomach dropped all the way to the basement.

The smell greeted him.

Sunrise was still hours away. His guards were at home, sleeping next to their spouses. He was alone. If he fell, he would call them. Despite his confidence, he managed to keep the depth of his concern hidden from his bride.

Reed is more than an anomaly.

Tyler went down the hall and put his hand on a metal door. Death and decay slammed into him like a hot cloud, licked his face with a humid tongue.

Tables were lined up.

Their metal edges dull and curved, their surfaces soft—each held a nude male. Tubes ran from their thin arms, trailing over their protruding ribs. Some of them were connected to respirators.

All of them had a needle in their forehead.

A lamp was positioned over each table, exposing each body with the spectrum of sunlight to stimulate vitamin D. They were a much higher form of plants. The bodies were necessary for the mind to exist.

One day that would change.

Tyler idly walked amongst his people. Green lights glowed at the head of each table, splashing the floor with an eerie effect. Some of the indicators were yellow instead of green, indicating stress, whether mental or physical. A few were red.

These were the ones that smelled the worst.

They would need to be disposed of in the furnace like annual flowers that had reached the end of their life cycle and fulfilled their duty.

These were his people. They were willing to send themselves into Foreverland, to sacrifice themselves to create a new reality. They were willing to die for him. Some did so consciously, others he convinced.

The justice system thought they had sentenced Tyler to prison. This was to be his punishment. But he chose to be here. Where else would he find so many lives that didn't matter? Where else would he find so many men that wouldn't be missed?

Men to build the next Foreverland.

Gramm rose from sleep.

His awareness floated to the surface like a hand gently lifted him from the sandy depths, a whisper that commanded he wake. His senses clouded, he nabbed the webbing of flesh between his finger and thumb and twisted until cold flames lanced into his palm.

He tasted the pain. And that was good. It was real.

Too often, he had awakened to find himself in the throes of reality confusion, not sure if he was indeed in the flesh or Foreverland. It was difficult to trust life when he didn't know where he was. Or who.

Pain, he had learned, tasted different in the flesh. It was immediate and fresh. It grounded him. Made him real. If he didn't taste the cold burn, he knew he had awakened in Foreverland.

Did that matter?

The cell door was unlocked. Gramm was still dressing as he skipped down the hallway and took the waiting elevator to the pool.

Chlorine stung his nostrils.

Gramm raked his thinning hair and watched Tyler swim another lap in the Olympic pool. His strokes were long and methodical. Gramm waited with a towel and an open robe. The old man climbed out of the water, his flesh soft and puckered, like soaked leather. It was gray and patchy, moles dotting his hairless chest.

Only his forehead was red and puffy.

"Thank you." He took the towel.

A pool of this size and quality was unheard of in a correctional facility. But the warden seemed to see it Tyler's way.

We all do.

An inmate met them at a small table against the wall, placed two mugs in front of them, poured coffee and slid a plate of fresh fruit toward Tyler. They watched three other men begin maintenance on the pool.

Tyler chewed like he swam: slow and methodical. “You are aware of what has happened?” he asked.

“Yes.”

Gramm sipped the coffee, watching the men untangle the hose and test the water. He didn’t meet Tyler’s eyes, but felt the tension emanating from the old man’s chest, felt the twist in his gut. Felt his pain, his fear.

It had been that way ever since Gramm had received biomite remediation. It was experimental, the state’s attempt at rehabilitation. He volunteered and would get time off his sentence by taking biomites. Days later, he sensed thoughts that weren’t his own, moved his fingers when he hadn’t wanted to.

Felt the probing of another mind.

And then the barrier between Tyler and Gramm dropped like a curtain. The illusion of their separation—that they were individuals—evaporated. Like fingers, they belonged to a hand.

The hand of God.

Tyler had synced their brain biomites. Gramm watched him do the same to the guards, the staff and even the warden, watched him slowly take control. The takeover happened years ago. *Seems like yesterday.*

“Alessandra is on schedule,” Gramm said. “She’ll sleep, I promise. She will become the host.”

Tyler hummed. Alessandra was happy. She was satisfied, drifting toward a blissful state of open awareness. Soon, she would be sleeping. She would become the unknowing host of Foreverland.

“And Danny and Cyn?” Tyler said.

He wasn’t asking. He knew what had happened. Gramm had promised that it wouldn’t. And now, for a second time, the kids were gone. He didn’t know how. Or why.

They need to be terminated. He wanted to say it. Instead, he let the thought linger for Tyler to see.

“There is an infection in Foreverland, Gramm. A virus.”

Tyler wiped his mouth thoughtfully.

“I’ve assured Patricia that everything is under control, that these complications were not unexpected. I don’t want her to worry, you see. But Alessandra has received information she should not be receiving.

She saw a photo of the child, you see, so let's not be naïve. Is that understood?"

"Yes."

"Good. I believe it is Reed; let's accept that. He has been communicating with them."

"But there's been no communication, I assure you. No email, phone calls, or texts. His presence has been nonexistent since his death. There's just no evidence he exists. It's just not possible. He's dead, sir."

"And mail?"

"Pardon me?"

"You've been monitoring the mail, as well?"

Gramm hadn't thought of that. A letter wouldn't be detected, it would have to be intercepted. That wouldn't be difficult to do, he just hadn't thought of it.

"Alessandra has been receiving dubious mail and photos of the island through magazines and false advertisements, correct?"

Gramm nodded.

"Our perpetrator is using outdated means. Surely he knows we've discovered it by now—a very audacious move to send her a photo of the child. He wanted us to know that, I believe. He wanted us to know that his pieces are in place. The question is, where is he? Mmm? Where is Reed?"

"I just...I don't see how he could be anywhere."

"You mean you don't see him?"

"Correct."

"So what you don't see doesn't exist?"

"That's not what I'm saying. It's just, there's no evidence he exists."

"The evidence is right in front of us, Gramm. Let's move past the doubt and accept that we've been outplayed and answer the question. If you can't see him, does that mean he doesn't exist?"

"Not necessarily."

"If you can't see him, then where could he be?"

The old man chewed the last cube of cantaloupe and waited for an answer. Waited for Gramm to say it first.

If you can't find someone in Foreverland, they can only be in one place.

"The Nowhere doesn't exist," Gramm said. "Not anymore."

"There is always a Nowhere. We can't be so arrogant to think that we have obliterated it. There will always be a boundary, a perimeter outside the realm of knowing, where nothing exists. And where nothing exists, everything exists."

Gramm felt nauseous. "I don't believe it," he muttered. "There is no Nowhere."

"What we believe does not shape reality."

"I beg your pardon?"

A wry smile curled the corner of the old man's mouth like the dry twist of a senescing leaf.

"What we believe doesn't shape reality?" Gramm stammered. "I thought..."

Belief was the basis of the new reality, the creation of Foreverland. The inner reality that Harold, Tyler's son, had created was based on his imagination. The inner reality that Patricia, Tyler's wife, had created was the result of her imagination. What she believed came true. The Foreverland she hosted was her mind; she made the rules of its existence. She invented the physics by which all of life had to abide.

What we believe becomes our reality!

"There are other forces at work, Gramm. In this case, I believe that other force to be Reed. And while our reality is shaped by our convictions, it cannot bend the unbendable truth, the true nature of existence, that Reed is throwing chaos into our well-laid plans. We need to deal with it. We cannot close our eyes and wish him away. In this case, we deal with life on life's terms."

"But how could he exist?"

"Ah, yes. How?" Tyler pushed his plate away. An inmate swept it up and replaced it with a fresh cup of coffee. "You recall how Reed was introduced to Foreverland when he was first brought to the island?"

Of course. Reed was the boy that refused to take the needle, the one that stole Harold's body.

"But Reed didn't destroy Foreverland." Tyler picked up Gramm's thoughts. "Who destroyed Harold's Foreverland?"

It was Reed's girlfriend. Lucinda.

That was the true anomaly. Her memory escaped Reed when he

was brought to the island. That memory was intact, a fully embodied awareness that woke up in Foreverland. She went from being a memory to a conscious being.

In Harold's mind!

She fled to the Nowhere, the gray static where nothing survived. She lived out there and watched the boys and girls arrive in Foreverland to play their games before they were sucked into the Nowhere themselves, where they were pulled apart, their skins left behind for the old men and women to inhabit.

"Is it not a coincidence, then," Tyler continued, "that it is Reed that haunts us?"

"What are you saying?"

"Maybe Lucinda didn't escape his memory in the first place. Maybe he was capable of sending her there, whether he was aware of it or not. And we underestimated him, Gramm. All this time, he was the one that ruled the Nowhere, not Lucinda."

They always thought Danny was the intelligent threat. Now there was the possibility that Reed had somehow survived in Foreverland without a physical body.

Could survive in the Nowhere.

If it is Reed, we have indeed been duped.

"The next question," Tyler said, "is what is he planning?"

"Revenge."

"Too shallow. Vengeance is for children, and a child cannot play this game. There is something larger at stake, a whole new universe. No, these are calculated disruptions. He's patient. And there's a pattern, I believe."

"Perhaps we're not looking at it from the right angle." The words spilled from Gramm's mouth as if they were not his thoughts.

"Precisely. We are not seeing the pattern because we are not looking at it the right way."

They finished their coffee.

The table was cleared. The pool was clean. Just the hum of the pumps filled the silence.

"What would Reed want, if not vengeance?" Tyler pondered.

"Lucinda."

The old man snapped his fingers, nodding with a smile. "True love is quite a motivator, yes. But what else would he want?"

"Justice."

"Yes, justice. His perception is that a great injustice has been done and he is the equalizer, that he will right the wrong."

"What injustice is he after?" Gramm asked. It was obvious, but he had asked it, the words tumbling out as if they did not belong to him, once again.

"Sacrifice, Gramm. Revolution requires sacrifice, it has always been thus. And who perceives injustice more greatly than the ones that have been sacrificed?"

"The children."

In the making of Foreverland, children had been forced to leave their bodies and were sentenced to the eternal Nowhere. *But don't they realize we are creating a new universe, an entirely new reality? Even the physical universe demands a price for its creation. There are black holes that gobble light, there are volcanoes and asteroids and predators and prey. Sacrifice is the nature of creation. Even children.*

"Bring her to me," Tyler said.

"Alessandra?"

"Yes. Grant her the interview she requested."

"Is that a good idea?"

"I want to make contact with her, see where she is, feel her out. See her from another angle. The sooner she sleeps, the sooner she is ready for Foreverland. We don't know where Reed is, Gramm. We don't know what he's doing, and time is not on our side."

"When do you want to see her?"

The old man stood. "Soon."

That was all he said. His guards appeared, the two he most relied on. His personal attendants.

"What if we fail?" Gramm said. "Contacting her could make her unravel into madness. Maybe Reed is planning that you'd do this."

"Maybe."

A cold chill passed through Gramm. It didn't emanate from the old man this time.

Tyler eschewed the wheelchair Melfy was pushing and shuffled away holding her elbow instead, like he had all the time in the world. But if time were currency, the old man was nearly broke. Yet he walked like a prince.

A prince that would become a king.

The old man stopped at the door. "Maybe we're already in Reed's Foreverland and don't know it yet."

He was joking, of course. They couldn't be in a Foreverland without knowing it. Certainly not in Reed's mind.

Gramm twisted the webbing between his finger and thumb.

The pain was good.

21

Alessandra

ADMAX Penitentiary, Colorado

The table was metal.

Cold.

Alex rubbed her hands on her thighs. But it wasn't the table or the metal chair that drove a shiver deep inside. It was the white light. It was the putty walls with hairline fractures. It was the smell of suffering.

This was the Alcatraz of the Rockies.

She'd been in federal prisons before, even the extant Russian gulags and Nazi gas chambers, where ghosts tugged at her soul. But this...this felt colder, like apparitions floated around the table, taking turns sitting in the empty chair across from her.

She'd flown out of New York the same day she got the invitation, and stayed in the nearest hotel for two days. Now she tapped her toe and rubbed her thighs for warmth.

She spread the folders on the table to get her mind off the chill and organized two stacks of photos that still smelled of new ink. In one stack, there were photos of a tropical island, the palms tall and bending, the grass green and lush. The other stack contained desolate hills and harsh living and gray skies.

The walls shuddered.

Momentarily, the floor jiggled like gelatin, the colors smeared. Lately things had been a little off, like a camera constantly trying to autofocus. She rubbed her eyes. When she opened them, a door was open in the anteroom.

Through the wire-mesh glass, Alex watched a guard enter, his belly filling the doorway. He was followed by an old man dressed in a saggy blue shirt and loose-fitting pants. The hunch between his shoulders caused him to look at the floor. He was followed by another guard, this one female. She held the old man's elbow.

Alex stood. The legs of the chair raked the concrete.

The big guard held the interview room door open. The old man's slippers scuffed the floor. He paused at the empty chair, wheezing. The guards remained until he waved his knobby hand.

As if dismissed.

"Dr. Ballard?" Alex said.

The old man blinked slowly, lazily. The gray eyes rested on her. His nostrils flared. He tipped his head, examining her as a collector might evaluate a new possession. His eyes appeared to smile, but his lips remained a grim slit beneath a lumpy nose.

"I'm Alex Diosa. Thanks for agreeing to meet with me."

She knifed her hand over the table. Dr. Ballard never took his eyes off of her. Neither did he move his hand.

Alex looked through the wire-mesh window. The guards sat in chairs as bare as the ones in the interview room. She wondered if Dr. Ballard could hear her, if maybe dementia had taken hold. She'd heard strange things about him, that he preferred long bouts of solitary confinements—sometimes weeks at a time. *Did I read that or see it on* 60 Minutes*?*

"Can you hear me?" she asked.

"Yes, Mrs. Diosa."

She had the urge to run, to leave the briefcase her father gave her twenty years ago for graduation, to abandon her notes and belongings like rubbish and flee through the wire-mesh glass. It was his voice, the way it resonated inside her. She'd heard it before. *No. I've felt it.*

Alex fumbled with the pictures, pulling the paperclips off of bundles Geri had assembled for her, bundles Alex took apart over and over late at night, reshuffling and reorganizing. She'd memorized every photo, every note, but now aimlessly looked through them.

Deep breath.

He was smiling—the corner of his mouth curled like a hook. He cocked his head curiously.

My grandfather used to do that. Alex jerked at the sudden realization, felt the warmth of familiarity soothe her flailing nerves. He didn't look anything like her grandfather. Still, she couldn't help but smile.

"I'm an investigative journalist," she started. "I wrote for *The Washington Post* as well as *The New Yorker*, *60 Minutes* as well as producing several documentaries. I've written books on crimes against humanity in North Korea. You might be familiar with some of my work."

She mentioned a few. He smiled.

"And what do you want?"

"I'm researching the Foreverland crimes."

"Is that what you really want from me?"

"I'm looking for the truth, yes."

"And what is truth?"

He didn't say *the* truth. He just said *truth,* like a Buddha searching for deeper meaning. She looked at the photos. Her hands were steady, but her heart fluttered. "I want to know how all this started."

"Is truth relative, Mrs. Diosa?"

"Let me be clear, I'm looking for facts."

"Ah, facts. That's different than truth."

"I don't believe so, Doctor."

His eyes flickered upward, looking just above her eyes, right in the middle of her forehead. A shiver raced beneath her scalp, a tingly net that wrapped around her head, microwaving her brain. There was a circular scar on his forehead, about the size of a chicken pock, where a hole used to be, where a needle used to go.

Now healed over.

"You're the inventor of computer-aided alternate reality," she said. "It was your technology that spawned Foreverland."

And your son.

His right eye twitched, as if he heard her thinking. He drew a deep breath and coughed into his fist. "I've been in prison for thirty years," he said. "What do you want from me?"

"I know you didn't have anything to do with it, but—"

"Then why are you here?"

He asked that question as if it had nothing to do with what she was saying, like a Zen Master asking his pupil what the true nature of reality is.

No, no. Why are you HERE?

She found a photo of a group of old women standing in a patch of dead grass. Young women, ranging in ages from twelve to eighteen years old, were behind them. "This was the second Foreverland, I'm sure you know. Your wife helped these wealthy women acquire the young bodies of the girls behind them. Your wife erased the identities of these young girls so that they left behind their living bodies."

He was nodding but looking at her in that examining way again.

"It's body snatching, Dr. Ballard. Murder. It never should've happened."

"Why is that?"

"Why is...it's *murder*."

"We are still human, Alessandra. We evolved to survive."

"We're talking about teenagers."

"Children die every day. In underprivileged countries, they die by the thousands. And you're concerned with a few?"

"I'm concerned that privileged men and women are kidnapping neglected children instead of accepting their own death. We're still human, Dr. Ballard, yes. Not immortal."

He stroked the tabletop, blinking slowly.

She hesitated before reaching for the briefcase and dropped a manila folder on the table and displayed newspaper articles dating back decades.

"Your wife, Patricia Ballard, suffered from schizophrenia. You invented CAAR in an attempt to stabilize her mind. You continued to do so even after you were arrested the first time."

He didn't look at the articles, didn't see the photo of a younger Dr. Ballard in his basement laboratory wearing a striped necktie, his thick wavy hair combed to the side. He didn't see the picture of the beautiful woman, either, or read about their only child, Harold Ballard.

"What did you expect to happen?" she asked.

The tone of her question came out all wrong. She only wanted to ask why he would take such a risk by sticking a needle in his wife's head. Instead, it sounded like she questioned why he would invent an alternate reality.

He sniffed briefly; his nostrils, like before, flared momentarily. He slightly craned his neck toward her.

"What," he asked carefully, "is love?"

"I'm sorry?"

"Love, Mrs. Diosa. What is love?"

"You're saying you did it because you loved her?"

"What would you do for someone you loved? Would you not have compassion? Would you not sacrifice everything for that person?"

"You loved her?"

"True love, Mrs. Diosa, has many faces. Some not so pleasant. Would you agree?"

"I'm afraid I'm not following."

"What would you sacrifice for someone you loved?"

"That's got nothing to do—"

"Would you sacrifice yourself? Would you?"

She shook her head. "Dr. Ballard—"

"Answer the question, please." His smile was as gentle as his words.

"Yes."

"Of course you would. And what if your sacrifice would save millions? Would you?"

She looked through the wire mesh. The guards looked asleep.

"Why are you asking me this?"

"I'm curious." Soft smile. "Would you give yourself to save millions of people?"

"You're talking about a biblical savior."

"Not necessarily. It could be any reason, perhaps a blood type or an antibody that makes you special. But you had to give yourself entirely, unconditionally. Would you?"

She shook her head. "Could you look at these pictures?"

He covered her hand with his. It was papery, but warm. He blinked slowly. "Answer me honestly. That's all I ask."

She wanted to put the newspaper articles back, wanted to shove everything on the floor, sit back and listen to him. His voice had a soothing quality, a vibrato that resonated somewhere between her eyes. In her chest.

"Yes," she whispered.

"Of course you would." He sat back and folded his hands in his lap. "Have you ever heard voices?"

"What?"

"In your head, have you heard voices? The chatter of another mind inside your head, arguing with you about everything, whispering to you at night? Have you?"

"I..." She clasped her hands under the table, swallowed and lied. "No."

"Have you ever scratched yourself until you bled, hoping if you dug deep enough you would let the voices out?"

Alex shook her head.

"My wife suffered, Mrs. Diosa. And nothing was helping her. I would do anything to help her. I believe you would, too."

"You're saying your wife was schizophrenic?"

"Have you ever wished for a better place?" he continued. "Have you ever closed your eyes and dreamed of a world where there's no pain, no suffering? A place many people call heaven?"

She swallowed spastically. Suddenly, she was sleepy.

His eyebrows pinched together. Lines wrinkled his forehead, the circular scar, the size of a BB, bulged on a crest of old skin. Sadness dripped inside her, as if emanating from across the table. So many emotions she couldn't explain, this interview was a carnival ride whirling through the night.

"Your son," she whispered, cleared her throat and tried again. "Did you teach him how to do it?"

He looked disappointed and clucked his tongue. *Who is interviewing who?*

"He must've seen you doing it," Alex continued. "Went down to the basement, saw Mommy with the needle in her..."

The wind ran out of her. Her throat constricted. Not another word could fight through it. The doctor looked at his hands, nodding while he recalled.

"He was still a child," he said, "when I was sent to prison."

"Then how did he know how to do it?"

"He was always bright. And he loved his mother."

"He loved her so much that he left her in the wilderness."

Something triggered inside her, a stone pulled from the bottom of the pile, a landslide beginning to tumble.

"You don't understand what he created—"

"He destroyed children." She slammed her fist on the table. She jumped at her own anger, while he merely sat back.

"The death of children," he said, "was not intended."

"Just an unfortunate side effect?"

"I was in prison."

"But you could've stopped him."

"Mrs. Diosa, unfortunate events happen every day. We call them unfortunate because they bring suffering. Now I asked you if you wanted to know truth."

"You haven't told me anything yet."

"God allows the world to suffer, would you agree?"

"You don't strike me as religious, Doctor."

"And yet God allows torture and death. Criminals savage their victims—"

"What defines a criminal, Doctor?"

"Storms strip people of their homes, natural disasters wreck their lives, disease takes away loved ones. This is the nature of the world we live in, Mrs. Diosa. Would you agree?"

Her throat tightened.

"Good and bad, Mrs. Diosa, are part of life. One event is deemed good if we favor it, bad if we don't. Without our interpretation, it is just life. Just God. And God allows it all to exist; He accepts the world as it is, allows it to exist. Can you be like that, Mrs. Diosa? Can you allow the world to exist?"

"They were children..."

"Can you be like God? Can you allow reality to be as it is?"

He blinked so slowly she thought she'd entered a time warp.

"What if you can do better than God?" he asked. "What if you can create a world without suffering, would you do it? The children wouldn't suffer anymore, Mrs. Diosa."

"What are you talking about?"

The slightest curl twisted the corner of his mouth. "What would you sacrifice to end the suffering? Would you climb upon the cross?"

She shook her head, tried to swallow.

She wouldn't say it out loud, wouldn't give him the satisfaction. Would she sacrifice herself for the world? Would she give up her family to end all suffering? Would she create Foreverland?

Yes.

He closed his eyes, nodding, as if savoring a moment, the taste on his dry tongue. It sounded like something was stuck in his throat. He was humming.

The interview door opened.

The female guard placed a glass of water on the table. Dr. Ballard drank as he looked through the tropical pictures.

A glass in prison?

This was all wrong. Paperclips, pens and glass were being passed around like Office Depot, not a supermax federal prison.

Alex felt depleted. She let her eyelids fall for a long moment. When she opened them, the old man had already reached the end of the pile. Both guards helped him stand before he made an effort. His right knee was stiff.

"Would you care to walk, Mrs. Diosa?"

"A walk?"

The ground was damp and the air crisp, the sun above the distant mountains. It had recently rained. The roads were dusty on the drive in. Now everything was clean.

How long were we in there?

The doctor stood on a concrete slab with a cane, his right leg still stiff. But he wasn't hunched over anymore. In fact, his complexion wasn't ashen, either.

Maybe it's the sunlight.

There were no guards at his side. Beyond, the inmates played basketball or sat on picnic tables. If someone meant to do them harm, there was nothing they could do. But none of them looked at Alex, the only female in the yard. As if she didn't exist.

"And how are you feeling now?" he asked.

"A little nervous."

"You looked a little pale inside. I thought a walk would do us good. You came so far to see me."

He gestured at the track that circled the chain-link fences and barbed wire. Guard towers with black windows were stationed in the corners. He patted her hand.

"I wasn't expecting this," she said.

"What were you expecting?"

This was supposed to be a hard-hitting interview, her one chance to unearth details the world had never seen about the man behind Foreverland. She felt like a little girl seeing the mountains for the first time.

The wonder.

"Are you happy?" he asked.

He was looking through her, like he'd done inside. His eyes were x-rays, seeing her thoughts and feelings. *What is he asking? Does he want to know about the hallucinations? The malfunctions? The nervousness? The vomiting and the uncontrollable grief that sometimes shakes me at night?*

"Are you disappointed in your son?" she asked. "For starting Foreverland and using it the way he did?"

He let go of her hand. And they began their walk. Her guilt for asking such a question was measured in small breaths. Dr. Ballard's steps were quiet, not once shuffling. The inmates on the track gave them a wide berth. He stopped and looked up.

"What do you see?" he asked.

"What?"

"Above us, what do you see?"

"Sky. Clouds."

"And why is the sky blue?"

"The atmosphere scatters more blue light than red."

"So you see blue?" Dr. Ballard smiled. "Your perception tells you that it's blue."

"I don't understand."

"You came here to know truth, yet our senses determine our reality. Perception is not truth, Mrs. Diosa."

"The presence of that spectrum of light is blue whether I perceive it or not. A tree that falls in the forest makes vibrations whether I hear it or not."

"You labeled it blue; therefore it is blue."

"Blue is just a word."

He raised an eyebrow. She shook her head. He was twisting words, molding facts, playing a head game, and she was losing.

Have I already lost?

"How do you feel about your son, Dr. Ballard?"

He raised a finger. "Is the sky blue?"

"Of course."

He didn't move, only smiled with finger raised. They weren't going anywhere until she answered the question, like a Buddhist monk required to answer a koan before entering the temple.

What is blue?

Alex learned to surf when she was younger. She lived on the West Coast until she was twelve and her cousins would take her out to Hermosa Beach and connect with the spiritual nature of the wave. *The wave is the wave and we cannot change that.* It was her responsibility to ride it.

Dr. Ballard was the wave.

"Perception is not the same as truth," she said.

"Very good."

"Therefore our reality is not truth."

"And why is that?"

"Because our perceptions determine our reality. And perception, by its very nature, is flawed."

"You're saying we create our own reality?"

"*You're* saying that," she quipped.

"Perhaps I am." His smile brightened.

They began walking again. She had passed the koan. She was exhilarated, like a little girl receiving her father's approval. Or a dog thrown a bone.

A misty cloud filled her head. It was light and cool and intoxicating. She wanted to close her eyes and lay down on it. Somewhere in that pleasantness, she was nagged by the queer nature of this conversation, like the words she spoke didn't belong to her, as if she was cheating on an exam or being fed lines through an automated teleprompter.

What she said made sense. *But this isn't why I came here.*

They stopped at a group of picnic tables and the inmates calmly left. Dr. Ballard fell on one of the benches with a satisfied groan and rested his hands on the crook of the cane. The flat ground beyond the fence was thick and grassy.

"A father," he said, "always loves his child."

Alex nodded, giving him plenty of space to reflect. He was answering her question from a few minutes earlier. *Or was that an hour ago?* The sun was so much lower.

"What he did with your technology, were you disappointed?"

"My son is dead, Mrs. Diosa. Dead or alive, that does not change my love for him, not one bit. He will always be my son. I will always love him."

"But were you disappointed?"

"He did his best to understand. That's all I could ask."

"So you approved?"

"Does it matter?"

"You knew it was possible, that Foreverland could be used to switch bodies?"

He pondered. His blue eyes seemed to glitter. *I thought his eyes were gray.*

"Are we our memories?" he asked. "Or are we our body?"

"That's irrelevant."

"You asked about switching bodies, who is switching?"

"Don't twist words, Doctor. Those boys and girls were taken against their will, forced to give up their bodies."

"They gave up their bodies, you say? So you agree that who we are is not our bodies."

"Who they are, Doctor, was thrown into something called the Nowhere."

His eyebrows pitched. He threw a hard glare at the ground, squeezing the cane until his knuckles were bone white. He nodded, tipped his chin to her and winked.

"You've done your homework," he said.

"Did you know what he was going to do?" A sudden realization trickled through her. "You wanted him to create Foreverland."

The air around them cooled, an invisible cloud falling over them like a chilled hand. He minced unspoken words, staring into the distance.

"What if we could live without the body?" he asked.

"You mean in Foreverland?"

"If we are not this body, Mrs. Diosa, then we must be something else. Something more essential."

"You mean a soul?"

"Perhaps."

"And Foreverland is heaven?"

"Foreverland," he said, grinning, "is just a word, Mrs. Diosa."

"Foreverland was built with the *souls* of innocent boys and girls, remember. And you approved of it."

"Lack of disapproval is not approval."

"Then your crime is inaction."

"I'm in prison, Mrs. Diosa." He stood with a groan. "How could I have stopped him?"

"Did you want to stop him?"

"I believe that is irrelevant."

The walk continued. His footsteps were still quiet and carefully measured. Occasionally, he would look up at the sky while she asked questions and he would answer distantly, as if the conversation had grown stale. The conversation was going in a circle.

Because she was chasing her tail.

They were on the far side of the yard, alone on the track. The distant shouting of a basketball game was small compared to the wind rushing through the barbed wire, blowing through the open field, carrying fragments of voices from beyond the fence. She closed her eyes, pinched her nose. When the static of voices frayed her attention, she had learned focusing quieted them.

The voices fell on her like pellets, pricking her cheeks and neck. She searched the sky. *The sky is blue.*

He took her by the elbow and silence returned. The thin skin of his fingers slid the length of her forearm until he held her hand. "I need to ask a question, Alessandra."

"How do you know my name?" She wanted to shout, but it came out as a whisper.

The words broke the downward spiral of thoughts, the eddy of confusion, and rooted her in the present moment with the wind on her face and the sky—the blue, blue sky—above and the smell of sweat and fear and suffering.

"Why do you care about Foreverland?" He waited for an answer. It was a formality, really. *He can see inside me.*

"The children..."

"Yes, the children. You care about the children. You care about all people, the old and the young, the innocent and the powerful. Why do you care?" His eyelids grew heavy but unblinking. "Why?"

She shook her head.

"Because you love, Alessandra. You love deeply, truly. And you have so much to give. You love."

She nodded. *Yes. I love.*

"Are you happy?" he whispered. "With all the justice and injustice in the universe, with the lion eating the antelope, cancer ravaging bodies, black holes trapping light?"

His hand was so warm on her arm.

"God allows the good and bad, the pleasant and the suffering."

She shook her head.

"Good and bad are just words, words that God allows. He allows it all to be as it is because He loves. And your love, Alessandra, is as big as His."

"How do you know my name?"

"Can you be a god?"

"I don't believe..."

"Something gave rise to all of this." He spread his arms. "Allows it all to be. Can you do that?"

The air was dense, like breathing water. The ground was soft and the sky—the blue, blue sky—was down and the mountains were up and the wind in her lungs—

A tear fell.

A raindrop smacked the dirt.

"It's the answer you came for. It's truth, Alessandra. You have truth. You can be truth. Only true love has space to allow for the saints and the sinners, the heroes and the villains. You are the truth and the reality."

His face was blurry through brimming tears.

"You are the words."

She was crying, but this time the tears were different. They sprang not from a mysterious emotional hole inside her, but from the wind and the sky and the gentle hands cradling hers.

And knowing that she could be all right with everything. Just as it was. She could be everything.

Everything.

The rain splattered around them. Spots darkened on the old man's shirt. A cart pulled next to them. The big guard, the man at the interview, was driving. The old man fell into the passenger seat and propped his hands on the cane. He looked straight ahead. The cart remained still. Alex felt the heat of a thousand eyes.

The inmates were staring at them.

The basketball games had stopped, the card games frozen. Their clothes were wet; the cards rain-soaked.

The cart moved forward, turning onto the track, slowly grinding its way back to the building. Alex remained at the far end of the yard, but she wasn't afraid. She wiped her eyes, sniffed a final time and walked back as they watched her. She felt their eyes, their hunger and fear.

Saints and sinners.

She could be with the saints. But the sinners...yes, she could be with them, too.

She walked to her car and drove down the road. When the hill ascended in her rearview mirror and the prison was no longer in sight, she stopped in the middle of the road and began to cry. A deluge smeared the world into blurry colors, pounding the hood, snapping on the window.

Alex cried tears of joy.

Because she loved.

22

Tyler

ADMAX Penitentiary, Colorado

Gramm was waiting. There were tears in his eyes.

"Temper your enthusiasm." Tyler sat on the edge of his bed, twirling the wet needle between his fingers. His head throbbed, an electric spike pulsing through his forehead. He dared not move until his heart rate settled.

The mere thought of speaking caused it to rise. In spite of the pain, even he couldn't suppress the smile. *Alessandra is the one.*

He knew what she looked like. Patricia had sent stills and video of Alessandra. He had heard her talk, saw her quickened pace when she was agitated, the furrowed brow when she concentrated, the tip of her tongue dragging over her teeth when she was curious. But to finally meet her, to be with her, all of her, was stunning.

She's beautiful.

He'd meant to calm her down, to sway her with dialog like a mythical siren. Half of what he said flowed out of him spontaneously, as if her beauty gave rise to inspiration. She was a beautifully tortured soul, full of pain and pleasure, suffering and joy. He spoke nothing but the truth—*she is love.*

And that's why they needed her.

Regardless of the disruptions, Reed couldn't stop the inevitable—Alessandra Diosa would close her eyes and dream a new reality. Humanity would join her.

Tyler and Patricia would lead the way.

He wished to immerse himself right then, to see his wife on the inside, in her mind, to meet her at the opera or walk the streets of her city, to share the good news and celebrate, but pain spread across his face.

The stent was done.

He had pulled the needle for the last time. The hole was swollen, nearly closed, like he'd used the prong of a pitchfork. Raw fingers scratched his brain. He would have to make the change; his next leap into Foreverland would be through biomites.

"Call the guards." He couldn't feel them out there, couldn't feel Gramm in front of him. To expand his mind would exhaust what little strength he still had and ignite the brain storm that had finally passed.

The rubber wheels of a wheelchair approached. He reached up and took Melfy's hand. He wanted to sit in the yard, feel the sun on his face before the good doctor injected more biomites up his nostril.

"Sir," Gramm said, "there's a problem."

The yard would have to wait. It would have to wait much longer than Tyler realized.

They went straight to the basement.

Yellow and red lights everywhere.

The guards dry heaved when they entered. Melfy splattered the floor before she could get out, the acrid smell of vomit steamrolled by the smell of death.

"What happened?" Tyler asked.

Gramm held a cloth over his face with one hand, spastically raking his hair with the other, hair follicles wedged between his fingers. "The health indicators," he said, "all started dropping."

"When?"

"When Alessandra left."

Tyler was too weak to stand. He waved forward until Gramm pushed, pointing when to turn. Half of them were still green, the ones he deemed most important. He didn't need them all. And when Alessandra was asleep, when she gave herself to hosting Foreverland—completely and eternally—he wouldn't need any of them.

He just needed her.

Tyler covered his face and had Gramm turn right at the fourth table. He raised his hand. He grabbed the edge of the nearest table, his fingers brushing the cool flesh of its occupant—a bald white man from the Arian brotherhood, his chest a canvas of ink.

The light was red.

The occupant was fat when he first took the needle, an obese man sent to the penitentiary for double murder. Now his ribs were showing beneath olive-colored skin. Wisps of remaining hair stuck to his balding scalp, swirling around a purple birthmark distinctly shaped like the state of Florida.

Santiago.

"What happened?" Tyler asked.

"He had flown to the United States this morning and arrived in Minneapolis. He met with Macy. That afternoon, just after lunch, he stopped breathing." Gramm stopped to rake his hair. "I can't explain it. There was no reason for them to...it was like they were just turned off."

Tyler held the Spaniard's hand. It was colder than usual.

Death usually is.

This was a time to rejoice, not mourn. Alessandra had nearly gone to sleep during their interview. It was only a matter of time, and now this.

"What's the biofeedback?" Tyler asked. "The cause of death?"

"Preliminary reports suggest...it's just..." Gramm pulled at his graying hair.

"What?"

"He stopped breathing."

"That's not an answer, Gramm! Goddamn it, it can't be nothing. No one stops breathing for no reason."

Gramm's breathing became shallow. He pursed his lips and took short stabbing breaths like a woman going into labor. If Tyler was twenty years younger, he'd snatch the pansy by the earlobe and drag him down to the table, shove his worried face into Santiago's clammy stomach and let him smell death until it was burned into his palette.

The pounding started again; this time his forehead was being stabbed with an ice pick in time to his heartbeat.

"The good doctor needs to see your stent," Gramm said.

Tyler clenched his teeth, driving the ice pick deeper into his gray matter. *Reed did this.*

It was a slap to the face, an insult. A warning. Santiago was a good soldier. He was meant to guide Danny, but when it was clear that the boy wasn't capable of supporting a Foreverland on the level Tyler wanted, Santiago watched after him.

But now that Danny was missing, it was irrelevant.

Damn him.

"The good doctor," Tyler said, "will perform a full autopsy—"

Beep-beep-beep...

The lamp next to them dimmed. The monitor was red lights.

Tyler reached for the table—the man's chest sweaty, pale and still—when another warning chimed. The next table, red lights signaling another loss.

And then another. And another.

Like dominos falling.

"Do something!" Tyler shuffled around the table. "Damn it, Gramm, stop this!"

Gramm's hands fluttered at his sides. He looked around like a bird sensing a predator, his brain stuck in a panic loop. His hands went to his scalp and locked onto his hair, gray tufts between his fingers.

Tyler took several short steps and grabbed a handful of the former chemist's shirt. "Puh the pugs," Tyler said, the words slurring past his swollen tongue. He wet his lips and slowly enunciated, "Pull... the...plugs."

More warnings joined the chorus.

Six tables had been lost, and now a seventh. They were dropping one after another. Tyler looked down the long row, looked for the one table they could not afford to lose. If the man in the back stopped breathing, all would be lost.

Alessandra would not sleep.

Tyler shoved off and began sliding his feet. When he reached the end of the table, he made a three-step lunge to the next table, and then the next.

The red lights were behind him, but they were gaining. The room was dimming. They were going to lose them all. Tyler kept his eyes on the back.

Three more tables.

His breath shortened. Darkness bled into the fringes of his vision.

His knees shattered like glass. Warmth spilled into the crown of his skull, spread over his head and face like oil, washing away the throbbing pain, and trickled into his burning chest.

One more.

He could barely feel the edge of the table beneath his cold fingers. The beeping was behind him. He reached out, focused on the table against the back wall, when warmth bled through his hips, into his thighs and knees, taking all his strength with it.

The floor began rising.

He took one big step and closed his eyes. The impact was dull, but a sharp crack cut through the numbing fog as his hip shattered.

The beeping was a distant warning. The red lights were still coming.

The table was above him, the lights on the panel still green. He reached up, his senseless fingers finding the buttons. He pushed randomly, pushed them all.

With every bit of strength, he pecked at the monitor, hoping to hit the button that would pull Samuel offline.

We can't lose him!

All at once, the beeping stopped. The room was quiet.

His wheezy breath scratched the silence. He tried to swallow.

"Doctor?" Warm hands were on his cheeks. "Doctor?"

Gramm was squatting in front of him. The good doctor was with him. Tyler's eyelids were so heavy, so tired. A green haze shaded Gramm's worried expression. Tyler barely moved his lips. Words would not fall off his tongue.

He tried to whisper his wife's name, but he couldn't feel his lips, couldn't feel his body. He'd run out of time and could only send out a thought and hope it would reach her.

I'm sorry.

AUTUMN

Dreams are strange.
Some never-ending.

The elevator descended with purpose.

The smell of manufacturing gave way to what was below ground: a distinct odor of burnt plastic and clay.

Jonathan pushed his hair back. His distorted reflection—his eyes still green, the bent bump on his nose—split in half as the elevator doors opened to reveal a long empty hall and an attractive young woman in a white lab coat.

"Welcome, Mr. Deer."

"Jonathan."

"Of course." She extended her hand. "My name is Dr. Jones. You can call me Julie. Watch your step."

The hairs on his head stiffened. An electrified field slowly rode down his neck, over his shoulders and arms until all the hair on his body was rigid.

"It'll take just a moment," she said.

"Aren't you certain by now?"

"Redundancy ensures our security, Jonathan."

The scan sank through his epidermal layers, vibrating through subdural layers until it reached his core, examining every cell that composed his body.

Julie paced around him, her eyes crawling over him like he was on display in the Smithsonian. "Remarkable," she whispered. "Simply remarkable."

They didn't know who he was. What *he was, though...they knew what he was. They were in the business of biomites.*

She took his hand, traced the veins forking over his knuckles, leaned close enough that he could smell toothpaste. He held his ground while the scan penetrated his chest. She looked at his eyes, his bent nose.

"You altered your face," she said.

"Anonymity is my ally as much as yours."

"Where were you done?"

He sighed. "Are we finished?"

Julie turned down the hall. There was no end in sight. The subsurface laboratory felt cool and damp. If he was correct, they were at least one hundred feet below the manufacturing plant. They passed heavy lab doors where vibrations leaked out.

"Can I ask a question?" she said. "Why come to us? Why on earth would you come here when you can have anything you want in one of those Foreverland worlds?"

She stopped at a set of double doors. Her hand hovered over a scanner.

"You have the secret to creating a Foreverland reality, why would you want to toil in the physical world?"

The doors opened.

The room was the size of a warehouse. They stepped between two long rows of glass cubicles that resembled side-by-side shower stalls, the glass black and reflective. The cold air settled around him and he shivered. He would count the stalls to make sure they were all present, they were all functional.

"To balance the scales," he answered her question. "I came to balance the scales."

23

Cyn

The wilderness of Wyoming

Her sleep was endless.

She swam in the ether of unconsciousness, where dreams came in fragments and images blurred into colors and sound smeared the background. There were snippets of waking, of seeing the landscape slur past her, of night falling. For the most part, her eyelids were too heavy and she remained in dream purgatory.

Until all was quiet.

She rolled her head off the glass, her chin wet with saliva. She rubbed the sleep from her eyes.

It was a truck.

She was in an SUV. It took a moment to notice the person in the driver's seat, a boy with long red hair. His name limped out of the fog.

Danny.

That was all she could remember. They were parked on an incline, surrounded by trees. Senescing foliage, in the grip of autumn's approach, was among needled evergreens. A single tree stood before them, one barren of life, wedged between two halves of a boulder, a tree with silver-gray branches, dead and gnarled.

She knew this tree. *Impossible.*

"No." She slammed her fist into her leg. Pain radiated across her thigh. This was no longer a dream.

"No, no, no..." She fumbled with the handle.

"Cyn."

"Don't touch me!"

"Let me—"

The door popped open. She tumbled from the SUV and slammed into the ground. A thousand memories rose to the surface.

There was snow here.

I was buried in the snow. The boy, Sid, on my chest, his hands around my throat.

The driver's door slammed. Cyn scrambled on all fours and stumbled through the thicket, away from the hill. Around the back of the SUV, she ran in the opposite direction. Away.

Away, away, away...

Run, Barb's voice whispered. *Run, run away.*

Cyn's throat hurt, her chest burned. She missed steps, fell and got back up, racing down the long slope, sprinting for the trees at the bottom.

She fell one last time, her palms scuffing through long grassy reeds, raking the rocky ground. She crashed hard, losing all her breath, rolling over with pain deep in her stomach.

She was here once before. She was here again.

In the wilderness.

Give me the body.

Cyn closed her eyes and wished it would all go away, that this was all over. She couldn't do this again, couldn't face the wilderness.

"Not again," she muttered. "Not again."

Barb's presence began to fade.

It receded into the background, far below the surface of her awareness, deep into her subconscious where Cyn no longer felt her, no longer heard her.

A shadow fell.

Danny reached out. She considered it. He brought her out here, took her to the last place on earth she ever wanted to see again, and now he wanted to help her stand. If he thought she would enjoy this, that she would follow him back to the SUV so they could tour the countryside and reminisce about the old women in their brick house, about their shaved heads and the cots and the needles in their heads, about waking up in an endless Foreverland loop without memories...

She raised a limp hand and let it fall into his hand.

He latched on and tugged. When her dead weight didn't budge, he relaxed.

And she pulled.

Danny's weight yanked forward, the toe of his boot catching her ribs as he tried to stop. She snatched his coat and pulled him over her as she turned, bringing his weight crashing down.

She hooked her leg around his waist to mount him, but the slope carried his momentum away from her. He was on his hands and knees. Too lanky and strong to take down, she threw herself onto his back and wrapped her arm around his neck. With the inside of her elbow over his windpipe, she secured the choke hold with her other arm and rolled.

All his weight fell on her.

He flailed like a flipped turtle, grinding jagged stones into her shoulders. She ducked her head, hooked her legs over the top of his and applied more pressure. Wildly, he tapped her arm. A few more seconds and the restriction on the carotid artery would black him out. She kept her head down.

His arms thrashed through the tall grass.

Paper began to rustle. He stopped prying at her arm and waved a piece of paper. She couldn't read it, but she saw the lettering.

Her hold relaxed.

He dropped the note and gasped for air. Cyn bucked him down the hill and spun in the opposite direction, sweeping the paper up as she jumped to her feet. Danny stayed on his hands and knees, choking a string of drool to the ground.

Green ink.

That was the color of the letters on the envelopes she never opened. The envelopes she stacked in a wicker basket, envelopes she threw in the garage.

"What is this?"

He put his hands on his hips, still on his knees. His cheeks were red; a scuff on his chin was finely lined with blood.

"Did you write this?" She shook it in his face. "Are you the asshole sending me letters?"

He shook his head.

"Then who?"

"A friend."

"Is this a joke? You were in on this sick joke the whole time?"

He didn't answer.

"What...what does this even mean?"

"I don't know."

"What do you..." She balled up the note and fired it into his face.

She regretted letting go of the choke hold and stormed up the hill, her thighs burning as she climbed. Not even halfway to the top where the dead tree waited, she stopped.

Pressure was building. *No, not pressure. Presence.*

Barb was rising from her subconscious like something lurking beneath the water. She ignored it, pumping her arms until she was halfway—

Give me the body.

Cyn turned around. Danny was on his feet, opening the wadded note, smoothing it against his thigh. Barb whispered in the dark.

She took a step back down the hill. Her head swirled with panic as Barb tried to find a handhold. With each step toward Danny, she faded away, disappearing like an apparition.

Danny was catching his breath. Blood was smeared across his chin and the back of his hand.

"Why do I feel...*different* around you?" She wouldn't talk about Barb, would never admit to it.

"We survived Foreverland."

He feels it. Does he have someone inside of him, too? "Why'd you bring me out here?"

He held up the wrinkled paper. When she narrowed her eyes, when the thought of ripping that page into little pieces crossed her mind, he began to read.

"Where once there was light on a dusted rim, when day followed day, now a night-filled *sin*." He emphasized the last word and paused.

Sin is the homonym of Cyn. But sin could mean Barb: the demon in my head.

"Turn back your sight to where your steps begin," he continued, "and return to the root and fall again."

He dropped his hand and, once again, paused. "This is about you," he said, "going back to where Foreverland started."

He nodded up the hill, at the dead tree.

"Where you fell," he said.

"You kidnapped me, dragged me out to hell because of a poem? A goddamn poem?" She grabbed two fistfuls of his coat and swung him around. "We're going back to the truck; we're getting the hell out of here."

"You feel different. You said so."

"I don't want to be here."

"Reed is how I found you. He sent me. I don't know why, I just know that something feels different when I'm with you. And he's telling us to be out here."

"Why?"

"I don't know yet."

"He told you to bring me back to my nightmare, to hell on earth? Are you out of your mind? How would you like to go back to the island?"

"I do." He turned his head and swallowed. "Every night. Except when I'm with you."

The pain was in his eyes. *Are we all doomed to relive the nightmare?*

"How old are you?" she asked.

"What's that matter?"

"You don't belong out here."

"But you do?"

"I didn't say that. Neither of us should be in the wilderness."

"You think we're too young for this? You think that's how it works?" He chuckled. "Age is relative. There's a time dilation between

Foreverland and physical reality; they're not synced up. Time goes much faster in Foreverland."

"I know."

"Think about how long we were in Foreverland." He spit blood and thumped his head. "I look young, but that's an illusion."

"I'm just saying we're over our head out here. You don't know anything about surviving in the wilderness and neither do I."

"We don't have a choice."

"I didn't choose this life."

"None of us did." He rattled the letter. "Something's happening, and this is all I got."

A chill wind streamed down the hill. Cyn wrapped her arms around herself. Her fingers were nearly numb, her nose leaking.

"So what then?" she asked. "What now?"

"There are supplies in the truck. We set up camp."

"And what? Search for another note?"

"We wait. Something will come up." He sounded too confident.

"You know how cold it gets out here?"

"Yeah."

"And you want to camp?"

"That's the plan."

"There are cabins." She pointed at the hilltop. "Over there."

He looked around, nodding. There was something else on his mind. She knew what it was. It was the same thought lurking in her mind, one she wanted to ignore before the vertigo of reality confusion dropped her stomach.

She followed him up the hill, past the dead tree, staying close enough to him that Barb didn't surface. By the time they reached the SUV, her legs were numb.

How do I know this isn't Foreverland?

They stopped in an open field.

The headlights grazed dying wildflowers. Beyond, in twilight's gray shade, scrubby trees and thick undergrowth were swallowing the remnants of three buildings: two log cabins on the left, a brick house on the right.

Somewhere between them was a lump of earth where Jen was buried. *No, that was in Foreverland. Jen died in Foreverland, not in real life. We all died in Foreverland.*

They all woke up in their bodies, but the memories of those deaths remained. Somewhere in the ethers of the universe, imagined or not, it happened.

"I can't go," she muttered.

If they were going to stay out there, the house would be more suitable than a tent. But there were memories in there. Memories, she feared, that were worse than the cold.

Danny turned around.

When night had fully arrived, he had set up two tents and stacked wood. He'd stopped for supplies somewhere between Minnesota and Wyoming, and stocked the back of the SUV while Cyn slept in the front seat. There was enough for months. She shivered at the thought of staying that long.

He heated tea and something to eat. They sat in silence and listened to wolves howl in the distance. A quarter moon hung over the mountains. Exhausted, she climbed into her tent.

She didn't stay long.

Afraid that Barb would return, she went to the only place she knew would keep the old woman quiet. Danny looked up from his sleeping bag when she unzipped the flap and crawled in. He watched her shove her sleeping bag inside. She could feel his arm between the layers of fabric.

"This doesn't mean anything," she whispered.

Barb didn't visit her dreams that night.

Cyn opened her eyes to the smell of smoke.

It was well past sunrise. Danny sat on a fabric chair with a stack of broken limbs beside him. A cup of coffee waited on an empty chair.

They drank in silence.

She felt foolish for crawling into his tent and couldn't look him in the eye. He was younger than her. Maybe sixteen? Cyn was eighteen, or nineteen. She wondered about the accuracy of her memories, and that included her birthday, a day she hadn't celebrated, ever.

But he was right: age didn't matter.

"How long are we staying?"

"I don't know." He kept busy breaking wood.

Cyn cleaned the plates in a bucket of ice-cold water.

"Can I show you something?" he asked.

"Depends."

"It's just something someone taught me. It helped me through, you know, the worst of it."

He didn't need to elaborate. The days that followed Foreverland were *it*.

"When I couldn't take it anymore, someone taught me that pain is unavoidable, but suffering is optional."

"Cute."

"What he meant was the thoughts, how I identified with them, believed them, let them spin stories in my head, take me out of the present moment where I didn't want to be. The present moment is all that exists."

He crossed his legs and closed his eyes. He didn't call it meditation. "Be here," he said. "Let the thoughts rise, let the thoughts go, and count your breaths without prejudice."

He didn't know her thoughts.

As long as he was near her, her thoughts were ordinary thoughts. But when he went to fetch wood or get water from a nearby stream, other thoughts surfaced.

Was there a method to meditate with another person living inside your head, someone that could pour a bottle of pills down your throat?

In just over a week, the nights were too cold to crawl out to pee. They slept together, always in their own sleeping bags. Sometimes she woke in the night to find they were holding hands. It was always his arm that hung out from the sleeping bag, as if he'd reached out.

She tried going back to the cabins, but the sight of the brick house racked her fear. Danny never pushed, giving her space.

Occasionally, they'd see something move in the trees. Just over the ridge, one morning, they saw the wolves that kept them awake at night. Five of them stared across the field before trotting into the forest.

"We need to be careful," Danny said.

There were nights she swore she could hear them walking around the tents.

It was mid-afternoon when he left with a towel over his shoulder. Tired of clinging by his side, she decided to stay at the camp. Ten minutes later, Barb began to whisper. The old woman's voice was weak and scratchy, almost exhausted.

Cyn didn't wait for her to reach the light.

She followed a path into the trees and up to a ridge. She saw a cliff ahead and hid in the trees. Down several granite shelves was a shallow stream. Danny was in the middle of it, his underwear clinging to his skin.

The water had to be just above freezing. His ribs jutted from his sides. He wasn't shivering, yet. His skin was fair, his shoulders freckled. He scrubbed his head with shampoo and rinsed it in the slow current.

"I know you're there," he said.

She ducked behind a tree.

"You should come in, rinse off," he said. "You won't regret it."

It had been weeks since she bathed—her clothes would testify—but she was already shivering, a cold that reached her bones, one that started on the inside, ignited by fear.

She didn't join him. But she didn't go back to the camp. She huddled against the tree, arms crossed, sitting on a bed of moss.

Barb was quiet.

Danny climbed the granite shelves and squatted next to her, fully dressed with the towel around his shoulders. Steam was rising from his head. She noticed the scar, the tiny starfish in the middle of his forehead.

Branded by Foreverland.

"How'd you do that?" Danny ran his finger over the raised scar on the back of her hand.

She jerked it away. "It wasn't suicide."

"I didn't think that."

He took her hand, his fingers icy cold, and tenderly traced the white line that went from her knuckle to the knob of her wrist. His touch tingled up her arm, embraced her heart, almost brought her to tears.

"Did it happen out here?"

She closed her eyes, remembering the big city, the tall buildings. She arrived at the airport alone, feeling so small and insignificant. Before she arrived at the Institute, she got so high that the sidewalk rocked like the deck of a ship and almost threw her into traffic when she fell off the curb.

Those days felt so distant and foggy. Almost like they weren't real.

"It was the last day I used. I was so messed up." She chuckled and shook her head. "Unlike now, right?"

"So what made you stop using?"

"This new recovery program paid for by the Foreverland fund. Hurray," she said flatly. "I didn't plan on cleaning up, really. It was a free trip to the city, and I wasn't doing anything, so..."

"What city?"

"New York."

He stiffened. "The Institute?"

"Yeah. How'd you know?"

"When?"

"Like, last spring."

He looked away, calculating; his lips moved slightly until he shook his head. "I was there, too, about the same time. I received an invitation from the director."

"Mr. Deer?"

He nodded slowly. Thoughts churning.

"What's that mean?" she asked.

"I don't know. Maybe it's just a coincidence."

He didn't sound like he believed that. Nothing, so far, had been a coincidence.

Danny pulled a stocking cap over his damp hair and gloves over her hands. "We should get back to the fire."

"How do you know?"

"Because it's cold."

"No. I mean, how do you know this is real?"

His smile faded, but didn't disappear.

"I mean," she added, "how do you know this isn't still...you know..."

Cyn's Foreverland looked exactly like the wilderness. There was no difference. That tree on top of the hill, the one they saw when she woke in the SUV, was in Foreverland, too.

The scar on their foreheads would always be there to remind them, but the real scar was the question they asked themselves every day for the rest of their lives.

How do you know this isn't a dream?

"I don't."

"What if we're dreaming again?" she muttered.

"I don't know how that would be possible."

"Of course it's possible." She woke up every day in that Foreverland cabin. Only when she woke up did she know it was the dream.

He fell against the tree, their shoulders touching. "Does it matter? Wherever this is, we can only be here. It's all we can do."

Her chin quivered. She clenched down, hated showing emotion, hated her weakness. It was something she couldn't control, couldn't throw on the ground and choke. She felt his hand reach for her, felt his fingers lace between hers.

"This is real," he said.

They held hands that way, listening to the stream until the cold chased them back to camp. They sat by the fire, warming their hands without letting go. Their clothes were saturated with smoke. Perhaps it was the wood they were using, but there was an odd hint of something fragrant. It wasn't cedar.

It was lilac.

24

Danny Boy

The wilderness of Wyoming

My demons are different than yours.

Reed wrote that in one of the poems. Danny remembered that every time Cyn ventured off into the trees alone. She'd return with a wide-eyed look and stare into the fire, rocking back and forth.

It had been weeks and she never left his side; then one morning she climbed out of her tent and took a walk. She didn't go far, just up and went. Her hands were quivering when she returned, but then she did it the next morning, going out a little farther.

Her demons are different than mine.

When Foreverland crashed, a lot of the old men died. They got what they deserved. But now he realized those bastards got off easy. They didn't have to deal with the demons that haunted dreams, the nightmare sometime lurking in Cyn's eyes. The ashes of Foreverland would never dust over them.

Death was too good for them.

And the ones that escaped—the old men somewhere out there in their young, new bodies—left the survivors with the bill, a debt Danny,

Cyn and others paid every day. He could only hope the old bastards would come back to wipe the slate.

The old women, too.

"I'm ready."

Danny looked up. Cyn's arms were stiff, fists balled against her hips. She'd left to fetch water from the stream and was gone longer than ever before; he was about to go looking for her, afraid the wolves had gotten too close.

Steely tension ridged across her brow. She sat in the passenger seat.

He didn't ask what happened, just got in the SUV and began to drive. *She's ready to face the demons. And the demons live just over the hill.*

It was early afternoon.

The sun was breaking through a cloud fracture, sunbeams gliding over the meadow, but darker clouds shrouded the three buildings ahead. The log cabins peeked through the overgrowth like relics from another era. The brick house was obscured by evergreens, as if hiding from shame.

Dilapidated wind harvesters leaned near the partially collapsed barn, blades locked in place.

Cyn's breaths had become clipped and punctual. Unblinking, disbelief filled her eyes. *The boogeyman really did live under the bed.*

"We woke in there," she said.

She pointed at the cabin on the left. And then she said it two more times, then nodded.

Danny put the SUV in drive and idled over the hill. She was still nodding and pointing when they stopped in front of the cabin and opened the door.

Six beds.

Steel shafts of sunlight came through the clouded windows, exposing abandoned spider webs. The mattresses were faded and frayed, soiled from a leaky roof or bodily fluids.

"We woke up." Her voice bounced in the exposed rafters. "And couldn't remember anything."

Danny remembered that feeling, of waking up on the island and not knowing who he was, where he came from. They told him he'd been in an accident, that he was going to be healed.

Did the old women tell the girls that, too? Or just feed them to the needle?

The wood planks were spattered with bird feces, their footsteps echoing in the crawlspace beneath. She stopped at the wood-burning stove. The clouds, for a moment, parted and a dusty spotlight cut across the room. A rogue gust of wind hit the building. The walls creaked and splintered. Outside, one of the wind turbines squealed for a moment.

She looked at the bed in the corner. The wall above the mattress had been clawed into lines. Cyn sank her knee into the mattress and dragged her fingers over the markings like Braille.

They were gouged in bundles of five.

She had been counting the days.

She woke up scared, alone and confused; she began counting the days when it would all be over, when someone would come for her, take her away, tell her it would be all right. That this couldn't be happening.

That someone loved her.

An enormous patch of weeds had grown next to the brick house. Dried sunflowers peeked above the fray like dying sentinels.

A slate of rain slid over the sky, casting a gray pall over Cyn's complexion. Her eyes darkened. The big bad wolves had lived inside the brick house.

She walked toward the sunflowers, disappearing into the thicket of weeds. The weeds had lain down where she walked, but he lost track of her. He exited near the brick house. He stood and listened, heard her scrambling like a rodent for cover.

Something began thumping.

It sounded like a bat dully pounding a bag of rice.

"Cyn?" He listened. "You all right?"

He marched back into the fray, plowing through the thickest parts, where thorny vines raked his hands and cut his cheeks, sharp grassy edges slicing at his forearms. Memories of the jungle jumped into his head and his heart beat as loud as the thumping.

There were whimpers.

"Cyn!"

Panic dumped into his veins. Nothing could happen to her. He brought her out here, nothing weird could happen, it would be all his fault. *Please, not to her.*

She was on her knees, as if praying.

Her fists were smudged with fresh earth. She raised them above her head and hammered the ground, again and again and again.

The first patter of rain touched the ground. The drops were cold. Danny knelt next to her and put his hand on her back. Welts were slashed across her arms from the weeds.

"I hate who I am," she said.

She said it after slamming the earth. Again. And again.

He put his arms around her. She hid her face on his shoulder.

"I hate who I am. I hate who I am."

He didn't know why she chose that spot to punish. But he thought he knew why she hated who she was, who the old women turned her into. At some level, she blamed herself for being dragged out here. If she just didn't run away from home, if she didn't use, didn't lie. If she was just a good girl, her parents wouldn't have hated. Wouldn't have left her. If she just wasn't bad to the core, none of this would have happened.

Danny knew why she cried and shook, knew what was inside her; the guilt she carried was the same as his. It didn't make sense, it wasn't logical. But there it was.

I deserved it.

The rain came down in icy bullets.

Danny ushered her out of the weeds. The SUV was parked in front of the cabin, but the wolves had arrived.

It was a pack of ten.

Their noses to the ground, they circled the truck. The pack leader trotted between them and urinated on the front tire. He locked eyes with Danny. The pack stood their ground, as if guarding the truck.

"This way," Cyn said.

She pulled him in the direction of the brick house. Danny held her hand and kept looking back. The predators watched their retreat through a blurry curtain of rain.

The trees in front of the brick house gave them some cover. Danny stood on the bottom step, still watching for the wolves. Despite shivering, Cyn took the stairs one at a time, laying both feet down before taking the next. The railing creaked in her hand.

Vines trailed from the soffits, moss clung to the brick. Somewhere under a tangle of vines was a porch swing. He followed her up onto the porch and out of the rain.

"You hear that?" she asked.

Danny remained still. Had he missed the crunch of a paw or the snap of a twig? He looked back and counted. They were all there, but what if one had been hiding?

The wind raked the trees and a swirl of leaves tumbled past.

He realized there was a chance they might be stuck out here for a while. Until the wolves moved, they weren't getting back to camp. But the brick house was a fortress, a rock-solid castle with security cameras and metal shutters that could withstand a military assault. Stones were scattered on the sloping porch. If the door was locked, they could throw one through a window.

It was a Southern-style porch that was wide and accommodating. Ceiling fans were above, their blades wilting from decay; small tables were surrounded by cushioned chairs, the stuffing ripped out and stolen by vermin.

There was even a tall glass on the far table, one that would hold a cool sip of tea on a summer day when the old women would sit and watch the girls blister in the sun. The napkin was still beneath it, the edges curled and shrunken.

Cyn twisted the knob. It took a boot to the bottom half to open. The house sighed a stale breath of rat turds and damp fabric. She stood in the doorway.

A breeze sprayed rain over the floorboards. The napkin fluttered beneath the tall glass on the table. He had assumed it was a napkin, but it sounded more like paper. He ducked beneath limbs and cleared heavy vines to reach the table.

It was an envelope.

The paper was warped with mildew, tainted green. He turned it over. The ink was the same color as algae.

Danny Boy.

He tore it open without hesitation, without questioning how it had gotten out here. *Had it been out here all this time?*

A single sheet inside, folded once.

Once the past uncovered,
And the demon cast out,
Only then forward you move,
To live without doubt.

The door slammed.

The porch was empty. Danny ran to the door, turned the knob and kicked at the bottom. It was jammed in the swollen frame.

"Cyn?" He pounded with his fist. "Cyn!"

He put his shoulder into it without luck and found a stone near the steps. The rain had stopped. It took both hands to raise it above his head and crush the doorknob. The door flew open on the third attempt, as if it had been open the entire time.

The house was silent.

He screamed her name and searched the house. All the doors were locked, all the windows shut. The house was empty. She was gone. Danny ran outside and discovered something else.

The wolves had also disappeared.

25

Cyn

The wilderness of Wyoming

She had reached the end.

The bottom.

There was no chance to give up the drug of choice until you bounced off the ground floor. Problem was, what you thought was rock bottom could be a false stage—you crashed through to find there was more falling to do.

But this is the end, she decided. *No more running.*

She had beaten the earth where Jen was buried. Even though it happened in Foreverland, even though Jen didn't really die, not in reality, not in the flesh, she still felt the old man's hands around her neck in Foreverland. Still fed the worms, in Foreverland.

Did that make it any less real?

Cyn had been hiding in fear ever since she left the wilderness. Now that she was back, she was still hiding—from the pain, from the voice in her head. And nothing was working. She was ready to face this. And she knew where the big bad wolves lived.

No more.

She walked up the steps of the brick house and heard music, something classical, cellos and flutes. "You hear that?" she asked Danny.

She twisted the handle and kicked the door open. She expected the smell of death to barrel its fist into her nose. What she saw was impossible.

The house was immaculate.

There was an oval carpet in the center of the room, credenzas to the right and left, a television directly ahead. The grandfather clock was tucked in the corner, the pendulum dutifully keeping time.

Scented candles burned on the coffee table.

The cabins were still dilapidated, the garden still a tangle of weeds. All was as it should be. But inside the brick house, dreamland waited.

Foreverland is alive.

Beethoven floated on the scent of vanilla-cinnamon. A shadow appeared at one of the doorways. Nerves tightened along Cyn's arms, across her chest. Cold fear gave way to a furious storm. Her fingers curled into her palms; fists clenched at her sides. An old woman stepped into the hall.

Barbara.

Her clothing was expensive, a brand Cyn couldn't name and didn't care if she could. A loose scarf—zebra print—was bunched around her neck where, undoubtedly, folds of skin hung loosely. Her gray hair curled around large earrings that were outsized by the rings on her fingers.

And her lipstick, bright red.

It was her. Only this time she wasn't looking in the reflection of a shattered mirror. She walked into the hall, a separate person. Their eyes met and they stood like cowboys waiting for a move.

The music ended.

The silence was meted out by the grandfather clock. Barb turned her back and walked into another room down the hall. Coffee cups clinked from a cupboard.

Cyn looked around.

She could break the leg off one of the end tables or shatter the glass on the grandfather clock, wrap a shard with a blanket off the couch.

The coat rack.

She wedged it against her hip, the polished pegs aimed forward like a rack of manufactured antlers. Barb returned with two cups and stopped.

Cyn's knuckles whitened.

"Piss and vinegar." A smile touched the old woman's painted lips. "That's why I chose you."

"I should run this through you."

"Sweet Jesus, child. You don't know where you are."

"I know who I am...I'm not you."

"I didn't say *who* you are. I said *where.*"

With that, the old woman sat on the wide sofa littered with throw pillows of the same floral print. She sank into the center, placed the mugs next to a thick binder on the table, and slid one toward Cyn.

"What's that mean, I don't know *where* I am?"

Barb sat back to sip the coffee, smudging the rim with lipstick. She indulged in another taste before leaning forward to open the binder.

With a steel grip on the burnished coat rack, Cyn could see the collection of photos of beaches with blinding white sand, impossibly long yachts, and tropical resorts. She kept her eyes on the old woman, waiting for her to fling scalding coffee in her face, or pull a weapon from the cushions. Instead, she leisurely flipped the pages over, one at a time.

As if she had just arrived.

"Your life was miserable before I found you," Barb said. "A street rat, a rag doll. A little sex toy for drugs. For you, death would be easy. You were already killing yourself, you just didn't have the courage to do it all at once. For me, it was quite the opposite. I worked hard to succeed at life, you see. I had a career and a family and a wonderful marriage."

The plastic pages crinkled.

"If you think I was born with a spoon of sterling silver, you're wrong. I was like you, Cynthia—beaten by my stepfather and hated by my mother. I made myself, I rose above it. I earned it, you see. And I wasn't about to give it up to death without a fight."

"*Where* the hell are we?"

"I had an opportunity to beat Death, you see. To start again, to keep what I earned. There would be one less homeless child causing trouble in the world, one less tick on the mane of society." She nodded at her, unaffected by the battering ram pointed at her head. "You didn't want the gift of life, child. I did."

"So you took it."

"I took it."

There was nothing for her to argue. Everything she said was true. Cyn was worthless. Long before Barb was in her head, little voices told her so. She had nothing to live for.

If you would've just asked for my life, I probably would've given it.

"No, you wouldn't." Barb answered Cyn's thought.

Of course she did. Somehow she was still in Cyn's head. *She's inside me, part of me. So is this room, this house...it was too real, the colors vivid, the touch, the smell. Where am I?*

"You're a fighter, Cynthia. Just like me, you refuse to let anything be taken from you. And that's why we're here, right now."

"*Where?*"

"I put a needle in your head and sent you to Foreverland, where you were tossed into the Nowhere and your empty body left behind for me to rightfully have. I put a needle in my head"—Barb rubbed a tiny scar on her forehead—"and left this cancer-ridden body to move into your body, child—your beautiful, healthy unwanted body. It's what you wanted; you wanted to die. And I wanted more life. We both got what we wanted."

"You know that's wrong."

"But then Foreverland crashed and I hadn't fully crossed over into your body. That was me that woke up in the cabin, in your body, I just didn't know it. That was me that suffered through Foreverland's endless cycle of birth and death because Patricia refused to let us wake up in physical reality. That was me that went to the edge of Foreverland and peered into the Nowhere. And that was you that came out of it, your memories, your soul that came back to *your body!*"

She slammed the binder closed, a moment of finality. Or acceptance. Those photos—her husband, her family—represented her life. And she would never have that life again.

"You're the only one to have survived the Nowhere, as far as I know. You should've been shredded and dissolved, but somehow you fought your way out of it and took your body back. Do you know what happened to me, where *I* went when you returned, mmm? I was plunged into your subconscious. It's dark in there, child. And very lonely."

"Then get out."

"That's what I'm trying to do." She sipped her coffee. "Maybe I was wrong, I should've chosen a meeker girl, a coward. But then I don't think I would've been at home. It is what it is, no arguing over spilt milk."

She was wrong. There were others that survived the Nowhere, that walked out of it. She was forgetting her husband, how he was caught crossing over when Foreverland crashed, how he walked out.

But it wasn't like that. I didn't walk out of the Nowhere. Something pushed me out. Or someone.

She remembered those memories being forced back into her body. No, more than her memories. Her soul.

"This is *my* body."

"It's *our* body, child."

Cyn slammed the coat rack on the binder; the table cracked and the pegs splintered. She swept the book into the television; photos fluttered out.

"That's why I like you." Barb didn't flinch. Her laugh had wicked notes, the husky crackle of tumbling cigarette butts. "Put that down before you hurt yourself. Sweet Jesus, have the coffee. I didn't poison it."

Cyn heaved the coat rack into the wall like a spear.

Outside, it was sunny and the weedy patch gone. The garden was back—straight rows of beans and beets and corn.

Am I dreaming?

"Of course you're dreaming," Barbara said. "But you're not asleep. And that's the problem."

"Then *where* am I? Tell me, goddammnit! Why the hell am I in the house like this, and the world is back to the way it was?"

"You can thank your boyfriend." She cleared her throat. "There's some connection with him, something that pushes me deeper into your subconscious when he's around. He forced me to discover parts of you that I'd never seen before, things that you don't even know exist."

"What are you talking about?"

"Beliefs, thoughts, the things that make you tick. Your psychology, child. I understand you far better than you ever will. Let's say I've discovered some truths that needed to be learned. And now I understand what I've done."

"What truth?"

"I can't tell you the truth. You'll have to see it."

"What do you want?"

"Peace. I want peace."

"Then go away."

The old woman's smile was grim. She stood with a slight groan and walked to the window, leaving a trail of expensive perfume. Birds fluttered around the corn.

"What is real?" Barb asked.

"Not this."

"And how do you know?"

Cyn started to answer, but nothing would come out. Everything that defined reality—eyes, ears, nose, mouth, touch—was all here. To her senses, the garden, the music, the candles were all real.

"Where am I?" she whispered.

"You're lost, Cynthia. Like so many in the world, you're lost. But we can find our way back. We can find the truth."

The old woman faced her. Her steeled eyes had softened. She looked kinder. There was no smile, but there was no resistance. No more *you should kill yourself*.

No more separation.

Barb had been in her subconscious. She knew the underworld of Cyn's thoughts, whatever was in there. What else did she know?

"Why now?" Cyn asked. "Why are you friendly now?"

"I told you, I learned the truth, down there in the dark subconscious. I suppose I have your boyfriend to thank for that, for forcing me down there and facing it. Let's say I know how to solve this standoff between us. I've had a change of heart."

"Tell me what to do."

A kind smile brushed her lips. Barb walked softly across the room, stepped over scattered photos and reached for the door. The music, the candles, the grandfather clock faded as she pulled it open. Outside, the wind howled across a gray landscape, branches scratching the weathered railing and the slumping steps.

"Remember how to fall."

"Fall?"

"Open your eyes, child. See what I see. Know what I know. I bring you the truth of where you are."

Barb offered her hand.

Cyn hesitated. It could be a trap. The old woman had fought her all these years and still lived inside her. Maybe this was a new attack: woo her with kindness before shoving Cyn into the dark subconscious.

As long as it's not the Nowhere.

Cyn was tired. With one fist clenched, she reached out.

She accepted Barb's hand.

Her body seized like she'd grabbed a hot wire, voltage gripping her nervous system.

"Open, child. Open and fall."

This was the moment of standing on the precipice, looking into the chasm of the unknown. This was how she escaped Foreverland the first time, by surrendering to the present moment.

By falling.

Cyn unclenched her fist.

She let go of the hatred, the piss and vinegar, the clinging to what was rightfully hers. She wiped away the separation in her mind so that there was no *Cyn*.

There was no *Barb*.

No *us*.

No *I*.

Just *Am*.

In that moment, Barb's thoughts rose to the surface, titans surging from the dark. They didn't have teeth or claws, didn't consume her. They simply told her where to find the truth.

The door slammed.

Cyn stood inside a dilapidated room with rotting furniture and a broken clock, the smell of mold and neglect. There were no pictures on the floor or coat rack stuck in the wall.

She opened the door and took the steps one at a time to find Danny. She knew where they needed to go, what they had to do.

You are the bridge.

26

Danny Boy

The wilderness of Wyoming

Danny woke up shivering.

The windshield was frosted. The rain had stopped sometime in the night. He heard sniffing and leaned against the driver's window. A thick mane of fur was investigating the crease of the door. The pack circled around the SUV. The pack leader stood in front of the brick house. One by one, they trotted around the house.

Danny looked through the brick house for the tenth time. He went back to the camp and sat inside the SUV until he stopped shaking, then started a fire.

What if I'm all wrong?

Doubt had punched him in the throat, convinced him that his delusion brought them out here to die. He read through the letters, held them up to the sky to reveal any hidden messages, imprints he may have missed.

Once the past uncovered,
And the demon cast out,

Only then forward you move,
To live without doubt.

He'd brought her to the wilderness to fall again, to face her demons. *But where the hell is she?*

The house was empty. There were no open windows, no back doors for her to escape. The door slammed like the house had swallowed her whole.

Danny examined the two discs that had been sent with the poems. His disc had a blue edge; Cyn's was yellow. Other than that, they were identical. They reflected the firelight across the beige fabric of his coat, the pattern mottled from the arrangement of pinholes and strange angles at which they were drilled.

Build the bridge.

That was the message, yet the discs didn't contain any directions on how to build anything. There were no images or messages in the reflection, no grooves that contained data. The pinholes could be some rudimentary code, some altered form of Morse code.

Or maybe they draw code.

He found a pencil in the glove box. Using a manual as a straight edge, he stuck the tip into one of the holes and rotated it like a wheel, producing a scribbled mess. He reached for Cyn's disc, the one with a yellow edge, and the discs magnetically stuck together. They were easy enough to pull apart. He rotated them until the holes were aligned.

The patterns were exact matches.

"What bridge?" His voice echoed in the distance. "Build what bridge? Tell me where you are, Reed! What the hell are we doing?"

He stomped around the fire, kicked up clods of mud, and heaved logs as far as he could. The pressure of survival weighed on him like stones. Somehow he'd lost Cyn, there wasn't much food left, and winter was almost on them. He had to keep moving to avoid letting the weight pull him deeper.

Pretty soon he was running.

He ran in no particular direction, zigzagging across the field, coming back to the fire, then up the hill, pumping his arms until his ankles burned and his thighs were numb and his chest was blowing up.

He fell on his knees.

The cabins and brick house were just over the hill. He wanted to throw the discs into the great wilderness, lose them in the obscurity of nature. If Reed wanted a bridge, he could mail plans next time. Danny curled his finger along the blue edge of the disc, tested the weight, imagined the sun flashing off the silver surface as it twisted into the gray air—

A wolf howled.

It was long and lonely, rising from over the hill. Danny turned for the campsite when the pack answered. They were striding around the SUV, all of them except one.

The alpha male howled from over the hill again.

Danny stayed on his knees, his heart thudding in his throat. There would be no running. No hiding. He had given in to a moment of weakness, took the bait, threw a tantrum. This was the end. He dropped his chin.

This is where it ends.

At least he found her. At least, for a moment, when he held her hand, he slept without guilt. In those moments, he left Foreverland behind and dreamed of a better life. He hoped Cyn felt that, too.

Wherever she was.

The howling had stopped. They were coming for him. The alpha male came into view and stopped at the crest of the hill, looking down on him while the pack snuck up from behind.

Danny closed his eyes. *I'd rather the wolves take me than the needle.*

The alpha male sniffed the ground. Eyes still closed, Danny felt the weight of the pack circling. Their footsteps grew louder.

A shadow fell over him.

"Danny."

She stood in front of him—short, ragged blonde hair and a baggy sweater billowing in a sudden breeze. She was calm and deep, as still as a midnight pool, yet he sensed the tension of a predator, one that could spring without notice.

"Is it you?" was all he could say.

She reached out and took his hand. Warmth flooded his arm, filled his mind. Her presence was as large as the distant mountains.

Doubt was vanquished.

She touched his face, dragged her fingers down his nose, over his lips, and drew him close. She smelled of sweat and things old, but her kiss was sweet. There was something else, something so intense that it tingled in his sinuses, something wafting out as they held each other near the crest of the hill—fragrant and floral, richly permeating everything that was her.

Lilac.

Somewhere, the wolves howled.

They slept in the SUV that night.

Danny did not dream, not of tomorrow or today. It was just a long blank dream canvas where all his hopes rested in complete silence. They woke with hands clasped, saints in prayer.

They packed the camp before the sun rose, left no trace of their existence.

"Where are we going?" he asked.

"To make a delivery."

She wouldn't tell him where she had been or what happened. She told him to set the GPS. The wolves stood across the meadow and watched them drive out of the wilderness forever.

Toward New York City.

WINTER

To have everything,
Is to have nothing.
The opposite is true.

Jonathan sat at a round table.

The man across from him was overweight and sweating. His eyes were set too close. He stared at Jonathan, unblinking, as his fingers rapped against the desktop like the tips of ten-penny nails.

Monitors were mounted side by side. Video, which Jonathan could only assume was streaming from other labs, was on display with bar graphs and dynamic charts and scrolling numbers.

The door opened. Neither Jonathan nor Beady-eyes looked up, holding each other's gaze. A man in a gray suit, jacket open, leaned over the table, red tie dangling. Beady-eyes spun in his chair and the two proceeded to whisper, occasionally looking over the table.

Jonathan waited patiently while Beady-eyes pointed at the screens and pecked at various keyboards. The suit stood back, arms folded, and watched. Beady-eyes turned his small eyes back on Jonathan.

The suit pulled up a chair.

"Mr. Deer." He sighed. "This is all very complicated."

"I understand."

"I'm sure you do." That was sincere. "You understand there is no room for error in what we're doing? We can't estimate, not one single item. Vagary will leave the result up to chance, and neither you nor we have the right to guess at what you want us to do. You understand?"

"Of course."

"So when you say you want to use your memory, we have a problem."

"I didn't say memory."

Beady-eye's knuckles whitened, fingers interlaced like a wrecking ball.

"I'm capable of carrying the data," Jonathan said.

"For two hundred and four fabrications?"

"I've given you the physical specs for each one."

"But not the personalities."

Jonathan nodded slowly. "I don't have them yet."

"And you want to start production without them?"

"I'll have them."

"Timing is critical, Mr. Deer."

"I understand."

"I don't think you do." Beady-eyes pounded the table. "When fabrication is

finished, there has to be a personality matrix uploaded immediately. If you're late or there's a problem, you'll stand by and watch them rot."

Obviously, Beady-eyes had seen this before.

"I understand the timing," he said. "And I'll be there."

The suit and Beady-eyes argued some more. In the end, they couldn't stop Jonathan. He'd paid for the service, their bosses accepted. Jonathan would make the delivery.

Or die trying.

27

Alessandra

Upstate New York

Drip. Drip. Drip.

Liquid sunlight dripped onto a desert in steady, even strokes. Like a clock. A metronome.

A heartbeat.

The beat measured the seconds of the day. But it wasn't sand that caught each golden drop. It fell into Alex.

Heavy, heavy Alex.

She floated in a dream, not knowing it was a dream—a nowhere of sweetness—until she neared the surface, close enough to taste real life.

Her eyelashes cracked.

She stared at a popcorn ceiling. Up there in the catacombs of her misty mind was her name, but she couldn't see past the fluffy grit, the swirly texture. It was just a ceiling.

There was no name.

There was a warm place beneath the covers. She reached under the downy comforter, expecting to feel a dark spot spreading across her midsection where she had wet the bed. She was nude, but dry. Her bladder, full.

The blinds in the window were dark. She began drifting beneath the surface again where nothing mattered, where her dreams would cradle her in a warm embrace.

What's my name?

When the bedroom door opened, she didn't recognize Samuel at first. It took a few seconds to recognize her spouse, then a few more to remember his name. He appeared fuzzy. Even after she blinked several times, he still appeared to be a double image out of focus.

"Hungry?" He placed a tray on the dresser.

He had gone away for a few weeks.

She seemed to remember a sudden business trip and complications, something to do with the government and CIA, top secret service that required his anonymity. He texted and emailed, but didn't have the service to call.

But now he was here, every day. He appeared when she woke up, always with food and a smile. Steam rose from a teacup; the scent of chamomile mixing with her body odor rising from beneath the covers. It wasn't a bad smell, but it made her wonder when she showered last.

Samuel sat on the bed; his musky scent, his manly allure pushed into her senses. He took her hand and massaged her fingers one at a time, kneaded her palms, rubbed her arms until her eyes began to roll. She smiled. It was impossible not to.

"What time is it?" she asked.

"It's about that time."

She looked around. *Where are the clocks?*

"I got to pee."

"Want a pan?"

"What?"

"Joking."

Samuel made shushing sounds, rubbing and stroking and caressing. If there wasn't pressure in her midsection, she'd have pulled him under the covers and let him do things to her.

She peeled herself away and urinated in the bathroom for what seemed like hours. Her head, resting on her knees, was a sandbag.

Thoughts and memories trickled through the fog, things she should be doing but no longer wanted to.

There were interviews and drafts to write, chapters to edit. Deadlines to meet. *It could wait. It could all wait. Even*, she thought while flushing, *personal hygiene*.

Samuel was under the covers. His shoulders were bare and bronze; muscles bunched along his arms. She slid next to him, fell into his embrace and forgot about those deadlines.

Life was too damn good.

Samuel was gone.

Sunlight cut between the blinds.

That side of the house faced west, which meant it was afternoon. Judging by the angle and length of the dusty sunbeams, it was late. Had she slept an entire day?

It was impossible to know.

She wrapped a robe around her nudity and bent a single blind. It was clear and sunny, the window chilled. A school bus rolled down the street, followed by laughter.

A pang of guilt struck her. *Or is it sadness? Or both?*

Somewhere in the endless blue sky, thunder rumbled.

The bed is new.

She couldn't remember ever sleeping in a king with comforters that thick. And she slept right in the middle, like it was all hers. She couldn't remember falling asleep, just remembered the rhythm of Samuel's embrace. Now it was mid-afternoon and there were things to do, but the thought of sitting at the computer, of punching those keys and staring at the screen was empty. She wanted to sleep, to sink deep into the mattress and into a dream where nothing hurt, and nothing bothered her.

Pots and pans rang downstairs. Samuel was cooking.

The front room was spotless. All the shelves had been dusted, the carpet cleaned, the throw pillows just the way she liked them. Samuel was stirring a warm pot of stew. She loved stew on a lazy winter day.

"Don't you have to work?" she asked.

"Working at home." He sampled the pot and stirred. "Skyping a conference a bit later. Thought we could watch a movie tonight."

The laptop was on the kitchen table, a background photo of Alex on the screen, her eyes closed, a slight smile. She couldn't remember that picture—maybe Samuel took it while she was sleeping.

It was strange to see contentment on her. Her photos were always intense, all business, get the job done. Even their wedding photos, like she was imitating joy.

A bad actor pretending to be happy.

But that picture on the computer—that was the real deal. She felt it in her toes.

A ten.

"Where you going?" he asked.

She had her hand on the back door. There was a little blank spot between staring at the laptop and going to the door. She couldn't remember that short little walk.

"Getting some fresh air," she said.

The leaves had fallen, but Samuel had picked them up. The flower beds had been put to sleep, the grass neatly trimmed. A squirrel or something squabbled in the bushes.

She pulled her robe closed, but the winter air rushed up her legs. It felt clean, the deck boards hard on her feet. She took a long deep breath through her nostrils and closed her eyes.

Somewhere a child laughed.

It wasn't far away. There were kids in the neighborhood, but this sounded like it was right in front of her. The backyard, though, was quiet, still and empty. A wave of voices passed overhead, like a speaker mounted on a passing drone—those fragmented pieces of language all mixed together like a pot of stew.

Thunder rumbled in a blue sky.

Her toes had become stiff. She wandered deeper into the backyard, walking like a monk, thinking about Tyler Ballard. She had never gotten around to transcribing her notes. It was probably the best interview she'd ever done. At the very least, the most revealing. And yet, she couldn't bring herself to pick up where she left off.

Not the best interview...the most satisfying.

She couldn't quite put her finger on it, though. *What had been so gratifying? Was it what he said?* But as she dragged her feet across the lawn, she couldn't remember anything he said.

Or was it the way he said it?

A door slammed.

Alex was on the driveway, the concrete colder and harder than the grass. Her knees were sufficiently numb, her fingers and nose aching. A brown truck had pulled up to the curb.

UPS.

The deliveryman stepped out of the open door. He rushed up the driveway with long strides just short of a trot with a box under his arm. It was wrapped in brown paper. He smiled at Alex.

"Bit cold today," he said.

There was writing on the box.

She didn't have to sign for it. He just handed it to her.

Her name was on the front. It was written in green ink. *Alessandra Diosa.*

"You're going to freeze." He took the box away. But it wasn't the UPS guy. Samuel put his arm around her. The truck was gone. How long had she been standing there?

Long enough that she couldn't feel her lips.

They went inside. They ate stew. They watched a movie. Later, they made love.

When Alex woke late the next day, she tried to remember her name and the day. She eventually did. But she never saw the package addressed in green ink again.

Never even remembered it.

She just wanted to sleep.

28

Tyler

ADMAX Penitentiary, Colorado

A headlight.

One bright locomotive.

Tyler was on the tracks. He tried to move, to look away, blink, but it only got brighter, only got closer. The ground didn't shake; the wind didn't blow.

Everything was silent.

The light went away and came back twice. It was after the second time he saw shapes. They emerged from the glow like Polaroid snapshots. A white coat.

A white man in a white coat.

The good doctor.

He put the silver pen in his white coat and stepped back.

Tyler saw spots. Tears rolled down his cheeks. His forehead was inflated and hard like the shell of a tortoise. His pulse thumped just above his eyebrows.

Sensation came back to his hands and feet first. His whole body vibrated with pins and needles, the kind that felt like a giant hand squeezing a lemon.

More tears.

Someone else was in the room. Tyler could feel him without turning. Gramm was off to the side, his arms folded, observing the good doctor. Tyler remained a solid object mounted on the examination table, but his mind was expanding like a net, capturing Gramm's thoughts like minnows. There were too many to make sense, silvery flashes that darted about in the ethereal mindspace.

But Tyler's mindnet went beyond the room.

It went out to the prison yard, where inmates squared up on the basketball court, walked the track or read books. He heard them all simultaneously.

Hundreds of them.

They chattered like the roar of a sporting event, the crash of a waterfall, a thunderstorm smashing across a flat rock. He covered his ears—

"You had a stroke."

Tyler turned his head. Gramm was near the doorway.

"Wheh?" Tyler slurred the word.

"Almost three months ago."

Three months?

"The good doctor saved you. I thought we lost you." Emotion strained the last couple of words. Gramm cleared his throat. "He maximized your biomite content and injected you with a new strain to repair the damage and restore your identity."

Tyler closed his eyes, working his finger and thumb around the bridge of his nose. Too much, it was too much. He closed his mind, withdrew until he only heard his own thoughts.

"Whah..." He worked his tongue and lips. "What happened?"

"A clot had formed around the stent." Gramm paused. "The good doctor thinks."

"Thinks?"

"That was the biofeedback. It was a miracle we saved you."

Again, the emotion in Gramm's voice.

They couldn't take Tyler out of the prison. If a doctor besides the good doctor were to see Tyler, the entire operation would be compromised.

Tyler agreed.

"From what we understand, the clot formed from overuse. Your last session was extremely long and stressful. And when we began to lose the basement network..."

Tyler lifted his head too quickly. Stars flitted through his eyesight. Memories reported for recall. He had just seen Alessandra for the interview, then went to the basement, where his carefully selected network of volunteers—all wired into Foreverland, all lending Tyler their minds to support the cause—began to fail.

All that red.

Gramm handed him a glass of water. "You're infused with maximum biomite capacity. Your body is now 49.9% biomites, as close to artificial as we can make it without the government coming for you."

The government's halfskin laws denied humans the right to exceed 50% biomites. At that point, the lawmakers claimed, people were more machine than human. And machines, the government decided, didn't deserve to live.

As long as he was breathing and thinking, Tyler didn't care how many biomites kept his heart ticking.

"There are special biomites we can use," Gramm said, "ones the government can't detect, if we need to increase your levels. There are advantages, Doctor."

Doctor? Who's he talking to?

Gramm was addressing Tyler, not the good doctor. It was confusing.

"It would halt some of your health concerns, but it'll take some time to locate—"

"No, thank you, Gramm. This is just fine."

Tyler caressed his forehead. It was senseless and leathery, without the deep wrinkles that once carved horizontal tracks from temple to temple. There was something missing.

"The stent was removed. No more needle, Doctor."

"Why are you calling me that?"

Gramm looked to the good doctor with concern. "Do you know your name?"

"I know my name, damn you. Why are you calling me 'doctor'?"

"Please tell us your name."

"Tyler Ballard."

"You are *Doctor* Tyler Ballard."

That wasn't it. He was calling him doctor. He never called him that. *Or maybe I don't remember it.*

"The stent," Tyler said. "You removed it completely?"

"Yes."

Tyler's sense of emptiness was confirmed: he was now a junkie without his needle.

"Reed was coming through the needles."

"Reed?"

"The volunteers. We determined it was Reed that killed them."

Tyler rubbed his jaw. Numbness was slowly fading. He was riding a wave of dull sensations into awareness, his thoughts becoming sharper and cleaner.

"The biofeedback suggested a termination command was initiated," Gramm said. "Someone or something simply told the bodies to just...turn off."

"We lost them all?"

Gramm shook his head. "No, we saved one. You saved him, actually."

Tyler had run to the back of the room. Samuel was the only one he needed to save. The rest he could lose, but that one volunteer he had to keep alive.

Alessandra depends on it.

"The Institute?" Tyler blurted. "Were they—"

"No, the volunteers at the Institute were unaffected. We took Samuel off the needle, increased his brain biomites, and converted him to wireless connectivity like you. He was offline for a short spell, but Alessandra didn't notice. Even if it's not Reed causing these problems, something's out there, Doctor. We can't risk you using the needle. We're too close."

The emotion got to Gramm this time. He rubbed his eyes and apologized. It seemed genuine.

"It's all right," Tyler said. "I understand."

"I thought we lost you, that all of this was...that Foreverland would just..."

"Now, now, Gramm. You did good. You and the good doctor, you both did good."

The good doctor, in a brief moment of clarity, nodded.

Perhaps Patricia was right: he should cross into her Foreverland and leave his body behind. Gramm and the good doctor would watch over it until Alessandra was ready.

Tyler held out his hand. They helped him stand. His legs were weak. Blood rushed to his head, thumped in his forehead. The guards appeared with a wheelchair.

"No, thank you." He waved them off. "Let's go to the basement."

"I don't think that's wise, Doctor."

"Nonsense. Time is short."

"You need rest."

"Apparently, I've been resting for months."

He made it to the elevator before succumbing to the wheelchair when the fuzzy static of the random voices buzzed in his head again. He assumed these were thoughts from the inmates, that the new biomites were spontaneously connecting with other minds, but they crackled in his inner ear like a stadium of angry spectators.

Gramm pushed him to his cell, where he closed his eyes and laid back on his bed to rest. The basement would have to wait.

Tyler spent weeks sweating on his mattress like a heroin addict gone cold turkey. The voices of static had become fingernails clawing through his scalp, pulling his brain apart a neuron at a time.

And Patricia...she was a snowflake in a blizzard of thoughts. If he couldn't find her, if he couldn't go to her, be with her, then none of this mattered.

He sat up and squeezed the sides of his head, as if that would quell the voices, but the vertigo caused him to vomit. Gramm assured him this would end, that he would return to normal. Occasionally, Tyler heard Patricia's voice rise above the din.

She was out there, waiting for him.

"Do something, Gramm." His voice scratched his throat.

It was another week before he was able to leave the room. The static of voices faded. Gramm and the guards came for him and took him to the basement.

The room was dark.

The lights had been turned down. The tables were empty slabs, red lights casting enough light to illuminate the aisles. The bodies had been removed and disposed of, all done while Tyler was in an induced coma.

Despite the emptiness, he opened his mouth to breathe, the heavy odor of decay and infection saturating the walls, clinging to the ceiling. Nearly a lifetime of work wasted in a single day.

These were the volunteers, the inmates that readily gave themselves to the needle. Their deaths would go unnoticed. They were lifers without family, men forgotten by the world.

It took great effort to make them disappear from the system—creating false documents, trails of paperwork, deleted notes. It had been over twenty years and no one had come looking for a volunteer.

And volunteer, they did.

Once Tyler showed them a way out of their suffering, a simple means of closing their eyes and going to a new reality, a way to leave their life, go where they could be anything they wanted, do anything they desired. They would never be imprisoned as long as their minds were free.

And Foreverland was the doorway.

Tyler's son, Harold, had learned this lesson from his father. He discovered that people would do anything to escape their suffering and they would take the needle willingly.

Harold found an island, found investors and collected the lost children that would never be missed. Their bodies would not go to waste, and neither would the minds of the elderly men that didn't deserve to die.

Harold made a great sum of money and funneled it back to the prison, where Tyler expanded his empire of volunteers. In a perverted way, Harold helped build the basement, helped bring his mother and father closer together. It was all in the name of science, a means of discovering a new reality. All the volunteers were potential candidates to become a permanent host of a boundless Foreverland.

But now they were gone.

As long as the volunteers at the Institute survived, none of that mattered. *And Samuel.*

All the lamps were off except one. It shined on a bleached and sickly body, like that of a drowning victim. His once olive-colored skin, the genetic trait of his Hispanic heritage, was pasty. Teardrops were tattooed on the side of his face; an enormous crucifix on his chest was etched in fuzzy blue lines.

Samuel was one of the first volunteers.

He'd renounced his affiliation to gangs and crime, had taken up a life of solitary study in the library, of assisting other inmates in their spiritual study. He taught himself law at night, reviewing case notes. Serving a life sentence, he would never practice, but his advice was often sound.

Next to Gramm, he was Tyler's most important soldier. Samuel was caring for the new host.

Alessandra's husband.

Tyler's last trip through the needle was to meet Alessandra for the interview. She was in her own Foreverland and didn't know it. And Samuel was making sure she stayed there.

"He's stable, Doctor." Gramm stepped through the green light. "Because of you."

Tyler touched Samuel's arm, the veins still pulsing.

"Samuel discovered Reed is behind this," Gramm said.

"How?"

"He intercepted a UPS package addressed to Alessandra. It was written in green ink. It's why we haven't been able to locate him. He's done nothing electronically—no email, no texts, phone calls or video conferencing. He went completely off grid. I suspect he's been communicating this way all along." Gramm cleared his throat. "Clearly, he's alive somehow."

"What was in the package?"

"More reminders of Alex's past and a poem of sorts. Cryptic. I assume he wrote that way in case we saw it. We could go back and search Danny's and Cyn's belongings, even Reed's old apartment. I still don't understand how he's doing it—"

"It doesn't matter now."

"It appears he's trying to jar her memories loose, create a disturbance in her acceptance pattern. If she remembers certain events, it'll set her back. I think he knows our time is limited. He's just trying to stall."

"We have more time than he thinks." Tyler lifted his hands above the body. In the bright light, they looked twenty years younger. The biomites bought him all the time he needed.

But with the noise in his head, did he want to?

"It's time to relocate, Doctor."

"What do you mean?"

"We need to leave the prison."

"Move?"

"Alessandra is nearly asleep. It's almost time."

Tyler felt dizzy. "No need to leave; I can do it from here."

"You need to be closer to Patricia."

"Distance isn't a problem, Gramm."

"We'll need to be out—"

"We can't be hasty!" He bridged his temples with finger and thumb, the voices spiking with his anger. "I need her fully asleep; there can be no instability."

Gramm knew this. If Tyler committed to the host, if he crossed into Alessandra's Foreverland and she woke up, there was the risk of being thrown into an expanding Nowhere. He had already taken that risk once when he went inside her Foreverland for the interview. To be sentenced to the Nowhere...that was worse than death.

"The feds are investigating the prison," Gramm said.

"What?"

"There have been inquiries by the FBI into abuse and lack of response by the warden."

"Why didn't you tell me sooner?"

"You were in a coma."

"Now, damn you!" He backhanded him across the table. "I've been awake all this time, and you tell me this now?"

Gramm dabbed the bead of blood swelling on his lip with the tip of his tongue. "We've been holding the authorities off. The trail of missing paperwork, missing prisoners is unmistakable. They suspect the warden has been involved in a ring of money for escape. They came to investigate a month ago, but the warden kept them out of the basement, kept you hidden. They're scheduled to come back in a week."

Fear radiated in waves. Gramm always cringed in the presence of Tyler's intense emotions.

He didn't flinch.

"There was no need to hamper your recovery, Doctor."

The feds were coming. All of these tables wouldn't matter, empty or not, when they stepped inside. The trail would quickly lead to the Institute. They had contingency plans, they could relocate all essential personnel out of New York within the day.

But Alessandra is too close. It could disrupt everything!

"We'll disassemble the basement, Doctor. They won't know what happened. All data can be erased and reprogrammed. Evidence can be planted to set the warden and guards up. We'll keep Samuel in sick bay. He'll continue his mission until its complete, and then we'll pull the plug."

When Alessandra is asleep.

Tyler pushed the black curly hair from Samuel's forehead. A red welt remained where the stent had been removed. Tyler had killed the connection just before his stroke.

Reed was coming through the needle.

"We transitioned him while you were out, brought his biomite levels up while he was still unconscious. We were able to explain his disappearance to Alessandra until he crossed back over."

"How?"

"I went in, placed a few calls. Explained he was recruited by the government based on his past service with the CIA. I implanted a few vague memories in Alessandra that he'd served in the military before she met him."

"It worked?"

"She's almost asleep, very open to suggestion. Now that Samuel's back, she's almost out."

Tyler rubbed his face. He had to check with Patricia. She would be worried; he hadn't seen her in months. Gramm would've kept her updated, but he needed to see what she thought.

But how do I connect without the needle?

He looked inward and the voices cranked up like the knob on a radio.

"I can show you the way, Doctor. I guided Samuel back inside, I can do the same for you."

Tyler's chest fluttered as he paced around the table, his hands against his head. It was all coming so fast.

Why didn't he wake me earlier?

"I've already arranged for your transfer to Attica in three days. En route, we'll detour to the Institute. We have time, Doctor."

Gramm put his hand on Tyler's shoulder. Peace and calm flowed around him.

"I'll show you the way."

The voices went quiet and still. As if they heard him.

And listened.

In the middle of the prison yard, the afternoon sun fell on Tyler's face, warm and radiant. He sat on the frozen ground, legs crossed, Gramm beside him.

The inmates wandered. *Breathe in.*

Birds overhead. *Breathe out.*

Snow on the mountains. *Breathe.*

There was only breath, only this moment.

Perfectly still.

He closed his eyes. In the darkness, the breeze whipped broken grass around his knees. Men shouted and birds called. The voices no longer haunted his mind. Across the great silence, one voice called softly.

And warmed his heart.

Without movement or effort, the cold vanished and the men fell silent. The breeze died. He crossed the vast space in an eternal moment of absolute perfection.

The breeze returned, warmer. The clatter of cutlery, the murmur of conversation.

He opened his eyes.

Gramm stood in front of him. Instead of the gray prison garb, he wore casual khakis and a loose-fitting white shirt unbuttoned at the top. His front teeth were still slightly crooked, but his hair was thick and past his ears. The surfing chemist was back.

A waiter cradled a padded menu, gold letters emblazoned on the side: *The Press Lounge.* Over his shoulder, the New York skyline glittered.

"This way, sir." The waiter gestured.

Patrons were just beginning their evening at the rooftop bar. The waiter pointed at a table near the edge. A woman sat alone, swirling a glass of white wine while she drank the city's view. Her dress seemed to flow despite the stillness.

Glowed, despite the darkness.

She turned. And smiled.

She fell into his arms, her essence melting through him, her floral scent swirling around him.

So warm, so soft.

All of this, everything was Patricia—the people, the buildings, the setting sun. This was her Foreverland. Perhaps he should forget Alessandra, live here the rest of their lives so that, when she died, they would go together. If death came at this very moment, he would not be disappointed.

But Alessandra could do so much more. Her Foreverland would be endless. She could network people into her Foreverland, bring all of humanity together. Alessandra would be the hub that established an immortal Foreverland, one that didn't rely on one person, one host.

The human population would become the host.

We would become heaven on earth.

With Alessandra, there would be eternal happiness, not just the fleeting moments of joy. It was what Tyler and Patricia had worked for all these decades.

He wanted the world to have this joy, too, wanted the world to believe that if death came in this moment, it would not be disappointing.

They swayed back and forth, dancing on the rooftop. The city light blazed like stars.

29

Alessandra

Upstate New York

Bing.

Alex had to go through a mental catalog to figure out what that sound was.

Doorbell.

That recognition lifted her from sleep, pulled her from a lifetime beneath the sand. Her eyes were open, but she didn't remember opening them. She was staring at an object.

Ceiling fan.

Her throat burned, her lips cracked, but the allure of the bed was greater than her thirst. Sleep was warm like the sun, those first few minutes on the beach before sunburn really set in, warmth that seeped through her, saturated every pore, tugged her beneath the sand—

Wake up.

There were voices. One of them was Samuel. The other was a stranger that told her to wake up. *Did I dream that?*

At first, they were downstairs. The front door was closed and muffled sounds were just below her window. She would've been content to lay there and let them lull her back to sleep, but this time her thirst won.

Her robe was piled on the floor.

She tied it closed, but not before seeing her hips jutting out at her waist, her ribs pronounced beneath her breasts. The window was a sheet of ice. The lawn was buried under snow, a fresh set of tracks carved to the front porch.

Everything so foggy.

Alex shuffled to the stairs, grabbing the walls and furniture for support. She couldn't quite straighten up, and her feet hurt. Her fingers were stiff. It wasn't until she reached the bottom of the steps that she moved less like an old woman.

Samuel had his hand on the glass door. He was talking to a kid all bundled against the cold, ice crystals coating his ski mask. A lock of red hair had escaped through one of the eyeholes. Large snowflakes, the biggest she'd ever seen, hissed behind him.

Snowflakes don't hiss.

The distant buzz of the voices was back, a radio playing static between her ears.

Samuel started backing into the house, waving the kid off, thanking him for stopping by, wishing him luck to find a house he could shovel, when Alex heard the tapping.

A fingernail on a pane of glass.

It came from the back door.

30

Danny Boy

Upstate New York

Danny rolled in the snow, getting legitimately cold before walking down Park Street, to the address Cyn gave him. Even though they didn't dare drive past it, she described it in great detail like she'd been there before. Like she knew exactly what to do.

"Just keep him busy for five minutes," she had said.

"How do you know all this?"

Ever since leaving the wilderness, that's how she answered questions: like she didn't hear them.

"You going to tell me what happened?" he once asked.

"I will."

Her unperturbed posture and her unblinking gaze were intimidating. She knew exactly where they were going, what they were doing. She didn't say how, one look was all he needed to know. *Did Reed come to you? Did he tell you how to build the bridge?*

When Danny's confidence wavered, the few moments his thoughts carried doubt into the foyer of his mind, she took his hand. As if she knew.

"We'll find the truth, Danny," she would say. "It'll set us free."

And doubt would be extinguished.

"His name is Samuel," Cyn had told him.

"What are you going to do?"

"Meet me at the truck."

He left the house on Park Street, a teenager in search of driveways to shovel. Danny walked down the sidewalk, a brand-new snow shovel over his shoulders. The truck was around the corner, the tailpipe huffing a steady cloud, the tires half-buried in the unplowed street. Cyn was turned in the passenger seat looking into the back.

The back windows reflected the drifting snowflakes and gray sky. Danny cupped his hands against the tinted glass. They had laid the backseats down before parking, and used their pillows and blankets to make a bed. She didn't say why. When he left her, it was unoccupied.

Now someone was in it.

We need to make a delivery, Cyn told him when they left the wilderness. And the *package* they were to deliver was lying in the back.

The woman's eyes were closed. He hoped she was sleeping and not dead. Cyn was holding her hand. Danny opened the driver's door.

"Take my hand," Cyn said.

The smell of lilacs was overpowering. His eyes began to water. Danny climbed in and did what he was told. He took her hand—

Blinding light.

A spotlight beamed through the windshield. It was like looking into the sun. A jolt of energy fired from her hand, pure sunlight beamed through every pore in his body.

He melted into ecstasy.

There was no separation.

He merged with everything around him. The silky essence of the universe flowed without friction, without boundaries, without resistance—

"She must stay asleep."

Danny was back in his body, back in the truck, the steering wheel in front of him. "What the hell just happened?"

"Don't let go."

"Who is she?"

"I don't really know, just don't let go," Cyn added. "They can't see her if she's asleep. Go now."

"Who are *they*?"

"Drive, Danny. And don't let go."

The GPS was set for New York City.

He didn't ask how she got the woman into the truck, or who she was or where they were taking her or why. But this was about Foreverland. It had always been about Foreverland, ever since he escaped the tropical island.

The faces might change, but there was always a *they*.

New York City

The snow had been cleared from the Brooklyn Bridge.

Traffic was unusually sparse. Danny drove with one hand on the steering wheel. His other hand was clammy; his fingers ached in Cyn's grasp. In the hours it took to get this far, her grip had tightened. She never looked away from the sleeping woman.

Lilacs were pasted to the back of his throat. It had never been this strong, as if the woman sleeping in the back was the essence of lilac.

"Alessandra Diosa," Cyn told him. "Her name is Alessandra Diosa."

Diosa? Danny had cringed. *Goddess.*

"Go faster," Cyn said.

He crossed the Brooklyn Bridge. The first light was green. So was the second one. They were all green, as far as he could see.

And traffic was thinning.

Cars were turning off Fifth Avenue, clearing a path for them to speed through the green lights. Even ambulances didn't get respect like that.

Alessandra moaned.

Cyn squeezed Danny's hand, their fingers grinding together.

"As fast as you can," she said.

Earlier, she told him to go the speed limit. They didn't want to attract attention. Besides, the roads were slippery and with only one hand on the wheel, they could just as easily have wrapped around a tree. But now they had a straight shot through the middle of the city.

And everyone, somehow everyone, knew they were coming.

But someone doesn't. We're hiding from someone with an all-reaching eye, someone that's looking for Alessandra.

"Do *they* know she's missing?" he asked.

"Not yet."

Danny flattened the accelerator.

The truck bounced over imperfections in the road, tossing them in their seats. Cyn's grip tightened. He couldn't feel his fingers anymore.

The flag on the GPS came into view. The destination was close.

Buildings towered over them, their shadows dissolving into the night. Broadway billboards looked down on them. The street was nearly empty. Only a few cars waited for them to pass; pedestrians watched from the sidewalks and inside brightly lit storefronts.

They turned on Forty-Sixth Avenue. There, on the corner of Seventh Street, the windows were brightly lit. The door stood open.

"Stop in front," Cyn shouted.

"There's nowhere to park."

"Just stop!"

He mashed the brake with both feet. The truck slid sideways before jerking to a stop. Alessandra slid forward, but her eyes remained closed. Danny opened his door.

"Don't let go!" She pulled him back. "You can't let go, understand?"

She crawled into the back and he followed. They moved slowly and methodically, keeping their fingers laced. He reached the latch and the back door whooshed open.

Headlights glared inside.

Traffic had resumed closer to normal and was starting to back up. People were shouting as they passed, windows down, fingers out. Whoever had cleared the roads and turned the lights green had waned.

Or maybe they were focusing on other things.

"Sit her up."

Danny pulled her into a sitting position. Alessandra's head wobbled. Drool glistened on her chin. *Are we committing a crime?*

The time to ask that question had passed.

"Take her hand." Cyn let go of Danny.

"You sure?"

"Take her hand!"

Danny grabbed Alessandra's free hand. It was limp and cold.

They held her up and took half-steps, her bare feet dragging across the pavement. She weighed as much as a grade-schooler. Danny could carry her with one arm.

Horns sounded off, cars stopped.

"Alessandra?" Cyn leaned in. "You don't have to open your eyes, but take a step."

Her head rolled from left to right, mouth open. They didn't slow down, but kept moving toward the open door on the corner of the building beneath bold letters, *The Institute of Technological Research.*

They reached the curb when she took her first step, flopping her bare foot onto the sidewalk, skin scuffed from her toes. Her eyebrows arched, but her eyelids were too heavy.

Car doors slammed behind them. Red and blue lights swirled across the building. Someone told them to stop.

"Don't turn around," Cyn said.

They were going through that door, even if shots were fired.

The police lights reflected off the letters above the door. Sirens came from the other direction.

Three steps left.

Two.

One.

A man in a white lab coat blocked the entrance. There would be no fight, not with a barely conscious woman in their possession.

Cyn looked at him, unblinking. And like the wolves, he stepped aside. They went inside the lobby. The man locked the door. Seconds later, a fist hammered it.

"Unlock this door!" a cop shouted.

The man in the lab coat crossed the lobby and pushed open the swinging doors. A harsh antiseptic smell rushed out. The soles of their boots squeaked on the waxed floor. Alessandra slid her feet until her knees buckled. They caught her before she crumpled.

"Alessandra?" Cyn shook her. "You can wake up now. We're here."

Her eyes fluttered but didn't open.

"Where are we taking her?" Danny asked.

"Just don't let go."

"Tell me where we're taking her!"

"Follow him." The man in the lab coat led the way.

"Why are we here?" He couldn't ignore the fear pounding in his chest. "Why are we bringing her to this place?"

"The truth is down there, Danny."

"But why Alessandra?"

Cyn stopped midway down the hall, clinging to Alessandra's thin arm. She panted like a cornered animal. *She feels the quiver, too.*

"It's the only way out of this?" she said.

"Out of what?"

"This mess, Danny. She told me she'd leave me alone if we did this."

"Who told you?"

Desperation pleadingly pried her eyes wide. "Just trust me."

She gently shook Alessandra until her eyelids fluttered again. An unfocused gaze peered through slits.

"We need to walk," Cyn said.

They took one step, then another. Alessandra's feet dragged and flopped. They held her hands like parents guiding their child to a very scary place.

The hall was long, the doors open and offices empty. The man in the lab coat waited at a metal door. Alessandra was walking on her own when they arrived, her eyes almost completely open. The man in the coat tugged the metal door.

Danny had been to the Institute in the spring, but none of this was familiar. He didn't remember the hall or what was beyond the metal door. He only had a vague memory of arriving. When the metal opened and the funk of wet fur and dung hit him, he remembered.

Coco.

The orangutan lay on a table, long arms at his sides, a needle in the forehead.

The walls weren't walls. They were dark, but he could see through the reflections, could see the cubicles with smaller animals strapped down.

And the wire. All the wires.

"She has to go back there." Cyn pointed at another set of doors across the room. The man in the coat waited.

"Why?"

"I don't know! We just have to go back there, Danny." She swallowed the lump cracking her voice. "We go back there."

"Why?"

"We have to fall."

Her voice faltered. She was tired of falling, and that's what scared him. He thought the falling was over. The way she emerged from the brick house, the confidence that brought them here had evaporated. They were two kids that kidnapped a goddess that someone would be looking for very soon.

But the man in the coat continued leading the way. Someone was expecting them. Expecting the goddess.

Cyn reached for his other hand. Even when he didn't take it, she left it out there. They were two steps from the doors, the man in the coat latched onto the handle. The sirens were still audible, the police still at the front door.

We have to fall.

He took her hand and nodded. They would fall together.

The man in the coat opened the doors.

They took the last two steps. Alessandra shuffled between them. Cyn's breath caught in her throat. There were two tables back there. A very old woman was on one.

Alessandra was on the other.

Alessandra crushed Danny's hand. She was standing between them, but she was on the table, too. Unless that was a twin.

That can't be her.

"You promised," Cyn said, "you would leave!"

Danny pulled Alessandra close to him, but he wasn't holding Alessandra's hand. He was holding Cyn's hand.

Alessandra was gone.

31

Samuel

Upstate New York

Alex hardly ate.

When she did, Samuel nuked a small bowl of soup. He'd spoon in a couple bites before her eyes started to roll, then dump it back in the pot. He did that for two weeks, same pot of soup. He never bothered to even put it in the refrigerator.

She never knew the difference.

Husbandry is easy.

Alex was a first-class bitch in the beginning. The old man had warned him. "She's a little difficult."

Difficult. Bitch. Same thing.

But Dr. Tyler Ballard promised him a reward no fool would turn down. He put the needle in Samuel's head and gave him a taste of heaven. "Get her to sleep and you can have that," the old man said. "Forever."

Samuel didn't understand how this world was in Alessandra's head, what it meant that she was a host or how she could dream something so real, a dream he was in.

He also didn't give a damn.

He punched that needle in his head and went to work. He smiled when she gave him that condescending look, turned away when she laughed at him. Where he grew up, you didn't walk away from that. He just had to keep his eyes on the prize.

He hadn't heard a peep on the baby monitor all afternoon. That was his idea and it was genius. He found the monitor in the attic, buried behind boxes where no one would find it. Instead of hauling his ass up and down those stairs, he just listened for her smacking those lips.

That meant she was waking up.

He ordered a pizza and decided to smoke a bowl. His stash was above the stove, tucked behind a jar of pennies. Just in case Sleeping Beauty came downstairs, he went out to the back porch. He only needed a puff or two because his stuff was potent. Everything in a Foreverland world, the old man said, was potent.

As potent as I want it to be.

He stepped outside without a coat. The flame flickered near the end of the pipe.

Footsteps.

Someone had been on the back porch. A second set of steps had followed. Those were bare feet.

He dropped the lighter.

Samuel ran upstairs three steps at a time. The bed was empty, the covers thrown back, the robe gone.

"Alex!" He went room to room. "Alex! Where are you?"

He leaped down the steps and crashed through the front door. Samuel raced down the center of the street without a coat. He shouted until his voice gave out, ran until his legs went numb.

Looked until the world turned dark.

And then he found himself nude on a table, staring at a bright light. The smell of death was all around.

He'd never see Foreverland again.

32

Cyn

The Institute of Technological Research, New York City

“You promised,” Cyn said, “you would leave!”

“Patience, child,” Barb said. “It’s been a long trip.”

She dragged her fingers along the edge of the table, her bracelets ringing. Barb was in the back room, as if she’d been waiting. She looked the same as she did in the brick house—the red lipstick, the thin scarf and large oval earrings with shiny stones.

She ran her fingers over the very old woman’s bent knee, across her knobby hand and up to her hunched shoulders, where the thinning hair—like that of a doll from a bygone era—spread out. Her body sank in a thick cushion. The simple white smock was bunched around her like a potato sack.

“Patricia,” Barb muttered.

Cyn recognized the very old woman—the curling body, the smell of old skin. How could she forget? She’d hosted the wilderness Foreverland that imprisoned Cyn and the girls. And now, with the needle in her head, she was hosting it again.

Cyn’s fist clenched involuntarily.

"You said if we brought Alessandra here, you'd get out of my head."

That was the deal. When she took Barb's hand in the brick house, her thoughts merged into Cyn and told her where to find Alessandra, where to take her, and where to find the truth.

And that she would leave.

Cyn wasn't concerned that Alessandra disappeared, but a small pang of guilt tugged at her. She didn't know where Alessandra was. When they stepped into the back room, there were two Alessandras—the one on the table similar to Patricia's, wearing a baggy green gown. There was also the one they brought to the Institute and disappeared. *What if we delivered her to the Nowhere?*

"You tricked me," Cyn said.

"We trick ourselves, child." Barb traced the wrinkles in the old woman's forehead, around the protruding needle. "When I first met Patricia, I had serious doubts that any of this Foreverland crap was true. I'd heard through social circles there was a way to cheat death, circles that only people like me are privy to, you know. Circles that run on money. I didn't believe it, of course."

She sighed.

"But stage 3 cancer will make you listen to anything."

Barb didn't look like a cancer patient. She'd abandoned that diseased body long ago. The image in front of her was a concept built on memories that only Cyn could see.

Barb flashed lipstick-stained teeth in a joyless smile.

"I wasn't excited about taking your body. I know you find that hard to believe, but it was murder, I knew that. But I was addicted to life, Cynthia. I wasn't willing to give it up cold turkey and told myself I was doing you a favor. How's that for rationalization?"

Barb raked the old woman's hair to the side and combed a part down the middle with her fingers. She smoothed the wrinkles on the white gown and stroked her cheek—a cheek so gray and thin that Cyn was afraid merely touching it would tear it like wet tissue.

"Do you remember your first taste of Foreverland?" Barb asked. "The freedom? The joy? I went there a few times, sort of practice for crossing over when your body was ready. I knew, right then, Patricia had bigger plans than swapping bodies for rich people like me. This body-switching business that she and her son had been doing was just practice for something much grander."

Barb looked at Alessandra's body.

"I was right."

Alessandra was set up exactly like Patricia. Was she her replacement? Was she already hosting?

Were there already boys and girls trapped inside?

Cyn squeezed Danny's hand, afraid if she let go, he'd take off running. He was watching her talk to empty space. Barb looked at their clenched hands and smiled—genuinely, sweetly. It reminded her of someone. Cyn sensed Barb's memory. *Her husband.*

Cyn's memories of that man were not so sweet—an old man that murdered Jen and buried her in the garden. He did it in Foreverland, but she woke up with the memory of the things he did to her.

"He murdered, but don't judge," Barb said. "He was a good man."

"He was worse. You know the things he did."

Her smile turned hollow. "You're too young to understand."

"Why are we here? You promised to tell me *where* we are."

"I promised to *show* you."

Barb looked across the room, over the tables, past Alessandra to the heavy curtain drawn across the narrow room. A stack of white boxes was on the floor and mail crates overflowed with envelopes. The Institute had been abandoned in a hurry.

The curtain that separated Patricia's and Alessandra's tables had been pushed aside. Cyn felt the room spin, confusion swirling beneath her. The truth was lurking just beneath the surface.

There are more tables back there.

"Why are we here?" Cyn muttered.

"Because I and others made a mess, child, but there's a young man that's going to fix all of it. He's going to balance the scales."

Cyn grabbed Danny's arm.

"I'm not talking about your boyfriend," Barb said.

Danny began spouting questions and tried to let go, but she wouldn't let him. He'd been patient with her talking to an empty room, but panic was setting in. The crazy train was at full throttle.

"Reed sent the letters," Barb said.

"Reed?"

Danny yanked her off balance. "What the hell is going on?"

She stilled him with a look, but it wouldn't last for long.

"Why send letters?"

"So *they* wouldn't see," Barb said.

"*They*...who are *they*?"

"Reed sent Danny to find you, child. There's a connection between you two, something that calms your minds, has something to do with your shared experiences, I don't know how. All I know is that when you were together, I was pushed deep in your subconscious. And Reed was waiting for me."

"You saw him?"

"I saw the truth."

She looked down, her expression sagging, her shoulders slumping. An emotional weight had been slung over her like a blanket of chains. *Was that guilt?*

"I am no longer blind to my blindness, child. I know what I've done, and what I need to do to balance the scales."

Barb looked up and half smiled.

Cyn hadn't noticed that Danny let go. She stood alone facing Barb. He went to the stack of boxes and began digging through the mail crate.

"What's back there?" Cyn asked.

"I think you know." She glanced at the heavy, plastic curtain. "I think you've always known."

"Reed showed me the folly of our situation, you and I. Even if I managed to possess your body and stuffed you into the dark subconscious, our fight would continue. One of us has to go." Barb held out her hands. "And it's your body, child."

"So you're leaving?"

Barb smiled.

"Where?"

"To visit some old friends."

This didn't make her feel better. She had the sense that Barb was going to haunt someone else's mind, that leaving only meant she would no longer be inside Cyn. After all, her cancer-ridden body was gone. She had nowhere to go.

And she wasn't keen on dying.

"I don't understand."

"It's all very complicated, child." Barb slipped her hand into Patricia's curled fingers. "You'll understand once you pull the curtain."

The boxes crashed. Danny stood in a mess of papers and large beige envelopes. Cyn trembled and wished he was next to her. The truth felt like a monster.

"If you don't want to know the truth, that's up to you. You'll be lost until you do. But that wouldn't be fair to Danny, now would it?"

"Fair?"

Her smile faded. Who was she to speak of fairness, the old woman that refused to die? But Barb's face was so heavy, her eyes slumped with guilt. A thief was no judge of fairness. Barb continued holding onto Patricia, and reached out her free hand and wiggled her painted fingernails for Cyn to take it.

"I'm sorry, Cynthia. This wasn't your fault."

Hesitantly, Cyn began to reach out but stopped. It could be a trick, all of this a bigger plan to throw her into Patricia's mind. Or Alessandra's.

"You didn't deserve this," Barb said.

Sadness stirred in Cyn's chest. To take her hand was to risk it all.

To fall again.

Barb let go of Patricia and offered both her hands.

"You won't hurt me?" Cyn's voice sounded as childish as the words, a little girl afraid of what an adult would do to her again. She hated the mist filling her eyes.

"You've hurt yourself enough."

Cyn finally slid her fingers into Barb's palm. Jewelry jingled.

Just like that, her hands were empty. No grand explosion, no insights of truth or fireworks. Barb just disappeared.

And the weight that held her down all these years had been lifted. She threw her arms around Danny and began to weep.

Alone, at last.

33

Danny Boy

The Institute of Technological Research, New York City

She collapsed like a windless sail.

Cyn had been speaking to herself, arguing with her imagination and pausing to listen. Danny let it play out, afraid an interruption would kick the legs of her sanity. She had been so stable since leaving the wilderness, so confident and powerful. But her sanity was a slippery slope. All he could do was watch her slide.

Lilac overwhelmed the medicinal scents and animals in the next room. It made no sense.

He tried to peel off her dead weight. He couldn't hold her up anymore. His knees were getting weak and the floor was spinning. He locked his knees and leaned against the door. The walls jittered, but the tables never seemed to move. He gulped at the thinning air.

"Breathe, Danny."

He focused on her face, expecting to see the haunted emptiness of a broken soul. Instead, the unblinking confidence was back. Her eyes, still puffy and red, cheeks slick with tears, were relaxed; the pupils large and calming.

The room flickered.

Sometimes it would turn then stop. Occasionally, an overlay of the same room was slightly askew. That's how Santiago sometimes felt, like a projection, an illusion.

A mask.

"What the hell is happening?" he asked.

"Foreverland messed me up, Danny."

"It messed us all up."

"My demon was different than yours."

Danny abruptly grabbed the table, his fingers accidently brushing against Patricia's arm, the skin like brittle paper. *My demons are different than yours, but we all have them, just the same.*

They were surrounded by beige envelopes with preprinted labels. He was holding one in a fist. He'd seen it from across the room when Cyn was ranting. It was beige, also. But there was no preprinted label.

Large green letters.

"What is it?" Cyn asked.

He held it up to the bright light. *Danny Boy, Cyn and Alessandra.*

It was addressed to all three of them, as if waiting for them to arrive. This entire experience—the traffic lights turning green, the empty Institute, the man in the lab coat waiting for them—was warped.

But nothing had made sense since that first letter arrived.

He slid his thumb under the flap. Three discs fell out. They were the same discs as before—weighty and perforated. The edges were different colors. There was the blue one and yellow like before.

The third disc was forest green, the exact shade of Alessandra's gown.

"Three discs," he muttered. "Three discs."

"What do they mean?"

He shook his head. He never figured it out. And now three of them had been mailed to the Institute. *What does he want us to see?*

A tremor inside him, a fault line breaking loose a current of fear. They were in danger. "Cyn," he stammered, "I think we should go..."

"We can't."

He could feel her pulse in his hand, could feel her chest rise and fall like the long easy strokes of the ocean. She looked at the heavy plastic curtain.

"Why?"

"We have to look."

"We can come back." He held the discs up. "I need some time to think."

"It's why he sent us."

"Who?"

"Reed."

"When did you..."

The tremor returned. This time he felt it below his feet, not inside his chest. The building shook like something very large fell on Fifth Avenue. *Was she talking to Reed?*

"What's back there?" he asked.

"We have to look."

"You know, tell me."

"I don't know."

But she did, she knew what was back there. Some part of Danny knew, too. He knew the truth was back there. That's why Reed sent them here. He didn't want to know the truth; it would be too much. He also knew that if they didn't look, if they didn't know, they would continue searching for it.

And it's right there.

Another tremor rattled items on the wall.

"It has to be now." Cyn reached out. "Because only now exists."

He took her hand.

Cyn clutched the curtain. She waited with her knuckles white, the heavy plastic bunched in her hand. Danny placed his hand over hers. Together, they pulled it aside.

The rings slid in the metal track.

Two more tables.

34

Tyler

Somewhere outside Philadelphia

Tyler!

The old man snapped upright.

He had fallen asleep in the transport van. The straight-back seats were rigid, but he hadn't slept in days. Exhaustion ran him down within an hour of leaving the Colorado penitentiary.

He wiped the spittle from his chin, using both hands since they were bound with plastic ties.

His head roared. *The voices.*

Someone had shouted his name above the fray.

Gramm was across from Tyler, his head leaning against the wall separating them from the drivers. His eyes were closed, lips parted.

Tyler heard a voice, though. A familiar voice.

He sat upright, his backbone rigid, and closed his eyes. He took a deep breath and, like Gramm had taught him during the days before the transport van arrived, reached out to find an Internet connection he could ride through the ethers to find Patricia. They were just outside Philadelphia. The voices wreaked havoc on his concentration.

The static roared.

A small wave of panic tossed him head over heels, like a surfer crashing through the undercurrent.

TYLER!

"Take the next exit!" Tyler slammed his fists on the wire-mesh window. "The next exit!"

Gramm jumped. "What's wrong?"

Tyler squatted in front of the window. He had agreed to the transfer orders that would take him to Attica, agreed to be shackled like any other prisoner in case they were inspected. All the papers were in order, nothing would stop them from getting close enough that he could make a detour into New York City.

He would lay his body in the Institute and, when the time was right, exit it for good.

"What's wrong?" Gramm asked again.

Tyler braced himself on the seat as the van took the exit. He locked eyes with Gramm. Their biomites synchronized, their thoughts mingled like salt in the ocean.

It was Samuel's voice.

Tyler never felt the transport van pull into the rest stop, didn't feel it jerk to a stop. He didn't bother releasing the driver's mind from his control. As a result, the driver sat like a mannequin. The authorities would eventually find him sitting in a puddle of piss, with his stiff hands on the steering wheel.

Tyler lay on the bench, eyes closed.

He pined for the quick slip of the needle, the direct pipeline to his beloved. But Gramm was there. He was already an expert at navigating the wireless connections. He carved through the cloud of voices like a missile guiding him through black cyberspace to find Patricia.

She was still in her own Foreverland, waiting for Tyler.

When he arrived at her side, she frowned.

Something was wrong.

35

Alessandra

New York City

The air had become gritty. It scratched Alex's throat.

Somewhere, sirens were singing.

She felt warm, felt full. She was almost asleep when the voices returned.

Hundreds of them.

Someone carried her through the white noise that stuck to her throat, crashed in her lungs. It was the breath of the universe.

I am the universe.

And that thought gave her comfort.

She was everything and wanted nothing more.

Just to sleep.

In bliss.

I love.

Perhaps it would have all ended there, she would've gone to sleep forever had the visions not come. She hadn't even realized that her senses were gone, that sight, smell, touch and sound had been replaced with the endless field of static, this amniotic world of voices.

It started with antiseptic—a distinct flavor of evergreen pine that clung to her tongue and sinuses beneath the ever-present smell of lilac. It reminded her of something, of somewhere.

There were halls. Long white halls.

Hard floors and open doors.

Wet fur.

The Institute.

Her eyes snapped opened. The white static evaporated in the present moment where two people, one on each side, held her hands.

A boy.

A girl.

They led her through the animal lab, past Coco splayed on the center table to the door on the other side, the door she had seen once before...

Pressure hardened between her eyes, in the center of her forehead. Pressure that condensed and hardened like a collapsing star.

The door opened.

She saw the table.

She saw the very old woman, saw the needle.

But on the other table.

The other table.

She saw.

The pressure burst between her eyes, filled the universe with scorching light, radiated pain to the hundreds of voices that cried out, that shrank into silence. The explosion released memories.

She knew everything there was to know. She knew the truth.

Alessandra was awakened.

Times Square.

Lights sparkled. The streets empty.

The buildings punched the gray sky.

Rain fell like heavy drops of mercury, snapping on the asphalt, pressing her shirt against her skin; rivulets raced down her face, dripping from her nose, tasting warm.

Salty.

The giant screens that advertised Broadway shows were blank, overlooking the heavy rain that filled the street, raced down the gutters. Trash drained into the storm sewers.

Thunder rumbled.

The screens came to life, flickering like lightning.

Images flashed in a blur of colors. She stood in the middle of the empty street, rain pouring down, watching the images slow like a roulette wheel. They weren't advertisements for Kodak or Virgin Records or a Broadway show.

They were memories.

Memorial Day. She was six. They were in the park, having a picnic. She was flying a kite with her cousins, holding the string as the plastic wings rattled in the wind, climbing into the sky. She was sucking on a Popsicle stick, watching her parents argue.

Watching her dad leave.

Drive away.

Forever.

Graduation day. She finished college at the top of her class, gave the honorary speech, and received offers from a dozen companies, one of which she accepted.

The Washington Post. *Where she met Samuel. He was short and stout, prematurely balding. Smart and funny. They married two years later.*

Lightning shredded the sky.

Samuel doesn't look like that.

They got married at Martha's Vineyard. They were career-minded, ready to change the world. They lived in Washington, DC. She covered politics for the paper. He was a lawyer.

But Samuel doesn't look like...

Alex worked ten years for *The Washington Post*. Samuel took a job in New York and they moved again. Alex continued investigative reporting. She wrote books, toured the country.

She got pregnant.

But Samuel...

They hadn't planned it, but things happen. Her career had always come first, but the pregnancy changed her.

Pregnant?

She never wanted to be a mother. She had seen too many bad things to bring a child into this world. But when she gave birth, everything changed.

Her world suddenly had meaning.

Rain gushed into the sewers. The heavens opened and dropped rain like a bucket, obscuring the birth of her little boy. He had a name. They were holding him.

Smiling and holding him.

Her little boy had a name.

He had a name.

Lucas.

A shiver ran down her back, kicked her legs. She fell on the dashed crosswalk, punched in the gut. Lightning splashed the gray sky that engulfed the skyscrapers, temporarily blinding her.

A solitary car was coming down the road.

The blurred headlights moved slowly down the side of the road, the reflection stretching over the asphalt. A streetlight turned red. The car stopped.

Alex stood.

Blood was smeared on her knees. Her hands.

Her leg began throbbing. She'd only fallen on her knees, but her whole body suddenly ached. She looked up; the car was still waiting on the light.

All alone.

You need to move, she thought. *Move!*

Despite the empty roads, panic gripped her. She wasn't thinking of herself. The car had to move. *It has to move!* She sprinted with her hand out, her bare feet slapping the pavement. On the screens, the memory reels displayed the present moment.

The car's at a stoplight.

She didn't watch the images, because she already knew.

The stoplight turns green.

She remembered.

The car eases into the intersection.

"No," she cried.

A truck blew through the red light; its front bumper crushed the driver's side door. Glass shattered.

The car spun away from the delivery truck.

The radiator hiss cut through the crashing rain. Steam poured from the grill. Fluid dripped to the pavement; glass scattered like ice chips.

The headlights askew, one working.

Samuel was trapped, the steering wheel wedged deep into his belly. There was blood on his bald scalp, his eyes blank.

Alex put her hand to her mouth and tried to stop the tears.

She tried to open the door, but the handle had been sheared away. She reached through the window and grabbed her husband's shirt, muttering his name as if she could wake him up because this couldn't be happening.

Because she forgot this was a memory.

It was happening again.

So consumed by Samuel—broken ribs poking through the shirt, the empty eyes—that she'd forgotten about the backseat.

Until she saw a yellow dump truck.

And a small shoe.

She backed away from the car and closed her eyes.

Lightning struck one of the buildings. She was on the ground. She'd fallen. Her legs too weak to stand, she pulled herself up the steel carnage to see into the backseat.

To see the little body.

"No."

Lightning struck again. It filled her with rage. The memory had settled in place. She remembered now. Remembered leaving the Institute, remembered it was Samuel that picked her up with Lucas in the backseat. They'd gone to the museum while she was touring the facilities. They were going to drive around and wait for her so they didn't have to park.

Coco opened her eyes.

She'd gone to the doctor, but the accident wasn't a hallucination.

"No. No, no, no, NO, NO, NO!"

Lightning. Thunder.

The creak of metal, the tinkle of glass.

She tore the back door off its hinges, flung it like a plastic toy, pulled her son from the backseat.

His body so small, so fragile.

The rain washed the hair from his eyes.

She cradled him while tears flowed. And the rain fell harder, muting her sobs, her cries. Her anguish.

The screens were blank.

She cried for the loss of her son and husband, but more than that, she wept for forgetting them. How could she let this happen? How could she go on with her life without their memory?

How could I forget his name?

The screens flickered and began to play forgotten memories. They played out what had happened after the accident, how she had survived, had gone home, how her parents cared for her, brought food to her bed, took her to physical therapy, moved into the house. Did everything a parent would do for their child.

But Alex couldn't carry the pain and loss. Life no longer had meaning and she wanted out. She wanted everything to go away.

The Ballards did that for her.

She'd gone back to the Institute and never left.

The images on the screens proved it: Alex on the table, a needle in her head.

Her past rewritten. The accident erased.

Too risky to ever remember having a child. She loved him too much. It was best to forget him. They erased it all.

Entirely.

Forever.

How could I?

The rain continued. She wouldn't let it stop.

Alex curled over Lucas's body until her back ached, her knees throbbed. Her eyes swelled. Her grief had no sense of time. Her tears flowed for eternity.

Shallow rivers coursed down the gutters, falling below the street. The city was still empty, cars parked at the curb. The accident was still in the intersection, the engine no longer steaming.

"It doesn't have to be this way." The screens were filled with faces. An older woman, her hair gracefully gray, cheeks rosy and plump and dented with a comforting smile. "Those are just memories." Her voice echoed down the empty street. "Thoughts."

"You're so much more than memories." It was an older man—handsome, genteel, hair graying like the woman. He looked so familiar. "You are much more than any man, woman or child. You've given birth to a universe, Alessandra."

"You are a goddess," the old woman added.

"We chose you because you are a strong woman that loves deeply; a woman with the potential to create new worlds, give rise to a home for millions of souls where suffering no longer exists."

Alex squeezed her son. He was so cold, so still. "Why did I forget?"

"He's not dead," the old woman whispered. "In your new world, he lives. Love, Alessandra. You are so filled with love. Even now, you can feel it swelling inside you. The memory of your pain only serves to hide that love. Put down your suffering, Alessandra. And be your love."

Thunder rumbled in the distance.

"This is your Foreverland, where anything can exist," the old man said. "Only you can bring heaven to earth. You, Alessandra. Only you."

Alex couldn't let him go. She would never put him down; she would hold him in her arms until her life ended. She would never forget him again.

"Don't end your life over a memory," the old man whispered. "You *are* Foreverland."

They weren't here; she could feel it. They were in another world. That's why they were on the screens—they were projections.

They did this to me.

They were the ones that put the needle in her head, rewrote her memories, made her life perfect. They were the Ballards. She hardly recognized the younger versions of their elderly selves. She was seeing their idealized forms. They wanted her to be here.

They erased Lucas.

And they needed her.

I am Foreverland.

She was the buildings, the pavement, the rain. When she was sad, it rained. When she was happy, it was sunny. The sky above, the air she breathed, the food she swallowed...*this is all me*.

But something was out there, something above the sky, far beyond the atmosphere. The noise was out there. The static.

The voices.

She had heard them ever since she woke up in this Foreverland, but now she could feel them. Out there—where the voices were calling from—that was where true suffering existed.

But this is my lilac world.

"Yes," Patricia said. "You are this world, Alessandra. You are the Foreverland no one could be. You have given rise to all of this; it is you that has sacrificed so much for so many. Even your son, your only son, will find life again in your world. He will live again."

There was nothing she could do to save them. She couldn't bring them back, not on earth. But here, where she was a goddess, where she, Alessandra, was the universe, where it would be her laws that physics obeyed. It would be her will that determined reality.

She could bring them back, will them into existence.

"Yes." Patricia's face loomed larger. "No more sadness."

"No more suffering," Tyler said.

"Only love."

"Love."

"If you sleep," Patricia said. "Sleep and give your love to the world."

Alessandra began to rock her boy. His face so perfect, so peaceful. She sang to him, promised she wouldn't let anything hurt him, ever again. If she had to sleep, she would sleep for him.

"Mama's here," she whispered. "Mama's here."

Her eyes grew heavy.

The weight began to lift from her. Lightness filled her heart. The gray sky parted. A beam of light fell on her like she was the only thing in the world that existed.

Because I am the world.

"Mama's here."

She would sleep for her son, for her husband. For the world.

A shadow fell over her.

Two strong hands gripped her shoulders. They coaxed her to stand and lifted her to her feet. The old man and old woman raged, their voices echoing throughout the city.

Alessandra wanted to sleep, wanted to take away the world's suffering, to soothe her baby boy. But she let the hands pick her up and put her on her feet. They held her upright and shook her until her eyelids—her impossibly heavy eyelids—became slits.

The voices grew louder.

"Wake up." A woman held her steady, jewelry jingling on her wrists.

Lips painted bright red.

36

Tyler

New York City

Tyler paced around the rooftop pool and splashed frigid water on his face until his shirt was soaked. He kneeled on the concrete deck. Water dripped from his nose, shattering his reflection in the pool.

It's over. Just like that.

A lifetime of work had come undone in a matter of hours. Was it Reed? Was he that far ahead of them?

He wanted us to see it.

It wasn't enough to destroy everything, he wanted them to see it unravel. Tyler and Patricia peered like voyeurs into Alessandra's world from the safety of Patricia's Foreverland. They watched her walk down the street, watched her memories come to life. They watched her wake up. She was going back to sleep, this time willingly. She would give herself to Foreverland, for her boy, for her husband.

And then Barb arrived.

"How the hell did she get there?" he said.

"It's over," Patricia said.

"I want to know how the hell she got there!"

"Don't raise your voice to me."

"One of your Investors, Patricia, waltzed into Alessandra's Foreverland like a goddamn revolving door!"

"Isn't it obvious? She was sent to wake her."

"I want to know how she separated herself from Cynthia!"

He ripped the sodden shirt from his chest and slammed it into the pool. It floated like a dead body.

How could Barb separate herself from Cynthia? And why? Barb shared that body; why would she leave it? It didn't make sense. At the very least, she should be helping the Ballards, not tearing down a lifetime of work. She would know the potential of Foreverland, would know that she could be immortal. It's why she went out to the wilderness in the first place, why she kidnapped Cynthia. If Alessandra went to sleep, Barb could have anything she wanted.

So why is she there?

On his hands and knees, he stared at his rippling reflection—the younger version of Tyler stared back. "Why?" he said. "Why is she helping him?"

Patricia shook her head. She didn't know. Didn't care. *Did it matter?*

She turned her back on him and went to the rooftop's ledge. The folds of her angelic dress fluttered. She laced her hands and sighed. Deflated of hope, she overlooked the traffic in the streets below, all the simulated people rushing to nonexistent jobs, to meaningless families.

They were alone. But it was more than that.

On the horizon, just past the setting sun, the crinkle of the Nowhere, the limitation of Patricia's Foreverland, shimmered. In comparison to Alessandra, this was a shoebox.

Patricia was feeling the claustrophobia.

Even with Tyler, they would be alone.

He went to her and stood on the ledge. "It's not over," he said. "We can still intervene. We'll have to bridge into Alessandra and throw Barb into the Nowhere. It's not too late, but we have to do it now."

"We can't."

"I'm not going to let a lifetime of our work go away. A lifetime, Patricia! This is our dream. We owe it to humanity. We can't turn our backs—"

"We can't risk it!" She spun around, her heels hanging off the ledge. "We can't go inside her world, Tyler. We'll invoke her rage and never leave. She has to be asleep!"

"We can still manipulate her thoughts, change her memories..."

She shook her head. A smile crept over her face, one of joyless acceptance. "She knows what we've done. She won't forget this time."

"There's still time."

"We walk away. We start again."

His physical body was doing well. With the new infusion of biomites, he could continue another five or ten years. If he could find the special biomites that Gramm spoke of, it could be longer.

Where is Gramm?

But it wasn't his body that made starting over impossible. They abandoned the prison. Federal agents would be looking for him very soon. They would discover his ability to transport his awareness. They would change that, make sure he never connected with Foreverland again.

He would never see Patricia again.

They had to abandon their bodies, exist in Alessandra's Foreverland. Their bodies were just vehicles. Their identities, their souls, were free to roam.

Reed had done it. So can we.

The breeze rose up the side of the building, chilling his bare chest. Patricia closed her eyes and breathed it in. He did the same.

His hand found hers.

He couldn't be a god without his goddess, couldn't live without her breath. The Institute was funded to operate in secrecy for another hundred years. Patricia's body would survive. He would abandon his body in the back of the transport van and stay with her until they found a host.

If not Alessandra, then another.

He wrapped his arm around her waist, lifted her hand and swayed his hips into hers. Soft music came up on the portico, a tune from the year they were married.

He inhaled the essence that was Patricia.

She laid her cheek against his chest. He rested his chin and closed his eyes. They danced that way—slow, close and loving.

Let Alessandra's Foreverland burn. Let Reed have his victory. Let them all wake up and go about their lives.

Tyler and Patricia would dance.

They danced until the sun set and the city lights speckled the streets and buildings. The pool glowed blue. All was perfect, all was happy. They ignored Alessandra, let their lifetime of work fall apart and swayed in each other's arms. They could live this way for quite some time.

Nausea crept in.

Tyler felt it in his gut. A queasy sensation, like he was falling.

No, not falling.

About to.

Like he was leaning over the ledge, his balance tipped too far, committing him to the fall. It was that feeling, just before it began, that he felt tugging his stomach.

Patricia pulled away. She felt it, too.

Her eyes went wide. She was looking at the monitor they used to peer into Alessandra's Foreverland. It was still projecting Times Square. The city was falling apart. The street had cracked open, the buildings were crumbling like rock slides, cratering the asphalt and concrete in clouds of dust and debris.

Alessandra was still there. She stood in the crosswalk, the enormous monitors scattered around her. Barb was at her side. None of this surprised him; they were literally destroying Tyler and Patricia's work. Reed had likely wanted them to see Rome fall.

What bothered him were the others. They were on the sidewalk, the wreckage all around.

And they were nude.

Where the hell did they come from?

They were old men and women, and tried to cover themselves, looking around in confusion, unsure of how they got there and why. Tyler didn't know, either. But he recognized them.

The Investors.

It was all the Investors from the island and the wilderness, the old men and women that Harold and Patricia had dealt with. With the exception of Barb, they were completely naked. It was as if they were pulled into Alessandra's Foreverland against their will.

If she could pull them...

And like a fish on the line, the hook was set.

The pool, the rooftop, the city floor blurred past them.

Tyler and Patricia would never see her Foreverland again.

37

Danny Boy

The Institute of Technological Research, New York City

Two tables, two bodies.

Danny clung to the plastic curtain, the eyeholes straining to rip through the metal clips.

"What does this mean?" Cyn muttered. "What does this mean, what does this mean, what does this mean..."

Danny's emaciated body was in a blue hospital gown, the cheekbones sharp, the lips swollen and cracked. It was sunk in the table's cushion. The complexion was pasty beneath the bright lamp, the needle in his forehead gleamed.

Cyn's body was on the other table, dressed in a thin yellow gown. Like Danny's body, it was too skinny, the eye sockets deep, the cheeks sunken. She picked up the hand and touched the forehead where the needle protruded.

Thunder rattled the walls. The lights flickered.

Danny walked around the lab, far away from the body, near desks crowded with stacks of folders, computers, centrifuges, and other machines to the curtain on the other side. He threw it open, the metal hooks scraping along the ceiling rail.

Another table, another body.

Another curtain.

He pushed past it. Table after table, body after body, men and women in various states of atrophy, all dressed in plain white gowns, all surrounded by desks, notes and instruments. Some with needles, some without. The ones without needles were dead, the light above them turned off like a plant no longer needed to photosynthesize. Danny could see the last body in the dim darkness of death. It was in a vibrant red gown instead of white.

The kind of red that spilled life.

"What does this mean?" Cyn asked.

He looked at his hands and felt the room shift below his feet, the ground surging through his stomach like he'd fallen off an unexpected step.

"But I left the island," he said. "I left the island."

"What does this mean, Danny!"

The room jittered, the overlay of reality faltering, the dream shaking. He'd experienced this before, when he saw Santiago like that he knew. He just didn't want to remember, didn't want to see the truth.

And now the truth lay in front of him.

He knew where they were.

But how did I get here?

Danny shoved a pile of folders off a desk. Papers spilled across the floor. He kicked them across the room, then pulled a computer over and cleared the desk with his arm.

Who the hell am I?

He heaved a chair through a plastic curtain.

Are these even my memories?

Smashed a monitor with his heel, flung a plastic mail basket against the wall.

Did I ever live in Spain?

Rain pummeled the outside of the building.

He stood over his own body.

Sweat trickled down his cheeks. He put his finger and thumb

around the needle. This was a replicated reality. This was what Patricia did in the wilderness; when the girls woke up in a cabin, the surroundings looked just like the physical reality.

This was the Institute; this was New York City.

This is Foreverland.

The needle was firmly planted in the body's forehead. That meant his physical body was lying in the Institute—the knees bent, the fingers curled, the ribs protruding—while he was here, standing over the replication. He could pull the needle out, but that wouldn't matter.

"I left the island." His fingers quivered. "I left the island."

Cyn put her hand around his. He let her gently pull it away. Her lower lip quivered. She knew, too.

"You left the wilderness," Danny said. "How did we..."

He remembered escaping the island, remembered Spain, remembered his life in the villa. His memories couldn't be trusted, but he remembered coming to the Institute last spring.

So did Cyn.

"We never left the Institute," he said.

Cyn nodded.

"They're experimenting," he said blankly. "The animals and all the bodies, they're looking for a host."

"Where are we now?"

He shook his head. *If this is Foreverland, who's hosting it? Patricia? Alessandra? Coco?*

Another round of thunder shook the building.

"Where did Alessandra go?" Danny asked. "The person we brought here, she disappeared. Where did she go?"

Cyn swallowed spastically.

"Why did we bring her here?" He grabbed her shoulders. "Why?"

"I don't know."

"Who told you to bring her here?"

She was shaking her head, quivering all over. "I think it was Reed."

She was hiding something, but it made sense. The envelope was waiting for them. He wanted Danny and Cyn to see their bodies. *To shock us into knowing the truth?*

Then the same would be true for Alessandra. He wanted her to see her body, for her to see the truth. But why? So that she'd wake up?

Lilacs. He could still smell lilacs, but it wasn't nearly as intense, not like it was when Alessandra was near. *This whole world smells of lilacs.*

The lights flickered for several seconds. The ceiling had fractured, debris showering the room. A light coating fell across the tables.

"We should go," Cyn said.

Danny spread his hand over the blue gown covering his body. "Where?" he whispered. "Where do we go?"

Cyn's grip tightened on his arm.

She pulled him away, dragging him through the papers and overturned boxes, around the plastic curtain when the next tremor hit. They braced themselves against the wall. A box spilled from the nearest bench, spilling envelopes across the floor. They were all addressed with green ink.

Danny Boy, Cyn, and Alessandra.

Thirty envelopes, some with the flap open, shiny discs peeking out. A lined square of paper was stuck between them.

Danny picked it up and unfolded it.

Where one to another is three,
In the dark there is now light to see.
Climb not the mountain nor the ridge,
But look inward, for you are the bridge.

"You are the bridge." Cyn read. No poem this time, just a statement. "That's what she told me, *you are the bridge.*"

"Who told you?"

"I don't...what's it mean?"

Danny stared until another tremor hit, this one mild compared to the others. *You are the bridge.*

That was different than *build a bridge,* but it didn't make any more sense. *How am I the bridge?*

It had something to do with the discs. He held one of them up to the overhead lamp that was still swinging. Thin filaments of light fired through the pinholes and drifting dust.

He shook his head. There was nothing different about these. They were the same weight with the same colors. His reflection was perfect, like polished steel; his eyes looked back through a galaxy of stars.

An oval of light raced over the ceiling. The disc's reflection danced on the dark ceiling. The outline was spotlight sharp, the tiny holes twinkled like stars. Danny held the discs side by side, beaming three spots on the ceiling. They were identical, the artistry and craftsmanship astounding, but told him nothing.

We're supposed to be here. He mailed those packages so we would get them when we arrived, after we saw the truth, once we knew where we were.

The next tremor hit.

"Come on." Cyn tugged at him. "Look at them later."

Now he says 'you are the bridge'.

He turned the reflections onto different parts of the wall, overlapping them in hopes that a symbol or words would appear. Cyn pulled more forcefully. The noises were getting louder, the building felt like it would come down any second. Foreverland or not, the pain of a collapsing skyscraper would be real.

He stepped away from the light and, at the last second, looked down instead of up. His shadow was sharply cast on the floor.

But the shadows of the discs were fragmented.

The light didn't pass straight through the holes because the holes were drilled at slight angles. As a result, the shadow was hazy. Instead of three sharp circular shadows, each disc cast a fuzzy shadow.

The floor lurched. The lights bounced on their cords. Cyn fell down. Danny hit the table and dropped one of the discs on the blue gown of his body.

"Danny!"

It was the exact color of the gown. And Cyn's body was wearing a yellow gown.

The same yellow on the disc.

He didn't need to compare the third one to the gown on Alex's body. They were both green.

Three discs. Three matching colors.

Where one to another is three, in the dark there is now light to see.

The walls didn't stop shaking. Large objects toppled in the dark end of the room; framed pictures slid off the walls. Cyn pulled him past Alex, past Patricia before he stopped. Her shouting was blotted out by another cataclysmic crash, this one knocking out the power.

"I need a light!"

"We have to get out!" she answered.

They went left to feel their way back through the animal room, past Coco and down the hall. Just as they reached the lobby, a generator kicked on. Emergency light shined from the ceiling.

Danny fumbled with the discs. He knelt on the floor—grit grinding into his knees—and stacked them on top of each other. The weak magnetic forces snapped them in place.

Cyn yanked him to his feet.

They lost their footing as the foundation cracked. Danny leaned against the wall, turning the discs until the holes lined up, and held them to the emergency light.

He looked down.

There's no shadow!

There was the shadow of his hand, but the space between his fingers and thumb was empty. The refracted light obliterated the shadow, as if the discs had disappeared.

Climb not the mountain nor the ridge.

The discs looked like galaxies, maps of the universe. But when lined up, they refracted light to leave no trace of a shadow, as if they didn't exist.

For you are the bridge.

"Danny!"

The front door was askew, the glass shattered. Danny kicked through it and ran as the building buckled and moaned.

The street was a war zone.

The buildings had fallen like metal boulders. I-beams poked out of the rubble like crooked fingers; craters pocked the uneven road. The pavement was still wet, but raindrops were rising off it like dewy drops of condensation, floating skyward like rain falling in the wrong direction.

They ran down the street wherever they could find an opening. A building fell behind them, the quake throwing them to the ground, a cloud of dust engulfing them. He was coughing on his hands and knees when Cyn dragged him to his feet.

A block later, they emerged from the cloud.

She pulled him down Seventh Avenue. The destruction seemed to be less frequent in that direction.

The sky was collapsing, but only faint wisps of smoke circled the crumbling skyscrapers. Above the clouds was a grinding white pall. It sounded like a mass of metallic insects, a roiling cloud of static that was deafening, that vibrated in their chests.

Danny knew what it was. He'd seen it before. So had Cyn.

The Nowhere is coming.

Something shattered.

Monitors were crashing in a heap of glittering glass and smoke. Times Square was coated with a thin layer of ash that fluttered like snowflakes. The ensuing sound of destruction was quickly swallowed by the grinding buzz.

The sky had morphed into a gray, gritty texture. It wasn't anything from this world; it was the absence of everything, a void in the fabric of existence. The closer it got, the more the sound transformed. It wasn't static or the buzz of some otherworldly insects that filled his head and hammered his chest.

Voices.

The last monitor fell, but the road through Broadway was mostly clear.

The discs were vibrating.

Something was missing, he hadn't unlocked the mystery. But he was close. A bridge connected two points of land, usually over a body of water or a chasm or steep drop.

Climb not the mountain nor the ridge.

A bridge allowed someone to go from one island to the next.

But look inward.

In other words, from one land to the next.

For you are the bridge.

"Cyn!"

She was running toward Times Square, ashy puffs splashing with each step.

Danny barely heard himself. His voice was absorbed by the great homogenous hum that cast a dull glow over the broken street and swirling dust.

A single beam of light cut through the falling ash and smoke, highlighting someone in the center of Broadway—severed marquees hung from the walls, streetlights bent, scaffolding scattered like broken toys. It was a dystopian Christmas.

Alessandra.

Her head was back, arms out. The sky was falling and the city collapsing, but the chaos didn't touch her. The closer they got, the stronger the scent of lilac.

She's the air we breathe, the ground we walk. And she's destroying it.

Now there is light to see.

But Alessandra wasn't alone. There were others huddled beneath the remnants of awnings and crooked doorways. And they were nude, not a pair of socks or a shirt among them. Ash settled on their shoulders and hung from their frayed hair.

Old, wrinkled, and saggy, they clung to each other. Some appeared to be shouting, but most were wide-eyed and frightened. He recognized one of them. His hair was the color of black that only came from a bottle.

Mr. Smith. Danny stopped running. *The Investors.*

These were the perpetrators, the thieves, the old men and women that refused to die. They were the ones that threw them into the Nowhere.

The Nowhere that now hovered over them with a menacing boil.

Somehow, Alessandra brought them here.

"Cyn!"

Someone intercepted her—an old woman, the only one clothed, grabbed her before Cyn reached Alessandra. She wrapped both arms around her and dragged her down, jewelry sparkling on her wrists.

Cyn struggled to get away.

Danny twisted the discs to keep the holes lined up as he ran. The vibrations quickly numbed his fingers. Alessandra wasn't standing in a beam of light.

She is the light.

Her light beamed through the discs' tiny holes like infinitesimal wires. With each turn they began to line up. With each turn, the wire of light became less intense. The circular shadow cast across his stomach became more opaque.

And then vanished.

The discs were aligned—blue, yellow and green. All three solid objects left no trace in the presence of light.

They didn't need to find a bridge, didn't need to build a bridge. The last package was addressed to all three of them. Danny misinterpreted the message—it wasn't *you* are the bridge.

We are the bridge.

38

Tyler

Foreverland

Monster.

They sought to create a new Foreverland, one for every living soul. Instead, they created a monster.

A black hole.

Alessandra could've ended their lives like meaningless ants. Instead, she bridged into Patricia's Foreverland and yanked them into her world, put them on the curb to watch the annihilation of Foreverland.

They thought they were safe. No one could bridge Foreverlands like that. *No one is like Alessandra.*

One moment, Tyler was standing next to the pool, dancing with his wife, and the next he was without clothes, shivering on the sidewalk, gravel digging into the soles of his feet, old age aching in his hunched spine.

What have we done?

It was hard to breathe, the air hot and gritty, thick with floral essence that coated his lungs. It was snowing, the remnants of a distant volcano drifting down from a gray sky.

The noise was worse. He didn't hear the pillar slam into the street, didn't hear the cracking asphalt. It was lost in the pervasive buzz, the sound of static that drowned everything, that scratched his ears, his eyes. The buzz drove a ticklish fever beneath his wrinkled, spotted skin.

Tyler put his arm around Patricia and attempted to cover her nudity. Alessandra could strip him of his dignity, but not his wife.

Not like this.

She hid her face. Her hair had thinned and grayed, her flesh hung from her shoulders. She aged the moment she was pulled from her world, no longer graceful. No longer angelic. She was a dried husk of a human being.

And the noise grew louder.

It was a jackhammer inside his teeth, picking at his organs and chiseling apart his joints. It shook loose his bladder. Urine ran down his legs.

There were others.

One by one, they fell out of the sky and landed with bone-breaking force—men and women just as nude, just as old. They emerged from a cloud of gray fluff, uninjured, and covered their ears.

Their shock was all too apparent.

They struggled to breathe the thick air, attempted to speak. Eventually, they backed away from the beam of light. Alessandra glowed like an angel.

Destroyed like a demon.

Patricia covered her mouth. Tyler felt her breath on his shoulder, her words against his ear. He couldn't understand her, but knew what she was saying. She recognized them, too.

The Investors.

These were the men and women that funded Foreverland. They were the ones that went out to the island, the ones that lived in the wilderness. They had moved into younger bodies, yet they were here.

They were old again.

Did she pull them out of their stolen bodies, just reach into the physical world and snatch them up like she'd done to us?

The biomites, of course.

The Investors had likely been seeded with biomites that allowed them to network with other biomites. Just like Tyler. Alessandra was reaching across all networks and grabbing their true identities.

Tyler could feel Patricia's tears against his arm. He moved to shield her from the others as they continued to fall. A puddle formed around his feet. Patricia's bladder let loose.

Don't do this to Patricia. She's given so much.

Alessandra could take Tyler, do what she wanted: embarrass him, ridicule him, march him naked in front of the entire world. He deserved it. But not Patricia. She was too loving.

Too good.

Tyler stepped off the curb and shook his fist to get Alessandra's attention. An invisible force pushed him back. His words were crushed in the heightened grind of static. He fell back, struggling to breathe. All he could do was mutter a prayer that never made it past his fluttering lips.

God, help us.

But their goddess wasn't listening.

All he could do was hold his wife. If it was the last thing he could do, he would hold her, protect her from the falling sky until the vibrations reached his bones.

The beam of light intensified.

Tyler shielded his eyes. Alessandra was a bleached, blurry figure. Barb was out there. Somehow that guilty bitch escaped the goddess's wrath. She stopped Cynthia from reaching Alessandra.

Reed sent her. She showed Alessandra the extent of her omnipotence. She should be on the curb.

The buildings no longer crumbled, but the blizzard of ash continued. The dark sky closed on them.

The hair on his arms stood up.

The grind of static popped his ears like hot needles. The old men and women covered their ears, mouths agape in agony. In silence, they screamed.

The static was inside him now. He felt it grind the inside of his body. His eyes filled with tears.

He looked up.

Please no formed on his lips.

In his liquefying bones, he heard the true nature of the tortuous sound. It wasn't static after all.

Voices.

Hundreds of scared and lonely voices, scattered like dust. They were coming for them.

We threw them out there.

Those were the voices he heard when he woke from the stroke, when Gramm saved his life.

Where are you, Gramm?

Alessandra wasn't just ending her world. She was making them pay for it. And the sins that built it.

The shadow collapsed around them.

The buildings disappeared.

The road.

Ashes filled the world.

Only a shaft of light remained, Alessandra a blurred vision.

Tyler whispered a plea that would never become more than a thought.

I love you, he whispered and wrapped his arms around his wife as the voices exploded like a sandstorm inside him.

His body went fuzzy.

The air corroded his lungs and softened his flesh.

He pulled Patricia closer and felt his arms merge into her as if she were dissolving.

Their molecules were letting go, spreading out.

Her heart beat into his chest. Her screams, silent.

With the last movement of his mind, the last thought that would ever be experienced by the human being known as Tyler Ballard was formed. It was a realization.

He saw the real monsters.

They burst into subatomic particles, the fabric of their minds stretched across the universe. The agony was unforgiveable.

This is the Nowhere.

39

Alessandra

Foreverland

Alex pulled down the Nowhere.

Barb had calmed her, got her to breathe, to feel just how big this world had become.

How big *she* had become.

This was all a product of her mind—these buildings and streets, the sky and clouds and insects crawling along the sidewalks. The realization was overwhelming, but Barb was there to guide her through it, to help her see the truth, that this reality—what Alex had become—was not solely the product of her mind.

They used children to build it.

And Barb was one of the guilty ones.

"I know." Barb closed her eyes and nodded. She was aware of what she'd done. That's why she was there. *To balance the scales.*

"I was an Investor," she said. "There are more like me."

The Investors lived in these younger, stolen bodies. In today's era of biotechnology, they all had biomites.

"And biomites interconnect minds."

Alex could network through biomites. And that's what she did. She created connections, starting with the Ballards. She found them in Patricia's Foreverland, a tiny universe in the ethers of existence. Having already established a connection, they were easy. The others took some time, but like an electromagnetic claw, she found them in the physical world and pulled them from their thieved bodies.

She brought them into Foreverland.

The Investors witnessed their true forms and were forced to see each other for what they were: naked, ugly and alone.

Alex closed her eyes and lifted her face to the sun.

It was not the sun that beamed down. She was the sun, the source of light, the center of this reality. She was a star that willingly collapsed like a black hole.

The warmth cleansed her of anguish, shed the sorrow and the pain. Her sadness transformed into acceptance.

And the rain rose off the ground and the ash fell.

The buzz of the Nowhere raged like a lumber mill, the voices becoming clearer. *The children...the children were fed to the Nowhere to build this. To support me.*

"Shhhhhh," Barb said, soothing the voices in the Nowhere. "Soon. Your suffering ends soon."

Alex drew the life force into a beam of light.

She let go of the guilt, the shame and sorrow. She let go of her past.

She looked out at the Investors, naked and alone in the shattered world. They were dim forms, vague figures lost in the blizzard of the approaching Nowhere. Their cries were endless and silent. Their anguish as deep as the Nowhere.

The Nowhere pulled them, cell by cell, into its entropic void. They fed the insatiable hunger with their being. Even Barb.

And the voices stopped, the ashes gracefully drifting to the ground until all was quiet, all was still.

The children hushed.

She didn't know where the children went, how they escaped or how the Investors took their place.

The scales were balanced.

40

Danny Boy
Foreverland

The Nowhere hummed at Danny's heels, ate through his ears and burned in his chest. The asphalt, once unforgiving, now softened beneath his steps like melting clay. Amidst the charred wreckage, the smell of lilac could not be stronger, as if the buildings were built of it.

He clutched the discs.

Alessandra was pure light, only a faint outline still visible. Barb had thrown Cyn to the ground. Hardly visible through the thickening ash, they rolled in puffs of dusty gray until they were coated. Barb saw him coming and yanked her to her feet. Cyn's hair stood out like fire. An aura encircled her as he neared.

The city had been swallowed.

The light burned Danny's eyes. He shielded his face, the discs glowing. Barb let go just as he grabbed Cyn's hand. The road turned to quicksand, eating their steps as they charged the beam of light.

Their fingers snapped together.

The Nowhere closed around them; the voices ate the ground, the air, the inside of their bones.

He didn't feel his last step as they reached for the light, lunged with all their weight and collided with Alessandra—

No sight, no sound.

Not even the ring of silence.

Nothingness.

SPRING (AGAIN)

Death is a doorway.
    To exit.
    To enter.

The office was silent.

Distant vibrations and damp, cool air were reminders of the subterranean laboratory. Production never stopped. There was always a need, always a want. As long as people could pay the price, they would.

They did.

Jonathan sat back in the chair. He focused on his breathing, harnessed his attention, brought his awareness to the right here and now.

The door opened.

Julie and others walked into the spacious office. Outside those doors, the warehouse was silent. Jonathan bolted upright. No one took a seat. He looked from face to face, searching for an answer. He'd given everything for this moment.

"We're ready," Julie said. "They're dressed."

Jonathan could hardly feel his legs.

The team of technicians was all present, all twenty-seven of them from different parts of the world, all sworn to secrecy, to operate in anonymity. They were compensated handsomely.

They walked into the warehouse.

A few words were said by the team leaders, this being the largest and most ambitious project of its kind. One of them held an object about the size of a cell phone. Julie handed it to Jonathan. His hand was shaking. She wrapped her fingers around his hand.

"You do the honors, Jonathan."

A single icon shone beneath the glass. He put his thumb on it and looked around. On eyes on him. Two hundred and four latches simultaneously thrummed. The doors released.

Movement stirred.

Jonathan didn't feel Julie take the control from him. He didn't see the team spread out and watch the doors, one by one, slowly open. No one moved, everyone waited, collectively holding their breath.

The warehouse grew quiet again.

Water dripped.

And then the first door swung open. A pair of large eyes peeked out. A child, a girl about the age of twelve, blonde hair damp and matted, stepped out.

41

Danny Boy

Foreverland

There was sky.

Danny didn't recognize it as sky. He was on his back, looking into the endless blue canvas. It could've been the glassy ocean at daybreak, but his mouth was dry and the air warm.

Pain flashed across his forehead.

He closed his eyes until the tension relaxed. His skin was warm and damp with sweat, tight where the sun had turned it pink. The grass crunched as he lifted his arm.

His elbow struck something hard.

It lay in the tall weeds, a half-buried circle with raised numbers. He pulled the grass aside and scraped the algae and matted leaves away.

A sundial.

The pain returned when he sat up, almost dragging him back into unconsciousness. He rode out the splashing white flashes inside his skull. Birds scuttled in the trees behind him. The briny scent of the ocean was strong.

Something is missing.

A three-storied dormitory was across the field, the windows punched out, vines clawing the walls. Beyond that, just above the trees, the cylindrical outline of another building was set against the cloudless tropical sky. The windows, once reflective, were now dull and chalky. It listed slightly to the left.

He knew where he was. *How did I get here?*

Something rustled in the grass.

Danny jumped up, regrettably, and fought the spots stabbing his vision, the pain lighting up his head as he scanned the trees and sky for predators. The tall grass was still matted where he was lying, the edge of the sundial—weathered and cracked—still exposed.

A path led away from it.

The sun reflected off the trampled grass. Danny bent down to pick up a disc—just one disc, the side smooth and reflective and perforated with a galaxy of tiny holes. And then the memories surfaced.

The three discs, the ash-covered world, the final beam of light. And then this.

The island.

A shiver trickled down his back, clinked in his stomach like cold cubes. It was just like he remembered when he woke up that first day with the old man telling him he was somewhere special, that they were going to help him. It smelled green and new. White birds soared with promise.

But the buildings were abandoned, the field overgrown. There were no old men, no boys being marched to the haystack. And something else was missing.

The lilac is gone.

The ever-present scent of lilac that had followed him for the past year had been replaced by the ocean.

He turned the disc over. The pattern of holes was the same as the others, but he didn't expect to find them. They wouldn't be hiding in the grass. This disc was different. The edge was red.

A moan behind him.

Danny spun and saw a depression ten feet away, the curve of a bended knee. Cyn lay on her back, her head cradled in a nest of bundled grass, her skin slightly pink. He fell on his knees and took her hand. Her repose was undisturbed, her hair fanned over the ground.

Her eyelids fluttered. Eyes unfocused, she gazed into the cloudless blue for several moments.

"Hey." Danny squeezed.

Her breath came in long, cool strokes. She started to sit up and scrunched her eyes. Folds wrinkled across her forehead. Danny could still feel a dull ache between his eyes, but the pain had faded. Hers was fresh out of the box.

"Where are we?" she asked.

"An island."

"How..." She swallowed. "Island?"

She lay still, eyes closed, breathing through the settling ache. He could see the subtle hints of memory returning, the details of Times Square covered in ash, running at Alessandra...*and then the light.*

"How'd we get here?" she muttered.

He held up the disc. She shook her head. Confusion clouded her pained eyes.

"*Where one to another is three, in the dark there is now light to see,*" he said, quoting the last poem found at the Institute. "The discs he sent, they were colored on the edges; each one matched the gown we were wearing."

A touch of vertigo swirled in his belly, the jiggling trapdoor threatening to drop him into a pit of reality confusion. They were in a Foreverland world looking at their bodies in the Institute that he presumed were representations of their *real* bodies.

"*Our bodies,*" he said, "were wearing those gowns: blue, yellow and green. Three of us, just like the last poem said, *where one to another is three, in the dark there is now light*. And Alessandra was the light."

He held the disc above her, the shadow falling on her stomach, a small galaxy of pinpoints.

"When the three discs were together, they vibrated. And then I noticed that these little holes dispersed the light in a way that made the shadow disappear, like the discs were just an illusion, like they weren't really there. Like the poem said, *look inward, for you are the bridge.* Only it meant all three of us. *We* are the bridge."

Cyn sat up and rested her arms on her knees. Her hair hung over her face like curtains. "But we were together before that."

"*There is now light to see*."

Alessandra wasn't the light when they walked into the Institute. That was the missing element. The pieces were in place so that when the time came, when Alessandra pulled down the Nowhere, when she'd brought the Investors back and transformed herself into a beam of light, there was a way for them to escape.

"She saved me," Cyn said.

"She saved all of us."

"Barb." The blonde curtains shook. "*Barb* saved me."

Danny sat next to her and gave her several seconds.

"Barb was...she was an Investor."

He thought so, but couldn't understand why Cyn was hiding her face from him. Why her voice quivered. The old woman had helped them become the bridge. She stopped Cyn until Danny arrived. Like she knew.

But she was the only Investor clothed.

"We all had an Investor," Danny said.

"Mine was different." She sighed heavily. "I never told anyone this, but something happened in Foreverland that was...different than everyone else when, you know, the time came for her to take my body."

She swallowed. Hard. *My demon is different than yours.*

"That cloud in Times Square," she said, "the gray coming down, I remember that, Danny. I remember the Nowhere. I know what it's like to be out there and pulled into a billion pieces. I remember having no body, no mind, just this...this shattered something...spilled all over the place like a...like a nothing."

She sniffed.

"And then I just got pushed out, like someone pulled me back together and shoved me back into my body. All of the others were still in the Nowhere and I was back, but..." She exhaled. "Barb was already there—I'm sorry, I don't like to...it's all weird and confusing. I know it sounds all, you know, impossible but, it's just...no one ever came out of the Nowhere except for me, I think. And, I don't really know why."

She quivered and stifled a sob. *Why me?*

She'd been in the Nowhere, tasted it. Danny was there, too, as a tourist. He didn't feel the separation, didn't dissolve. Maybe it would all sound impossible if she didn't say someone had *pushed her out.* Danny knew someone that survived the Nowhere, someone that could come and go as she wished.

Lucinda.

Reed's girlfriend came to Danny when he first went to Foreverland. She was the one with candy red hair, the one that knew the Nowhere, the one that took Danny out there to see and hear. She destroyed herself when Foreverland crashed.

But not before she found Cyn.

"Was Barb the one you were talking to?" Danny asked. "At the Institute?"

She nodded. "I'm not crazy, Danny."

"I know."

"She's been in my head since Foreverland ended. Every day was a battle. Until you showed up."

He remembered how it felt when he held her hand the first time, the way his body shook with relief, how his nightmare went away.

"When you showed up, she just went away, sort of. For the first time, I couldn't hear her voice. But she didn't disappear. When you were gone, she came back, she poured the pills down my throat, tried to take back my body. If you hadn't showed up that night..."

She took several cleansing breaths.

"But then she changed," Cyn said. "Said Reed was behind it all."

"Told you about Alessandra."

She nodded. "And when I saw Times Square and the sky falling, I thought she was sending us all to the..."

She sighed and didn't finish.

"I don't think that's what she was doing."

"That was the Nowhere. She was pulling it down, I could feel it. I can't go back there, Danny. I can't."

"We're not going back. I promise."

"How do you know?" She looked up, eyes wide, red and glassy.

He didn't want to lie to her, not ever. She didn't deserve that. He didn't know where they were going; he could only tell her what he thought Alessandra did, what made sense.

She destroyed Foreverland.

It was more than that. Somehow, Alessandra brought the Investors back and made them pay. How she did it, he couldn't explain. He even wondered if they were real, maybe they were just illusions. It was impossible to tell if anything was real.

Their fear, though, that was real. They stood with wide-eyed panic on the sidewalk as the ashes fell around them, cries lost in the descending static that ate up the world. And all those voices intermingled with that tortuous noise, all those fragmented voices that haunted the Nowhere. And just before Danny and Cyn hit Alessandra, just before the light swallowed them, he heard the voices go silent.

"You all right?" he asked.

"Head starting to hurt again."

Danny's forehead had settled, but there was still a throbbing knot between his eyes that he massaged with his thumb. Her headache appeared to go away, too, but now it was coming back. She rubbed tiny circles between her eyes.

"Where is she?" Cyn asked. "Where's Alessandra?"

Danny eyed the path. Maybe she woke up before they did and went exploring. Judging by their pink skin, he and Cyn had been lying in the sun a while.

"Where are we, Danny? If Alessandra destroyed Foreverland, where are we?"

"We're not awake."

"Why?" Her eyes pleaded, still wide, panic on the rims, reality confusion nipping at her heels. Thoughts of the Nowhere lurked behind her eyes.

He exhaled sharply, searching the sky.

If Alessandra was no longer a host and this wasn't reality, then where were they? Who was hosting *this? And why the island?*

A warm breeze rushed over the field. The grass rustled and brushed against them. Blonde strands stuck to Cyn's damp cheeks. Danny brushed them away, her face warm.

Once again, the smell of the ocean was strong, like they were bathing in it, breathing the salt spray, the taste lingering on his lips, stinging his eyes. And yet they weren't close enough to hear the waves.

And not a hint of lilac.

He searched the blue sky in the disc's reflection, the pinpoints dotting his eyes. The blood-red edge on his fingers. It wasn't blue or yellow or green. It was a different color.

Then he realized.

Something about the ocean, something about the red edge told him where they were.

Like we're breathing the ocean.

The path led to the beach. That was where Reed spent all his time when they were on the island. That's where they buried his body. *And this is what he smelled like.*

Maybe Alessandra didn't walk away from the sundial after all. Or maybe someone led her away while they slept. Danny knew where the answers would be.

"Let's go this way." He walked several steps down the trampled path. "I think we'll find something on the sand—"

She was gone.

Danny ran back. The grass was still matted, the bundled pillow still in place. There was no path leading away from it, no footsteps or broken stems. Cyn was just gone.

His smile faded, and he took a deep breath.

He walked in a large circle, looking through the grass like she was an object that fell out of his pocket. He tripped over the sundial.

This was the center of Foreverland when they were on the island, where everything started. Danny pushed away the debris and placed his hand on it. There was no tingling, no surge of power.

It was cold and dead.

Danny's head began to throb. The sky was still blue, the air still salty. If this was still a dream, if his physical body was still in the Institute, then he hadn't awakened. *And maybe Cyn's opening her eyes.*

"She's all right," he told himself. Then, "Please let her be all right."

He waited in case she reappeared. He couldn't stand the thought of her coming back alone. When the sun was directly above him, he decided to follow the path to the beach. He crossed the dunes out to the hardpack, where a set of barefooted tracks still dented the sand, slowly melting in the sliding waves.

The footprints walked straight into the ocean.

Danny stared at the crisp line of the horizon, remembering a time when he sat with Reed, when everything was bleak and hopeless, wondering what was out there. He took off his boots and socks, dug his toes into the ground, the water cool around his ankles.

Pain hammered a beating rhythm across his forehead.

He went back to the soft sand of the dunes, sat down, and turned his face to the sun that was still high, still hot. He closed his eyes, letting the salty air fill him. The thrumming pain shrank until it was a spot between his eyes going boom-boom, boom-boom.

The smell of the ocean faded.

The water went silent.

And Danny opened his eyes to a bright light.

42

Alessandra

The Institute of Technological Research, New York City

A thorn.

It was wedged between her eyes, probably no larger than a sliver. Felt like a railroad spike.

She blinked. Colors smeared across the landscape. She distinctly remembered seeing everything, being everything. She didn't need eyes. There was no separation. She was the city. She was everywhere.

The light.

But now she lay in a sterile room, the smell of antiseptic mingled with the rank odor of wet fur and mucus.

She blinked again.

Pain flashed between her eyes. The sliver was a double image, a gleaming rod extending somewhere between her eyebrows. Each breath sent it deeper into her head.

She lifted her hand.

Fire ignited her elbow, muscles screeching along her forearm. Her fingers hovered above her face, careful not to bump the metal sliver, pinching it between finger and thumb.

A deep breath.

It slid from her like an icicle, tickling her inner ears, raking the back of her eyes. Tears pooled. She turned her head and let them roll over the bridge of her nose.

Another bed.

It was on a white stand. An old woman was sunk halfway into a green cushion. Her arms and legs were bent. Her hair as white as the stand. She was a mummy pulled from the belly of a pyramid, her flesh wrinkled like ancient leather. Her mouth was slightly open.

The beds hummed.

Roller pins massaged the back of Alex's legs, buttocks and shoulders. Pain radiated all over. It took three efforts to get up. She sat in a hunched position, catching her breath, waiting for strength to return...

When she remembered who she was, where she'd been.

What she did.

The room began to turn. It was too much—the dream, the reality—and the walls began to shrink. She wished for the peaceful light that swallowed her, that eternal existence where she rested after bringing back the old men and women.

After silencing the voices.

Peace.

She ended their suffering. She sat in the middle of the empty street, bemoaning her own fate, when the woman named Barb showed Alex her destiny. She was the one that would bring peace to the children.

You will balance the scales, Barb told her.

Alex let one of her bare feet touch the floor. It was hard and cold. Pins and needles crawled up her leg as if struck with an aluminum post. She let the other one down and rested. There were tubes in her arms that burned when pulled out, clear liquid dripping on her toes.

Images were scattered over two computers.

She reached out and took one large step to the one nearest her. Data scrolled along the margins. A picture of her was set in the upper left-hand corner. None of the script made sense except one flashing word.

AWAKE.

She was no longer dreaming, back in her body, her flesh. It seemed so obvious she wasn't asleep, now; the density of her body was like a shrink-wrap of flesh, her identity contained within.

The image fractured into static. Data blazed over the screen and then went black. A single line appeared on a blue screen.

DATA CORRUPT.

Something broke.

Her reflection looked back from the blank screen—frizzy black hair, dark eyes. A red spot glistened on her forehead. She brushed clear liquid from the hole. It ached with each pulse.

The room resumed a slow spin.

She latched onto the computer and closed her eyes. *I'm awake now. I'm awake now.*

The monitor nearest the old woman showed a different status. Alex stumbled over to it. The photo hardly matched the shriveled husk behind her. It was a younger version, a healthier time.

Patricia Ballard, it said.

And the word below it brought the room to a standstill.

DECEASED.

She remembered her on the oversized monitors in Times Square, an image that more closely resembled the picture on the computer. But on the sidewalk, she was naked and old and hidden in the arms of her husband. Her husband, Tyler Ballard, the man she interviewed at the prison, was enraged.

That was in the dream. I interviewed him in the dream.

He had shouted at Alex, but the voices—the poor, distorted voices, the children that had been thrown into that gray static—filled the air, blotting out the crashing buildings that fell in plumes of ashes. Tyler was responsible. They both were.

Patricia wasn't angry. She was sad, resigned. Accepting.

She knew her fate. And when the Nowhere collapsed, she went willingly.

Of course, Alex hadn't meant to murder anyone. She only brought the ones responsible for the crimes she witnessed. Patricia and Tyler had kidnapped Alex like all those old men and women had abducted the children. The Ballards inserted Alex into her own dream. They wanted her to be the sleeping host that would keep Foreverland alive.

And they had already hurt so many.

But now there was silence. No more voices, no more pain. No ashes.

Machines began beeping on the other side of a curtain. Alex needed to leave. Her gown was loose, her feet bare. She needed to be less conspicuous and pulled open all the drawers and found a box of bandages. Gently, she covered the oozing hole in her head.

Her clothes were beneath her bed.

She ran past Coco, down an empty hall, all the offices open and vacant. She stopped at the front doors. Outside, it was dark, the streets empty. A light rain fell in slow motion.

Two cabs were waiting.

She pulled a hood over her head and ran. It was late, the city asleep. But the night was warm. Winter had ended. She could smell the green of new growth.

And no lilac.

Alex jumped in the first cab, lay back and watched the city pass by. The streets were slick and shiny. It was perfectly quiet, beautifully silent.

The voices no longer cried.

43

Cyn

The Institute of Technological Research, New York City

Thirst came in waves.

It was a pebble, a tiny stone that rose and fell. Cyn was reaching for something to stop it from rising and falling, rising and falling. But it wasn't a pebble, not something she could touch.

It throbbed.

Something beeped just out of reach, auditory spikes between valleys of silence, reminding her of a rooster that woke her after long, dead nights in the cabin.

Her eyelids cracked.

The light was harsh, slapping her into the cold tight ache of her body. She blinked back the fluorescent light and smacked at the thirst on her lips. Something was between her eyes.

She yanked it out too quickly, throwing a switch on an internal tuning fork. When the room stopped spinning—her head still singing—she was looking at a boy with red hair, sunk halfway into a green cushion. His arms and legs were slightly bent.

"Danny," she croaked.

She sat on the edge of the strange bed, her feet dangling just above the floor. Her knees, exposed below the hem of the yellow gown, ached. So did her fingers and elbows. Most of all, her hand throbbed like her forehead. It was wrapped in gauze. She peeled off the tape, exposing a slice across the back of her hand, thick whiskers of black stitching poking out.

I cut myself so long ago. Why does it still look like that?

The time dilation.

Danny was right: time went much faster in Foreverland. If she still had stitches, that meant—

Her knees buckled when she leaped, catching herself before coming down hard. Pins and needles shot through her feet. She lowered herself to the floor and crawled. The curtain that separated their beds had been pulled aside. She passed an open cabinet and noticed the box of clothing as she pulled herself up to Danny's bed.

She grew faint.

Closing her eyes, she slowed her breath. It came back to her now—where they were, where they'd been.

This is real.

"Danny?" she whispered. "Wake up, Danny."

His lips were parted; his breath shallow and warm. She pressed her ear to his chest.

Another computer beeped.

It was against the wall. Each step burned; the muscles and tendons contracted. Danny's photo was in the corner. The status flashed below it.

WAKING.

The cardiac monitor began to spike.

She stumbled back to his side and clawed at his shoulders, held his cheeks. His eyes moved beneath the eyelids.

"Come on, Danny." She looked around, hoping no one would hear her, no idea if someone was just beyond the curtains. She just knew they needed to get out. "Wake up."

If she pulled the needle too soon, would he be trapped in Foreverland? His eyes continued dancing. She squeezed his hand, fingers weaving together.

His eyes opened and stared into nothing.

"Danny?"

Tears welled up. She hovered over his face, stroking his cheeks. He blinked several times. Cyn pinched the needle and waited.

Waited for focus to return.

Waited for him to see her.

And when he did, when he blinked, when a tiny smile bent the corners of his mouth—

She yanked it out.

He bolted upright and couldn't catch his breath, huffing like he was dumped into a bucket of icy water.

"Danny." She rubbed his arm. "We've got to go, Danny."

He looked around, the pieces of reality falling in place too slowly. She pushed him up and pulled his legs over the edge.

"Easy."

She held him while he slid his weight onto his feet. He stared down and looked at his hands, turning them over like she'd seen him do before, his barometers of reality.

"We're back, Danny. This is the skin."

He was nodding, but still turning, needing to believe it, not just hear it. She retrieved the boxes of clothing while he sorted out this layer of reality. *Is he wondering the same thing I am, wondering if this is the last layer?*

She was only wearing panties beneath the gown. Danny grabbed a sweatshirt and a pair of sweatpants, tenderly walking around the curtain. She quickly pulled on a pair of pants, tucking the gown inside them and throwing the hoodie over it. Danny was still dressing.

Cyn peeked around the opposite curtain. Patricia lay still on a bed. She didn't appear to be breathing. The other bed was empty.

The building was silent.

"Danny?" she whispered. "You all right?"

His bare feet weren't beneath the curtain. A dreaded wave settled in her chest. Cyn shuffled around the tables.

"Danny?" She tugged the plastic curtain.

Several curtains were pulled back. Danny was ten tables back, still dressed in the gown, clothes in hand. He stared at an older man, his beard shaggy, hair wild. There was a hole in his forehead, but no needle.

"It's him," Danny said hollowly. "It's Reed."

She thought Reed would be younger, then remembered that wasn't his original body. Reed migrated into Harold Ballard's body when they overthrew Foreverland and escaped the island.

Reed's original body was dead. *So is that one.*

"I thought he sent us the letters," Cyn said.

"It was him. It had to be. It just..."

He started to sway, reality confusion tilting the floor. She let him take his time, but more computers were beginning to beep. They needed to go. They could figure this out later. Besides, it didn't matter who sent the letters.

"Danny, no. This way."

He slid his bare feet over the floor, went to the other side of Reed and pulled back the curtain. An overhead light flickered to life.

Another bed, another body.

"Oh, man, no," he moaned. "No, no, no...not you, Zin."

Cyn read the name on the computer. *Eric Zinder.*

He'd escaped the island with them. Now he was there, in the Institute, a hole in his head but no needle. He wasn't breathing.

There were more curtains.

Danny rushed through them, tearing them off their hooks, dropping them on the floor. The lights turned on one after another, bed after bed.

Body after body.

The first three were boys. She wasn't sure he recognized them all. The fourth one, though, was a dark-skinned woman.

Macy. She was helping them. She was working for the Ballards.

This time the floor tipped beneath Cyn's feet.

"They were searching for a host," he said. "They were bringing us here, searching for a host."

"She's gone." Cyn looked back toward the front. "Alessandra's bed is empty."

"Zin's the one that saved me," he said. "Kept me from going insane on the island."

"We have to go." She clutched his elbow.

He resisted. "They lured us into the Institute, somehow put us back here and then, they manipulated our memories so that we didn't remember...we didn't know we were..."

The room was spinning on him. He hung onto the bed.

"Danny! We have to go!"

He tried to yank away from her.

"Don't do this. We can't help them now. We don't know what's happening, someone might come back, we're not supposed to be awake, they'll put us back in...we have to go now!"

Danny was shaking his head. He went back to Zin, took the boy's hand, and continued shaking his head as if he just couldn't take it anymore. No more layers.

No more lies.

Cyn gently wrapped her hand around his. Danny remained unfocused as she took the clothes wedged under his arm and began dressing him. She put her hands on his cheeks.

"We're alive, Danny. And we need to leave. Do you understand?"

She pressed her lips against his, her body against his body.

"We have to go."

He nodded.

There wasn't time to lament, no time to understand where they were or why. There was only time to escape. She pulled him away, but Danny paused at Reed's body, his head cocked to the side. His thoughts, like hers, were obscured in the fog of waking.

He clutched Reed's gown and shook it. It was red.

"Come on."

They made it past the beds where they woke, past Patricia Ballard. The last time Cyn saw her was in a small cabin hidden in the woods. There was a monitor with Patricia's picture in the upper left-hand corner. *DECEASED.*

Danny was in front of another computer, this one near the empty bed. The cabinets below it were open. There was an image of an attractive Hispanic woman. *AWAKE.*

She made it out.

They passed through the animal lab and paused at the front door.

Brake lights glowed in an otherwise black and empty street. Rain drifted in tiny droplets, throwing red halos around the back end of the car. The driver stared at them through a blue cloud from an electric cigarette.

The back door was open.

Instinctively, they pulled their hoods up and walked out. It was late, the city still asleep.

"Wait." Danny held the door. "We don't have money."

"Fare's already covered," the driver said. "Get in."

"Who?"

"Somebody called, paid in advance. Come on, already."

"Where we going?"

"JFK."

Cyn and Danny traded empty stares, trying to cut through the mental fog, to calculate whether this was a good idea. Maybe they should walk until things cleared up.

Cyn saw the envelope on the backseat. She reached inside and pulled out two tickets. "Spain?"

Danny ushered her inside the cab.

44

Reed

New York City

It unfolded below.

The third-story window was spattered with tiny droplets that, over the hours he had stood there, coalesced and eventually ran in jagged lines. The man pushed brown curly hair off his forehead and checked his wristwatch. Thirty-two minutes past four.

The taxi pulled away.

It was the second car to pull up to the Institute of Technological Research, this one instructed to take an envelope taped to the front door and wait for two people. The driver would later be interviewed by police. With their hoods up, he wouldn't be able to help them with identifying the boy and girl other than remembering they were young.

The first car was different. That was a private driver, someone Reed paid handsomely for confidentiality. He took her to a home in the suburbs.

There would be no trace of Alessandra.

Rain continued drifting into the empty street. Occasionally, a car passed below, but no one noticed that the door to the Institute was open, that all the lights were on.

He took a deep breath and closed his eyes.

At 4:45, he reached into the front pocket of his white lab coat and pulled out a phone. The glass was cool against his thumb. He touched several icons, then sent a message. He waited for confirmation that all relevant data had been downloaded from the Institute.

It's done.

Even he was surprised by the weight falling off his shoulders, like a beast stepping off. It had been such a long journey, so many people had been hurt. He didn't plan it to happen like this, but the Ballards had already been so powerful.

But it was over. It was finally over.

Reed took off the white coat and placed it on the receptionist's counter. He punched a code into the phone and placed it on top like a paperweight as the self-destruct code erased all trace of the biomite doctor.

At the glass doors, he set the alarm and stepped out as the countdown beeped. The elevator doors squealed open. He pulled a hood over his head and stepped onto the sidewalk, drizzle beading on his hunched shoulders. The early morning chill cut through layers of clothing as delivery trucks began their morning routes.

He walked nearly two city blocks when the first police car passed him. They were heading for the Institute. The eerie news of the empty research facility would be all over the world by lunch.

By then, Reed would be far away.

45

Alessandra

Upstate New York

Alex grabbed for something, a ledge or a rope or a helping hand, but nothing, black nothing slipped through her fingers—

Asleep again. This time at the computer. Had her Madre seen her jerk her head off the desk, she would've fretfully wrung her hands. "*¿Otra pesadilla?*"

Si, Madre. Another nightmare.

It was those moments just after she woke, when she wasn't sure if the dream had ended or was just beginning, that disturbed her most. Her forehead always reminded her. She parted her black bangs and touched the tiny hole.

This is real.

Something was dripping.

The coffee cup lay on its side, a brown stain spreading over a mess of papers. She must've knocked it over when she lurched into wakefulness.

"Damn!"

She pulled old papers and tissues from the trash but stood too quickly and grabbed the desk to keep from falling. That was the second time in a minute she was glad Madre wasn't around. When the vertigo settled, she dabbed up the mess.

The doorbell rang.

She looked out the window. The lilacs had faded. Spring had passed. The neighbor was mowing his front yard. Spring blossoms had completely fallen from the cherry tree, replaced by foliage that blocked her view. The taillights of a black SUV were barely visible.

The front door opened. "Yes?" Madre said.

The voices were muffled, but Alex heard the word "agent" somewhere in the exchange.

Surprised it took so long.

She dropped the sopping papers. Coffee bled through the photo on top, the image of the white transfer van had been found in Pennsylvania, en route to New York.

The catatonic drivers made full recoveries. They were transporting one passenger to Attica Correctional Facility when they pulled into the rest area with no recollection of why or how long they'd been there.

Dr. Tyler Ballard.

It wasn't long before a full-scale Foreverland operation was discovered at the prison. Dr. Tyler Ballard had just left. He'd arranged the transfer, but the investigation suspected he was planning to be discharged at the Institute, where a similar Foreverland was in full swing. That's where his wife awaited him.

She was found dead, too.

Tyler Ballard was still in restraints, alone in the back of the van. The drivers claimed he was a little loco. When he wasn't sleeping, he talked to himself. "What was really weird," one of the drivers said, "was when he'd pause, like someone was answering him."

No one in the prison remembered anything. They were all fully loaded with brain biomites that had been rebooted. The only exception was an inmate named Gramm Hamilton, a former chemist serving a life sentence. He claimed to have been trapped in his cell by an intruder, that he had nothing to do with Tyler Ballard's escape and subsequent death.

The coroner couldn't explain how Tyler Ballard died. It was eventually written up as "old age and biomite complications."

"Right on the line," the coroner said. "He had the most biomites allowed by law, and they were experimental, too. I suspect this had something to do with his delusions."

The press eventually concocted an image of Dr. Tyler Ballard the mad scientist that hijacked a prison and tortured inmates with delusions of Foreverland.

Alex knew better.

In the months since she'd walked out of the Institute, no one had called or come knocking. Even when the investigation revealed a cab taking two unknown people, a young man and woman, from the Institute shortly before the alarms went off, no one ever contacted Alex.

There was no mention of a cab that picked up a middle-aged Hispanic woman.

Alex went to the top of the steps and listened.

"I'd just like to speak with her, ask a few questions," a young man said.

"Unless you have a warrant—"

"Mrs. Diosa is not a suspect, ma'am. I just have some questions about one of her previous visits to the Institute."

"I don't appreciate your implications," Madre said.

"Any information she could give me—"

"Bring a warrant."

She's been watching too much TV. "What's going on?" Alex stopped on the bottom step.

"Mrs. Diosa?" he called through the screen.

"You don't need to talk to the police," Madre said.

"What does he want?"

"It doesn't matter." It would take a crane to move her.

Three months earlier, the cab had dropped Alex off at a dark and empty house. Exhausted, she fell asleep on the couch and didn't call her parents until that afternoon. Madre shouted at her on the phone, but they drove over to the house immediately. They were both sick with grief. She'd disappeared for two weeks.

Only two weeks.

Alex later learned of the time dilation between reality and Foreverland. *But an entire year?*

Her parents noticed the wound on her forehead, but never said a word about it. Even when the story broke about the Institute and Tyler Ballard—the story about all those bodies, all those people networked into a computer—they pretended not to know that their daughter had gone there. And they never mentioned needles.

Madre moved into the spare bedroom. She had already lost a grandson and son-in-law, she wasn't going to lose her daughter. Alex didn't argue.

"I just want to talk," the man shouted through the door.

"Madre."

She took Alex's hand, pressed it against her cheek and kissed it. Then she went to the kitchen to make some coffee.

Alex leaned closer to the mirror and pulled strands of black hair over her forehead. The hole had healed, but she preferred to keep her bangs just in case someone looked too closely.

When she came out of the bathroom, Madre was sitting at the kitchen table with her cell phone. The agent stood at the back door, admiring the garden where Alex spent most of the summer, sometimes getting lost in the weeds, expecting to find a forgotten yellow truck.

"I'm recording this." Her mother put the cell phone down.

"That's not necessary, Madre."

"You never know."

"All right, okay. You never know."

Madre remained at the table like a mediator.

"Beautiful backyard," the agent said. "You do it all yourself?"

Alex pulled a chair from the table. "Want to sit?"

"Okay." He raised his cup. "Thanks for the coffee, Mrs. Diosa. Better than I deserve."

Madre nodded once.

"So what can I do for you?" Alex asked.

"Right. You're familiar with Foreverland?"

"Yes, of course. I'm writing a book. You know that."

He smiled sheepishly. *Let's cut through it.* "Like I said, you're not a suspect."

"Why would I think that?"

He eyed the phone. "If there's any way you can help, anything you can say, we'd appreciate it. I know you're well aware of the children involved."

The voices.

She heard them at night sometimes, woke in a sweat to silence. Dreams, that's all they were, memories of that dreadful event. It seemed like years ago, but the voices were nails that had scratched grooves into her memory.

"I don't know any more than you," she said.

"Right."

"The Ballards started all of this, correct? You found their bodies. What else is there?"

"You were at the Institute."

She clutched her hands. They were below the table, but the tension extended past her shoulders. "I've been there, yes."

"When?"

"In the spring. A group of journalists were invited. I can get the exact date..."

He shook his head. "That's all right. You went to a biomite doctor across the road shortly after that?"

"Some time after that, yes."

"He's missing."

"I think he left the practice."

He grimaced. "Leaving your coat and phone on the counter isn't how most people retire."

"I don't know where he is, if that's what you're asking."

"No one has been able to locate him."

"What do you want me to say?"

He paused for a long sip, swirling the remains. "You went to see him because of the incident at the Institute, right?"

"More coffee?" Alex asked.

Madre began to stand. Alex stopped her, went to the coffee pot and poured a cup. He looked at her forehead when he asked that. Not just a glance, but a question with his eyes.

"Why are you asking questions you already know the answers to?" she said.

"Helps me keep my thoughts straight."

She put the cup in the microwave and watched it go around.

"I lost my balance while I was there. The smells, the lab...you know, it wasn't what I was expecting."

"What were you expecting?"

"Not that."

"I understand you were in a car accident. I'm very sorry for your loss."

"Thank you."

He muttered condolences to Madre, talked about how proud she must be of her family and she had every right to be. The death of a child was a terrible loss.

"Have you sought treatment for your grief?"

"I'm sorry, what?"

"Since the accident, have you done anything to process your emotions?"

"What are you suggesting?"

He cleared his throat. "Have you gone back to the Institute?"

They stared for a long moment. "No."

"Not even to research for your book?"

"No."

"What happened with Coco?"

"The orangutan?"

"Yes. There are reports you said Coco opened his eyes."

"When did this turn into an interrogation?"

"I'm just following trails, Mrs. Diosa. Anything that will help."

"Look, I don't think I can help you. The Institute was performing illegal research. They were kidnapping suitable hosts to create an alternate reality and, thank God, someone stopped them."

"How do you know someone stopped them?"

"Don't play that. Those facts are all over the Internet. Someone woke up the hosts and wiped the computers clean. Some of them escaped before the alarm sounded and a car was recorded on a nearby security camera picking up two kids."

"Kids?"

"The footage is on Youtube."

"No one said they were kids."

"If you can't tell those are kids by the way they act, then you should turn in your badge."

He grinned and shrugged.

"I'll tell you what I don't know," Alex said. "What happened to all the employees that disappeared?"

"What have you heard?"

"The place was empty. And what about Mr. Deer?"

He cocked his head curiously.

"He was the one that organized these tours and invited the journalists," she said. "We heard he was a major part of the operation."

"I can't share that with you."

"And Patricia? Is she really dead?"

He nodded.

Alex sat down, cradling the warm mug for comfort. "And the unidentified hosts, the ones that woke up. Did you find out who they were?"

"Why do you ask?"

"I'm concerned, hope they're all right."

He leaned forward. "I thought this wasn't an interrogation."

"I just want to know that the children are safe."

She flicked a knowing glance at his forehead. It was unblemished, apparently untouched by a needle. But he knew the depth of the crimes committed in Foreverland. Maybe he didn't hear the voices, but he knew that children paved the way to Foreverland. Alex wanted to be sure she wasn't imagining she had quieted the voices, that she took away their suffering.

That she ended the Nowhere.

"They're safe," he said, unblinking. The tone suggested he answered the unspoken question, the real question.

"Safe?"

He nodded. "Thank you."

"For what?"

He held up his mug. "For the coffee."

That felt like a lie. The *thank you* meant something else.

A grin broke across his face. Madre's arms were crossed, her head hung down. Soft little snores rattled in the back of her throat. They got up quietly and left the kitchen without disturbing her or the phone recorder.

"Tell your mother it was nice to meet her." He stopped at the door. "It must be nice having her here."

She nodded suspiciously. He seemed to know more about her than he should. Or maybe he was just a better detective than she'd thought.

"Be careful," he said.

"What?"

He held out his hand. They shook. "With your book."

"Yes, of course. The book." She cocked her head, careful not to disturb her bangs. "Are you telling me not to write it?"

"Not at all. The world needs heroes."

"Is that what you think I am?"

He cupped her hand with both of his and gently squeezed. His tone softened, his eyes relaxed. He said, "I'm very sorry for your loss, Mrs. Diosa. I truly am."

She watched him get into his SUV, watched him drive away. She'd never seen him before in her life, she was sure of that. But he seemed so familiar.

Madre was rinsing the coffee pot. Her phone was still on the table. Next to it was a business card. It looked legitimate, an agent from the Biomite Oversite Agency. It was just his last name.

Johnstone.

She'd later remember that name and call the number and get the office of her biomite doctor, the one that mysteriously left the practice. But she right then, as Madre took chicken from the freezer, as children laughed somewhere in the neighborhood and birds squabbled at the feeder, she turned the card over.

Her breath caught short.

The agent had written something on the back.

She pinched herself, hugged her mother and wept.

The sky was clear blue, not a cloud in sight. She wept and the birds continued to sing and the sun continued to shine. She wept because it didn't rain.

"Thank you" was written on the back of the card.

In green ink.

46

Danny Boy

An island off the coast of Spain

The sea breeze blew through the house.

Danny slapped the papers against the table. Santiago rushed to close the doors, the curtain fluttering around him.

"Just close one," Danny said.

The portly Spaniard hesitated, knowing one door would only make it worse. But Danny smiled, and Santiago nodded. Danny didn't like the house closed up. *The breeze should always blow through the house*, Danny said. *I want to smell the water.*

The smell of this ocean was different than the Foreverland scent. This was more authentic, natural. And it reminded him where he was. *I am here.*

Santiago stood in the doorway, as if his rotund frame would block the wind. He held his mesh hat down, tufts of black curly hair escaping his open collar, the breeze carrying his musky scent into the room.

Santiago, the overweight Spaniard with crooked teeth and always a shadow of whiskers. How could I forget?

His compatriot. His business partner.

The Foreverland imposter resembled him, could pass as a twin. But he didn't have the mannerisms, not in the flesh. And now that Danny was back, it was all too obvious. The integration into Foreverland had been so seamless, his memories so well manipulated that Danny couldn't remember at what point he had been inserted.

The Institute.

That was the turning point. Something happened when the scientists brought him into the lab, when they had explained the experimentation. Danny had shuddered, appalled at their disregard for the animals' suffering. Mr. Jonathan Deer, the man that had invited him, the man that arranged for Cyn to visit, wasn't there during that trip. He was going to hear from Danny, though.

Danny remembered flying home, remembered crafting a tersely worded email on the plane, remembered landing in Spain and Santiago picking him up at the airport.

The other Santiago.

There was no plane ride, no coming home. They inserted Danny right then.

"Daniel?" Mary tapped the table with her fingernail, a clear coat of polish and tailored business suit revealed her impeccable taste. "Everything all right?"

"Yes. Sorry."

Danny turned his attention back to the contract, a stack as thick as a roll of dimes. He signed where there were Xs, taking the time to read sections he could understand, jotting notes in the margins. Santiago eventually looked over his shoulder, grunting each time Danny scratched out a line or made a comment.

It feels so good to be back.

Danny had returned to the villa after mysteriously disappearing for almost a month. The Spaniard didn't ask why or where Cyn came from or why they had covered their foreheads; he simply explained the state of his affairs.

Normality returned.

Danny tabbed each page he edited. When he reached the last page, the margins were littered with plastic strips.

"Jorge tendrá que leer a través de él de nuevo," Danny said. *Jorge will need to read through it again.*

"Of course." Santiago patted his shoulder.

Someone crossed the open doorway, the curtain dancing around her. A lithe young woman was squeezing water from her hair.

"Is everything all right?" Mary asked.

Even Mary looked familiar, the client he'd met at the diner, when the Nowhere oozed out of her left eye. Danny still couldn't understand how it was all accomplished, how Alessandra could absorb the details of the physical world and build a Foreverland world. Her mind was like a substance, a sponge that permeated the planet.

We were even discussing the same deal at the café. Or maybe my memories are corrupt and I only think she looks familiar.

He couldn't reason his way through the experience. In fact, the memories (false or not) put him at ease, like he'd practiced this negotiation already. Still, he was tempted to ask her if they'd met before.

"Daniel?" she asked.

"You will have to excuse us," Santiago said. "There have been late nights."

Danny was watching Cyn on the portico. "I changed some of the language that I'd like my attorney to look at. If you'd like, you can look it over first."

Danny slid it to the man on Mary's right. He efficiently scooped up the brightly flagged document.

"We can have it back to you in the morning," she said. "I'd like to conclude business before flying out tomorrow night."

"I don't see why not."

"Well." They stood. "Thanks for meeting us in person. It's not that we don't trust projection rooms. We'd rather meet face to face before investing in people."

"Ironic, don't you think?"

They didn't trust the very thing they were investing in: technology. *I don't blame them.*

"The irony's lost when you're giving millions to a seventeen-year-old."

"Time is relative." Danny smiled. "Einstein proved that."

"We're not flying through space."

They shook hands across the table. He could've sworn she glanced at his forehead.

"We prefer to shake hands," she added. "In person."

"Even that's not reliable," Danny said. "Not if we both have biomite-created hands."

"If the government continues restricting biomite technology, we might be looking for work."

"It should be none of the government's business," Mary's companion said. "If a man needs more than 49% biomites to save his body, he should have the right to do so."

"Can't have people turning into robots," Danny said.

"Halfskin," Mary said.

"What's that?"

"It's what they've termed the condition when the body is more artificial than human."

"Arbitrary, if you ask me." Her companion snapped his briefcase and dropped it on the table. "Man gets two prosthetic arms, two prosthetic legs and he's just fine. Make those prosthetics out of biomites and the government wants to turn him off. You know the story about the diver? He found an illegal strain of biomites, ones the government couldn't track."

Danny had heard of them and wanted no part of it.

"He dove to the bottom of the ocean, almost three miles below the surface, and came back unharmed because his body was almost entirely biomites. You know what the government did when they found out, right? Turned him off, like a light." He snapped his fingers. "Imagine what we could accomplish."

"That's the world we live in," Danny said. "So let's change it."

"Let's do so." They shook hands again. Mary caught him glancing at Cyn and smiled. "I'll let you get back to your business."

"It's been a long year," he said.

"I understand."

She has no idea.

Cyn was tone and tan, one leg pulled onto the lounger while she painted her toenails bright red.

Danny stood beneath the portico with two glasses of iced tea.

"Meeting adjourned?" she asked.

Her skin was perfect, barely a scar where the needle had pierced her flawless forehead. The cut across her hand had healed nicely, a white slash that would always remind her of the Institute.

He was grateful she woke up first, that he didn't see her with the needle in her head. It would've hurt to see her so helpless, so prone.

She stopped painting. "What?"

"Nothing."

"We going back to the States?"

"No, not yet. Best we stay here a bit longer."

A year, he was thinking. *Maybe more.*

The ripples from the Institute were still moving. Several months had gone by and the investigation was ongoing and would be for some time. Nothing had been solved. The Ballards had been found, but they had to have had help. An operation that expansive required men and women in high places.

Jonathan Deer disappeared. And Zin, Reed, and all the other victims in the Institute...they no longer have a living body.

There was nothing he could do for them. Cyn wanted to do something, but what? All they could do was follow the case from a safe distance. When things cooled down, maybe then they could find who was helping the Ballards.

Danny felt like it was his fault, the survivor guilt returning. He was convinced Reed had written the notes, that he was the one that put the pieces together. But Reed was dead. Was it possible to untether from the body and live in Foreverland?

That's what happened to Lucinda.

Cyn held out the sunscreen. She pulled her hair forward. Danny rubbed the lotion on her shoulders and across her back.

"What are we going to do?" she asked.

"We stay, maybe a year. Maybe longer. We can improve biomite production and efficiency, fund lobbyists to ease government restrictions, help those that really need it."

"No. I mean what are we going to do right now?"

"Oh, you mean now? As in now-now?"

"As in now-now." She wrapped her sun-warmed arms over his shoulders. They swayed like the ocean was an orchestra, paradise their dance floor. She nuzzled into his neck and sighed, her hair pressed against his cheek. It was an intoxicating mixture of the roses and ocean.

"Do we just live happily ever after?" she asked.

"Was there ever a doubt?"

They danced until their skin was hot, their bodies thirsty.

They swam in the sea, the water warm and buoyant. Danny floated on his back, staring at the blue sky, looking for the gray static to eat a hole through it, to fall on them. It would take some time to get out of that habit.

No more lilacs.

Somehow that fragrance pervaded Alessandra's world. The lack of that scent, oddly enough, kept him grounded in the physical world. Because of her, the Nowhere was no more. The children were quiet. No more dreams. No more suffering. They helped her with that.

And that eased the survivor's guilt.

Cyn swam into the deep and stayed under for a full minute. She emerged next to him and wrapped her arms around him. He thought about the diver, the one with the biomite body that went to the bottom of the ocean. He was the man that converted his body into biomites.

Like he built it.

And despite the bathwater temperature of the ocean, Danny felt a chill. He'd been missing the obvious.

That night, he found one of the invitations he'd received from the Institute, the one that lured him in to be captured. It was from Jonathan Deer.

Danny held it up to the mirror and read the last name.

And began to laugh.

EPILOGUE

ANOTHER DOOR OPENED; this time a boy about the age of thirteen stepped out. One by one the children of the Nowhere stepped out of the fabricating tanks, their eyes wide with wonder. Born again into the physical world, their bodies just like they left them on the island or in the wilderness.

Only now they were better.

They were made of biomites, no different than flesh. Special biomites the government couldn't see. The same biomites that composed Jonathan's body, the body he fabricated himself so he could leave the body of flesh he despised. This one, the fabricated one, the body of biomites, felt more like his body than Harold Ballard's body ever did.

And Jonathan could use this body to look like anyone he wanted. Become whoever he wanted. He had morphed his face and body to look like many different people, had taken on many different names to make this day happen.

But inside, he had never changed.

The technicians went to the children, welcomed two hundred and three children to the world. Jonathan remained in place, eyes on the last tank at the end of the line, the door still cracked and unmoving. His heart thudded like falling stones.

He drifted through the crowd, not hearing, not seeing, watching only one tank, the only one not to open.

His legs had become numb. He locked his knees to keep from falling, afraid to reach out, to look inside and see the failure. Of all the fabrications, this was the hardest. This was the most difficult one to piece together.

She'd been through so much. So fragmented.

She was the one that saved the children, that kept their existence in the Nowhere bearable. She was the one, of all of them, that deserved to step out of that tank.

He swallowed and reached. The door swung open.

He fell back half a step and saw only her, standing inside, head bowed.

Candy red hair.

Damp gown stuck to her perfect skin.

Her eyes closed, he watched. He held his breath, vowed never to take another until she—

The eyelashes fluttered.

Big green eyes, vivid in color, sharp in contrast, looked upon the world. Big green eyes seeing it for the first time in what seemed like forever and fell on the young man in front of her.

Jonathan Deer was no longer the green-eyed stranger with the bent nose. He let his true features return, showed his true face. His hair brown, long and curly.

She stepped out and reached up. Her fingers brushed his cheek.

The world blurred through his tears. "Lucinda," he said.

She whispered in his ear what he'd longed to hear since the day he woke on the island.

"Reed."

WHAT TO READ NEXT?

Continue the journey of biomites.

HALFSKIN

An Underground Reviews 2015 Best Books

http://bertauski.com/halfskin/

REVIEW FOREVERLAND!

If you enjoyed this ride, please drop a review on your favorite vendor. It doesn't have to be long and complicated. Throw some stars on it and write *Loved it!* or *It was really, really okay!* or *Meh*.

Reviews make the difference.

Find all the vendor links at

http://bertauski.com/foreverland

This book is a work of fiction. The use of real people or real locations is used fictitiously. Any resemblance of characters to real persons is purely coincidental.

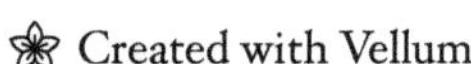

www.ingramcontent.com/pod-product-compliance
Lightning Source LLC
Chambersburg PA
CBHW051009180726
48291CB00006B/2038

9781951432188